POINT of BETRAYAL

Ann Roberts

Bella
BOOKS
2013

Bella Books, Inc.
P.O. Box 10543
Tallahassee, FL 32302

Printed in the United States of America on acid-free paper
First published 2013

Editor: Medora MacDougall
Cover Designer: Linda Callaghan

ISBN 13: 978-1-59493-324-0

Other Bella Books by Ann Roberts

Acknowledgment

I'm thankful to my editor, Medora MacDougall, for her keen knowledge of Chicago style, mastery of all grammatical rules I tend to break, and a wonderful ability to tighten my sentence structure and dialogue. It was helpful to have someone who was unfamiliar with the series remind me to put in details for new readers and avoid assumptions about characters.

Linda Hill continues to answer my emails and put me on the publishing schedule. I'm very grateful to her and all of the Bella staff.

Without the support of my partner Amy I wouldn't ever finish a book. This last year has been especially difficult, and her continued love and patience were critical to this novel's completion.

I am lucky to have family and friends who always ask about my writing and at the very least *pretend* to read my manuscripts or books: Susan, Morgen, Judith, Josh and Tiff, Patricia, Alexis, Debbie, and Sue.

Most of all, I am grateful to all of the readers who have faithfully and loyally followed Ari and Molly on their journey of love and discovery through four novels (assuming you're about to read this one). I appreciate all of your emails and words of encouragement more than you could ever know.

About the Author

Ann Roberts lives with her partner and their Rhodesian Ridgebacks in Phoenix, Arizona. Please visit her website at *www.annroberts.net.*

PROLOGUE

The beach was Nina's psychologist. While she spent her days as a social worker listening to children and adults divulge their secret sins and fears, it was the strip of sand at the edge of the continent that counseled her each night during her run. She often talked out loud, reviewing moments of her day, knowing the crashing waves muffled her voice as they built to a crescendo, claimed the shore and repeated the pattern.

She quickened her pace, the pure sea air purging her lungs of all she had withheld during the day. She'd lost track of the numerous times she had to swallow her words or stifle an angry comment she longed to hurl at the ignorant parents who weren't meeting the needs of their children.

She glanced at the water and smiled. There was something incredibly comforting about the ocean resting over her shoulder as she cut a path parallel to Highway One, the most scenic drive in California. Laguna's great beach, wonderful shops and chic restaurants were tourist magnets during the summer, but the season was long over and only the locals remained. She ran later in the evening after most of the other joggers had gone home, the welcome solitude a byproduct of her long hours as a school social worker.

"Bobby Arco is a complete asshole!" she shouted, thinking about the boyfriend of her favorite student's mother. Michaela was the sweetest kid, and Nina had never understood how her mother Eden had hooked up with such a loser. He'd left her a threatening message that morning after being questioned by Family Services for another suspected incident of child abuse she'd reported the day before.

"Stay the hell away from my family," he'd hissed into her voice mail.

Only after she'd deleted the message did she realize she probably should've saved it and played it for Evan, her assistant principal.

She saw the Montage Resort in the distance while her mind latched onto the other key moment in her day.

"Celia would definitely benefit from a support group. I'll call her church's outreach coordinator and see if there's one here or in Laguna Niguel," she murmured, recalling a teacher who'd spent her planning period crying in Nina's office about the death of her brother.

She took a deep breath and cleared her head, determined to run as far as the resort before turning back, her legs limber and her muscles attuned to the effort. She was ready for the marathon in January but now... *It's out of the question*, she thought.

Besides it was supposed to be something she and Sam did as a couple. They had motivated each other to train, and she would've given up after the first two kilometers without his support.

Maybe *that* was the reason he'd left. He was sick of playing cheerleader. She could get down on herself, and he'd constantly said she was her own worst enemy. Often their conversations focused on her lack of self-esteem and ended with him delivering a rousing speech, the kind he would write for his father, the city councilman. Sam often joked she got his best stuff and his dad had to live with the verbal scraps.

Her mind drifted to Evan, who was her superior but also Sam's twin brother. It was a bit awkward around him lately. Before the breakup she'd efficiently compartmentalized her personal and professional lives, telling herself the two relationships were unrelated.

"Yeah, right," she mumbled, acknowledging he had become the most important person in her life, a true confidant. But she'd made it clear to him he was only a friend and wouldn't be a rebound from his brother.

She took a sharp left and sprinted up the Crescent Point path to the gazebo that overlooked the Pacific, her ideal site for a wedding. It was 360 degrees of beauty, the Pacific Ocean and the San Joaquin Hills, embracing some of the most expensive real estate in the county. She wanted a wedding on the cliff and a house on one of the jutting plateaus that faced the water.

She'd need a much larger paycheck and a guy who wasn't Sam. He'd made it clear the last time they spoke. "*Nina, it's not going to work. It can't.*"

That part had hurt. He was the most important person in her life, but he couldn't say the same. Clearly his family came first. She took a long swig from her water bottle and replaced it in the holster, grateful she had the entire point to herself. During the summer Crescent Point was packed. She re-tied her customary ponytail and wiped the sweat from her forehead. She'd worn the style forever and she didn't care if anyone else thought it was childish.

Maybe that was part of the problem. She was a true creature of habit and lived by her patterns. If she found a way that worked for her, she never deviated from that route, but it meant she was highly predictable. Sam was the exact opposite. He was spontaneous. In the two years they'd been together, he'd never wanted to plan a vacation, insisting they just *go*. It drove her crazy, but she'd been willing to compromise as had he. Perhaps there was still hope. They definitely needed to talk again. She owed him the truth.

She gazed up the hillside and for the millionth time wished for a beach house, a dream that would never become a reality if she remained in the public sector. Of course, if she joined First Point Medical, she'd inch closer to owning prime real estate. She still had another two days to make her decision. They'd wooed her with a great salary, the promise of an office with a window and her *own* secretary. That would be a real bonus— no more typing notes or reports. She would be the only social worker in a growing medical practice that wanted to expand its clientele to include family counseling. She *had* the job if she wanted it. Juan Bojorquez had made the offer last spring after she'd coaxed his fourteen-year-old daughter into a drug rehab program. She was improving and he was grateful.

She loved her job at Brayberry Elementary School working with kids like Michaela and helping their families, but she had to think about the future—a better paycheck and benefits. She wanted to get back together with Sam, but what if that didn't work out? Still, would she like working in corporate America?

She closed her eyes and leaned over the railing, entranced by the show below. The powerful waves were no match for the side of the jagged cliff, and their continual confrontation resulted in a shower of foam dancing high into the air. She glanced at her watch, barely able to decipher the silver numbers in the darkness. The moon was only a sliver, affording her no extra help. She squinted and read eight thirty. The cold breeze blew off the Pacific; the chill reminded her it was November first, yet she wore only a tank top and running shorts—a definite benefit of living in Southern California.

She'd sprint back to her car and head home to the delicious salad, hummus and warm pita bread that awaited her. She'd write in her journal and weigh the pros and cons of the job offer.

A shadow moved on her right and she turned toward it, suddenly aware she wasn't alone. Hands pressed into her shoulder and propelled her over the railing. In a flash it became too difficult to scream and save herself at the same time. She grabbed the space between and found purchase before her arms flew skyward and her feet were strangely above her head.

Then she screamed.

CHAPTER ONE

A persistent mourning dove woke Ari Adams from her inaugural sleep in her new home. She'd covered her head with the extra fluffy pillow, thrown a slipper at the small window above her bed and turned on a soft jazz radio station, which almost worked until an annoying commercial overtook the airwaves. She imagined if she got up and gazed at the tall branch, she'd see the pesky bird making faces at her.

"I give up."

She threw back the covers and headed for the closet. Since she was dressed only in a T-shirt and boxers, the crisp November chill immediately gave her goose bumps, but she savored the feeling since it meant the end of the vicious summer heat. And the summer had been physically, mentally and financially vicious.

She stretched her arms and shook her head. She'd wanted a change, and Tina, her stylist for the past decade, had convinced her that a drastic haircut would be the ultimate symbol of her new life.

"Aren't you tired of looking like Morticia?" Tina joked.

Ari knew she was kidding because they'd often discussed Ari's Mediterranean features—oval face, regal nose, rich brown eyes and flowing black hair—and how well she could wear the long mane. But she agreed and ordered Tina to chop off nearly a foot, leaving her with a shoulder-length cut that required much more attention and time than she'd ever allocated to her morning preparation. It was a new look for a new life in a new house, yet it still felt like a part of her was missing.

She tousled her remaining locks and stared up at the ceiling and the beautiful crossbeams that matched the dark pine doors leading to her balcony. She loved the Spanish revival bungalow, and it was impossible to believe it had been nearly destroyed only a few months before, much like her personal life. Staring at the freshly painted walls and the new bedroom set she'd chosen, she realized she and the house had been reconstructed together, albeit very quickly.

She'd hired Teri, her best friend's handy dyke, to do the remodel, and she'd worked exclusively on her project, called in favors with subcontractors and suppliers. She'd completed in nine months what would've taken most contractors over a year.

"I know how much this means to you, Ari," she'd said. "I know how much you need this."

That was the truth. The house had become her life and the garden her sanctuary.

She stepped onto the small balcony that overlooked her expansive backyard and studied the various planters and walkways her landscaper had installed. She was sticking primarily to indigenous desert landscaping, but she'd wanted some color and insisted that brick planters be built for her burgeoning gardening hobby. If she wasn't at work she was out in the back either making compost or planting flowers and shrubs.

Now that fall had come, it was time to move forward with her vegetable garden. She studied the rectangle at the western side of the yard where a garage used to sit. The foundation had been jackhammered out and only the scarred earth remained. She smiled, grateful for the project. She liked being busy and the yard was a powerful distraction since her career as a real estate agent had flat-lined in the tough economy. Clients were hard to find and commissions were fleeting, so she'd found a hobby, convinced it was more therapeutic than the shrink her best friend Jane had dragged her to see. She didn't need to talk. She needed to work.

She threw on a pair of shorts before descending the winding staircase to her quaint kitchen. While she'd been determined to preserve the original light blue tile counters and white cupboards, she'd installed a Sub-Zero refrigerator and a stove that looked retro but was self-cleaning and boasted a delayed baking feature.

She flipped the cold water spigot on and was greeted by moaning in her pipes. When it stopped after a few seconds of water flow, she made a mental note to call Teri, brewed some tea and retrieved the paper, already planning a trip to Harper's Nursery.

The phone rang and she glanced at the display. *Dad.* She debated whether or not to pick up. If she didn't, he'd trek across town from his leased condo to see if she was okay, which would lead to a lunch invitation and several hours of father-daughter bonding time. That wouldn't be awful, but it wasn't what she wanted today. She just wanted to plant.

"Hi, Dad."

"Hey, sweetie. I hope you were up."

"Yup, I'm just getting started with the paper and then I'm off to the nursery."

"Why am I not surprised?" he said and she could hear a trace of sadness. He didn't like that she spent so much time outside.

"Dad, this yard certainly needed help after having a bomb go off in it."

Both of them knew she wasn't exaggerating. A bomb had literally exploded in the original garage before she'd purchased the bungalow. Her shrink had suggested that her commitment to landscaping sprang from a desire to change the entire look of the place as she first came to know it, back when it belonged to the previous owner.

"Well, I have some tickets to the Suns' game today and I thought you might like to go."

"Oh, that's nice," she said absently, already thinking about the rosebushes for the side of the house and how many tomato plants she'd purchase. "Maybe next time. I'm really busy."

"That's what you said last time and the time before that," he said. "Honey, I came out of retirement and moved down here to be closer to you, but I barely see you."

No one asked you to do that, she thought. She still considered their relationship strained, even though it was the best it had ever been. She'd never forgotten he'd disowned her during her twenties when he learned she was gay. Although fourteen years had passed, the memory of that long night remained, and neither of them could discuss her banishment or what followed—a suicide attempt.

"We just went to lunch together on Thursday," she said. "I think that counts as seeing me."

"Yeah, but I need your advice now. A lot's happened since Thursday."

She set down her tea cup. She knew what was coming. "They offered you the promotion?"

He paused before he said, "Not yet, but I think it's highly likely. I'd like to discuss it with you."

She sighed. "What do you want to do? Do you want to give up *retirement* indefinitely and go back to the force? I mean, you've been gone from Phoenix PD for over five years."

She'd put the emphasis on retirement, the part of the proposition she thought was most important to him. What she didn't mention was the reason he'd been rehired in the first place. He had accidentally stumbled into one of the biggest cases in Phoenix police history during his vacation, one that resulted in the resignation of her former girlfriend, Detective Molly Nelson, and the death of her godfather, Police Chief Sol Gardener. When the dust settled, the mayor had asked him to abandon retirement and head a task force investigating police corruption. Now the bosses were trying to make his return permanent by promoting him to lieutenant.

"Maybe," he said simply. "C'mon, hang out with your old man for a while."

She rubbed her temple and stared at the yard longingly. All she wanted was peace and quiet, but if she didn't say yes to him, she realized her friend Jane would be calling shortly and making her own offer. And she knew Biz would eventually call. She always called.

Everyone was worried about her since the breakup with Molly. Ironically Ari was far more worried about Molly, who'd lost the only job she'd ever wanted. She'd vanished. Ari imagined only her family knew where she was and no one would tell Ari.

"Okay, Dad," she relented. "I'll go."

"Great, sweetie. I'll pick you up at two thirty."

She could hear the enthusiasm in his voice. She knew he equated each visit as a step closer to filling the gap in their relationship, but while he saw that gap as a gopher hole in the backyard, she envisioned the Grand Canyon. Still, she appreciated him trying and she knew it was important.

She glanced into the solarium, toward the two photos sitting on the built-in bookcases—one of her mother and the other of her with her brother. Both were dead. That meant Big Jack Adams was the only family she had left.

The lump that filled her throat whenever she thought of family returned and she wiped away tears. It was harder now since she'd lost Molly and her wonderful family, who'd enfolded

Ari into the clan immediately. That was the worst part about breakups. You lost everything, not just your lover.

After she'd read the paper and finished her tea, she headed for the nursery. Glancing at the holes and stains that covered her shorts and T-shirt, she couldn't believe any man or woman would find her attractive, yet Kip Harper, the owner's son, was at her side less than two minutes after she arrived, suggesting several types of rosebushes and showing her the array of vegetables she could plant in late fall.

"This is my favorite," he said, stopping in front of a beautiful bush covered in fuchsia-pink petals that turned apricot at the center. "It's quite colorful and hardy enough for the heat."

She nodded her agreement and bent down to smell the blooming flower, cognizant that his gaze was most likely on her derriere. When she stood up, he was grinning.

He was buff with a short crew cut that made his ears stand out. She guessed he was at least ten years her junior, and when he smiled his gleaming teeth only made him look younger. She enjoyed walking through the nursery and talking with him since he was quite knowledgeable about horticulture even if he was entirely clueless about her lesbianism. He flirted with her as he loaded her cart, dismissing the questions of other customers with only a quick answer or pointing down an aisle toward another employee. He was helping her and wouldn't be pulled away to heft mulch into a car or explain the water needs of desert plants.

She knew he gave her extra attention in the hopes that she'd pick up on his interest, and she felt slightly guilty about withholding the truth but not enough to do anything about it unless he formally asked her out. Then she'd tell him and things could become horribly awkward, so she kept him talking about gardening.

When he loaded her car and waved goodbye, she thought he looked glum, as if he'd missed an opportunity.

She sighed, thankful she'd avoided a conversation about dating, which was the last thing she wanted to think about. Even her shrink knew to leave it alone for now, allowing her the space to sort out her own feelings and discover why she'd allowed Biz into her life at the expense of her relationship.

After nine months she had no answers. She had just let it happen. Maybe she knew it wouldn't work with Molly, who was an insecure, jealous, raging alcoholic. She was also the most amazing woman she'd ever met.

As she turned onto her lovely street, she saw Jane's Porsche sitting in front of her house. *My intervention group needs to communicate better*, she thought. There was no reason for Jane to babysit since her father was already on her agenda.

She pulled into the driveway and Jane traipsed across the lawn. She wore pedal pushers and a smart purple blouse that exposed much of her cleavage. She always looked sexy even when she wasn't trying. Her dark brown hair was pulled back in a gold clip. Ari couldn't tell if she was dressed for work or play. It was often that way with her. Whenever she left the house she looked chic, regardless of whether she was grocery shopping, clubbing or previewing houses. Ari knew she was the opposite; no one would ever confuse her errand attire of jeans and T-shirts with the power suits she wore for clients.

"Hi, honey," Jane called.

She offered her a peck on the cheek and carefully avoided the twenty-pound bag of manure Ari lifted into the wheelbarrow.

"You know, there are people you can hire to do that for you," she said, her nose crinkled in distaste.

"But I like doing it myself," she replied. "I feel like I'm one with the earth."

"Truly the sign of a sick mind. I'm one with the earth as well, just not the dirty part."

She laughed. "Then I guess you won't stay and help."

Jane shook her head. "I'm meeting a date for brunch. I just stopped by to show you this."

She handed her a printout of a news article from the *Laguna Beach Independent* with the headline: "Local Woman's Death Ruled Homicide." Surrounded by the story's text was a headshot of a woman Ari vaguely recognized but couldn't place.

She glanced at the caption beneath the photo—Nina Hunter. Nina was Jane's first love and one of the few women who'd ever turned her down.

"Oh, Jane. I'm so sorry."

"I'm okay, I think. We really weren't that close anymore, just Facebook buddies, but I can't believe she's gone. Who would kill such a nice person?"

She skimmed the article, which provided few facts about the murder. She quickly learned that Nina was a social worker at an elementary school in Laguna Beach. Teachers, parents and the administration sung her praises for her dedication to children and families. Initially the police thought she'd accidentally fallen over a railing at a scenic spot, but for a reason that was not disclosed, they had changed their minds.

"How could someone so admired be murdered?" Jane asked.

She shook her head. "There's obviously more to her life than what you know from Facebook. It says the prime suspect is Sam Garritson, the former boyfriend whose father is a city councilman."

"They'd broken up recently, but Sam swore to me that he didn't have anything to do with it. He's terribly distraught. He still loved her."

She raised an eyebrow. "And how do you know all this?"

Jane took a deep breath as if she was preparing for a speech. "Don't say no."

"Jane," she said sternly. "What's going on? You spoke with Sam?"

"He called me. He friended me a few months ago when we both commented on one of Nina's posts and then he poked me."

She nodded, well aware of the Facebook lingo. As a real estate agent, she'd learned to navigate Twitter and Facebook in order to survive with the under-thirty crowd, but Jane was the queen of social networking. She boasted two thousand Facebook friends and nearly as many followers on Twitter. *And I'd have that many too if I was willing to discuss my sexual activities in a hundred and forty characters*, she thought.

"So what am I not supposed to say no about?" she asked as Jane followed her into the backyard.

When Jane didn't answer right away, she dropped the wheelbarrow and faced her. "What did you do?"

Gazing down at the manure in the wheelbarrow, Jane pulled a tissue from her purse and wiped the smudges from the face of the bag. "It's just so dirty."

"Honey, focus. Why are you here?"

She set the tissue in the wheelbarrow and fished two airline tickets from her purse. "I think we should take a little vacation."

"A vacation? Now? I just moved in."

"Yeah, but you need a little time away. You never really took a break after everything that happened, and the last time you took a vacation was at least five years ago."

"That's not true," she argued. "Molly and I went away on long weekends a few times."

"That doesn't count. It's not a vacation if you don't cross state lines. That's a *fake* vacation that people call a *staycation*. That's B.S. I'm proposing that we get out of town, but in deference to your fragile state, I promise we won't go too far."

"Like Laguna Beach," she said dryly.

"Okay, that's a great idea! Let's do that."

She narrowed her eyes and resumed her wheelbarrowing. "I need to stay here and work. I've just started planting."

"God, honey, you make it sound like you're a farmer and the crops will die if you don't make the harvest. You can plant anytime. I really could use your help with Sam. You could put all of those great former cop instincts to work. The family wants someone else to look into the case, somebody who isn't local and won't arouse suspicion. Sam's dad, Steve, has to keep a low profile. This could hurt his chances for a political appointment with the governor. It would mean a lot to me, and I know you don't have any clients to woo right now."

"Don't remind me," Ari hissed. She dropped the bag into an empty flower bed and ripped it open. If Jane insisted on having a conversation with her, she'd have to endure the *dirt*.

"It sounds like Sam needs a private detective. You should ask Biz, not me."

"I thought about that and I'm guessing that if I invited her, she'd be happy to accompany us to California."

"Why would she do that? She's got a lot of clients who need her."

She snorted. "Honey, if we called her right now, she'd run over her own mother in that cute little Mustang if it got her here faster. She'd do anything to be close to you. Besides, I thought she was the reason you broke up with Molly."

She winced, but fortunately Jane couldn't see the tears in her eyes as she spread the manure with a rake, her mind wandering back to last Valentine's Day and the look on Molly's face when she'd found her lying in Biz's arms.

"I'm sorry I mentioned her," Jane said quietly.

"Have you heard anything lately?" Despite Jane's strong ties to the lesbian community, she hadn't been able to learn of Molly's whereabouts for the last nine months. It was as if she'd dropped off the face of the earth.

"Actually I just heard she went into a facility after she recovered from the gunshot and now she's out."

"What's she doing?"

"I think she's working for her dad."

Nelson Plumbing was the family business, but Ari couldn't imagine Molly would be happy repairing toilets or installing sinks. Her life was police work, and she'd been an amazing detective until she'd investigated the death of an informant and inadvertently stumbled into the crosshairs of a Mafioso with ties to the police department. She'd been forced to resign and Ari's father had essentially taken her place in the department and her office. Her career was over.

"I'm glad she got help." Ari dropped her rake and stared at Jane. Until she left, Ari couldn't enjoy her gardening. It was a solitary experience, as was most everything in her life now, and she relished being away from people, a fact her shrink found disconcerting.

"I don't want to go to Laguna," she said. "I'll be happy to call Biz if you want. She can probably help Sam in some way."

Jane rubbed her arms, and Ari imagined she was removing the imaginary dirt that clung to her two-hundred-dollar blouse. She hated the outdoors, and Ari knew she was at her personal tipping point.

"Okay, never mind," she said, defeated. "I might call her if Sam wants me to." She started up the brick path and added, "I'm using your bathroom before I go."

She smiled slightly. She was glad Molly was okay. Her dozen emails had been met with some harsh words and she'd given up. She'd worried Molly might commit suicide over everything that had happened. Ari was certain her brother Brian had saved her. She'd called him the day after Molly had resigned, begging his forgiveness, which he gave, and he promised to help Molly through what was undoubtedly the worst part of her life. For old times' sake, Ari had insisted Brian be hired to do the plumbing work on the house, but she was careful to be conveniently absent whenever he was on the job. She hoped he'd eventually call again, but it hadn't happened. She imagined Molly had forbidden him from keeping in touch. She understood why.

"Um, Ari, sweetie, you need to come inside *now*," Jane shouted from the back door.

She dropped the rake and wiped her feet on the mat before stepping across the threshold—into a puddle. Jane held up her red Manolo Blahniks with two bright pink lacquered fingernails and pointed to the water dripping from their pointed toes.

"I'm not happy."

CHAPTER TWO

Molly pulled up behind the Nelson Plumbing van. "Your Expert Plumbers!" The letters were fading from the harsh weather and the van needed a paint job. Her fingers were clamped around the steering wheel as if she were suspended in midair and hanging on for life.

Wasn't she?

She couldn't get out of the truck. She couldn't even look over her shoulder at Ari's new house. She'd been here once before—to investigate a murder on the last day she was Ari's girlfriend and the last day she was a cop. Valentine's Day.

When she'd strolled through the destroyed rooms with Andre that day, it had been with an enormous sense of relief: Ari was unharmed and justice had been served in a most efficient way. She'd had no idea what would happen a few hours later. It had actually been her suggestion that Biz drive Ari home. The images of them together filled her head, and she licked her lips.

I want a drink.

For the first time in nearly a month she needed a scotch. She tried to see the positive side, just as Linda, her mentor, had advised. She'd been sober for two hundred and sixty days, and the cravings had lessened. She fumbled in her pocket for the smooth stone with GRACE etched across its face. She rubbed her thumb against the word. She didn't need to stare at it anymore as she had during the first few weeks. She'd memorized its shape and the rounded script. Linda had taught her that control was about visualization—first the stone, then the moment and, finally, the desired outcome.

Her phone rang. She knew it was Brian. He'd tried to talk her out of coming, but she'd insisted since he was shorthanded on a Sunday. He'd done so much for her during her recovery; she was certain she could do this for him.

"Hey," she said.

"It's too much, huh?"

He was probably watching from the front window. She slinked down in the seat.

"Look, go home," he said in his casual voice. "I've got this covered. It's not half as bad as I thought. Water's only an inch deep. She might lose some of her flooring, but she did the right thing by turning off the water so fast..."

He stopped himself, realizing *she* was his sister's ex-lover.

"Go home, sis. You don't have anything to prove."

He was wrong. She had plenty to prove. For years she'd shown the entire Phoenix Police Department she was a great cop. Through her skills and detective work she'd amassed hundreds of collars and reversed the general prejudices about women and lesbians. She wasn't weak—even in her personal life.

"I'm coming in now," she said with determination.

I want a drink.

She didn't recognize the house. Without the address she probably would've driven right by. That day had been a hysterical nightmare, and she was much too focused on the job to notice the chili pepper tree in front or even the red door Brian had left slightly ajar.

Only a half-inch of water had scaled the Travertine tile step that separated the foyer from the rest of the downstairs. The living room was empty. She knew Ari didn't own a lot of things and she probably had just moved in. She imagined the renovation had been massive; much of the western side of the house had been gutted in the fire.

She found Brian wading through the flood in the kitchen, setting up various pumps to extricate the water. She grabbed a hose and started for the back door, all the while studying Ari's home, the choices she'd made and the colors she'd favored.

"Don't go out there," he said. "Take it through the front. She'll kill me if anything happens to the garden."

She stared at the paradise outside the kitchen window. "My god." The twisting brick walkways, large wooden planters and marble fountain reminded her of an arboretum. Everything was in bloom and the petals and buds blended like a large color wheel. She was enchanted and fascinated at the same time. She knew the yard had been nothing but a flat space of grass six months before. The metamorphosis was Ari's doing.

"You have your therapy and she has hers."

She offered a sharp glance and pulled the hose through the front door. Wherever Ari was, she would return to a muddy bog for a front yard. She cracked a smile at the thought of her distress.

"Serves her right," she said.

Instead of returning to the kitchen she wiggled out of her waders and gloves and climbed the winding staircase to the second floor. She told herself she was just curious about the renovation.

The loft area was Ari's tidy office where everything had its place. She'd raided IKEA for boxes and plastic bins to store her supplies, which were labeled and organized on a shelf. Only her laptop sat on the desk, along with a mouse placed perfectly in the center of its pad.

Skipping the guest room, she crossed into the bedroom. She was surprised to see new furniture, although it was arranged exactly as it had been at her condo. The dark pine bed frame faced east while her dresser faced west. An old rocking chair her mother Lucia had used at the end of her life remained in the corner with her lace shawl draped over it. Next to the dresser was the antique wood and brass umbrella stand that had belonged to her dead brother Richie. It held his sports equipment—street hockey stick, bats and tennis racket. His baseball mitt was looped through a bat handle so he wouldn't forget it when he ran out of the house for the next game.

The fact she'd kept such personal belongings in her bedroom had always bothered Molly, but she'd never said anything, not thinking it was her place and certainly not understanding what it was like to lose a parent and a sibling. Despite the amount of bluster the Nelson clan could generate during a dinner discussion, she knew she was lucky to have her family intact. And she knew Ari had loved them. She imagined it had pained her to lose that connection, perhaps even more so than their relationship. She added a point to the scorecard in her mind. Ari was still ahead, but she was gaining ground.

She realized there was something missing from the bedroom—a framed photo of the two of them, the one that usually sat on her nightstand.

She chewed her lip and resisted the temptation to look for it. Was the picture put away in a convenient location where she could reach it handily, or had she tossed it into the garbage? She really wanted to know, but her cop instincts told her she didn't have a warrant or any right to search Ari's things.

She split the difference and only opened the nightstand drawer. When she found nothing but the usual detritus of nail clippers, bookmarks, scissors and safety pins, she was disappointed. She sat on the bed, certain she could smell Ari's strawberry shampoo wafting from the pillow.

The whirr of the sump pump sent her back down the stairs, and she joined Brian in the kitchen.

"Find anything?" he asked with a crooked grin.

She ignored him and straightened the hoses to increase the flow while he examined the wall behind the kitchen sink, the source of the burst pipe. Her gaze strayed to a doorway and the solarium beyond it.

She sloshed to the center of the room, noting the built-in bookcases and vaulted wooden ceiling. She imagined Ari curled up on the window seat, her gaze alternating between the pastoral garden and a good book. If they were still together, the far corner would be perfect for Molly's piano. It would be just out of reach of the strong rays of the sun. She wondered for a fleeting second if Ari had thought the same thing.

The bookshelves were filled with all of her books, many of which Molly had never seen because they'd been kept in storage. It was one of the reasons she'd wanted a bigger place, to have a library. On a middle shelf were two framed photos Molly had seen hundreds of times, one of Lucia and one of Ari with Richie a few weeks before he was murdered. Nowhere was there a suggestion of her father's existence in her life.

"Okay, I think we're done for a couple hours. Fortunately she doesn't own any rugs and only a few pieces of furniture. Let's move those outside and then we'll go." He glanced at Molly, still lost in the beauty of the room and the depth of her musings. "Thanks for all of your help," he added sarcastically.

She looked away, embarrassed. "I'm sorry. I just…"

"I know. Let's get this done so you can go home and change. I'll pick you up in a few hours for our workout."

He grinned and she groaned.

CHAPTER THREE

Biz read the scrawled message for the tenth time. "Pay me or you'll be sorry." It wasn't signed, but that didn't matter. She'd found it under her office door that morning. She was surprised it had taken so many months for it to arrive. She didn't need her private detective skills to know who wrote it or what it meant. She smiled wryly. The lady got points for being succinct.

She'd worried this might happen. She hated employing amateurs, and the woman who called herself "Lola" and whose real name was Wanda, had helped Biz end Molly Nelson's career and contributed to Molly and Ari's breakup. Biz couldn't have scripted a better ending, but it had been so easy. Ari was so vulnerable and once she started drinking...

She smiled, remembering Ari's soft lips. Now that Molly was gone, she knew it was only a matter of time before she could win her affections. Ari would belong to *her*.

She'd given Wanda more credit, figuring she would realize Biz's situation was precarious and she was vulnerable since she was the only remaining link to Vince Carnotti, the crime boss who'd infiltrated the police department. Fortunately, Biz's police connection, Sol Gardener, was dead. As long as Wanda stayed quiet, she knew Jack Adams and his task force would never know her name. She'd broken no laws in the downfall of Molly Nelson, except using illicit drugs, but whatever. Everybody did that.

Wanda *had* to stay quiet. She tapped the blackmail note on her desk, wondering how much money it would take for Wanda to leave Phoenix permanently.

"She'd always want more," Biz whispered, voicing the truth.

She frowned, thinking of the possibilities she didn't like. Before he died, Biz had told Sol Gardener she was done. She'd been in his pocket for four years, doing light crimes like B&E, stealing cars and running drugs. The pay was incredible, far better than she'd ever made as a PI, particularly since so many of her clients were victimized women who didn't have any money. She rationalized that her work with battered women justified her criminal activity with Vince Carnotti. She had a right to a posh home, a hot car and a great girlfriend.

She'd finally arrived and now this. She crumpled up the note and shot it across the room against the wall. She couldn't let her ruin everything, but she couldn't fathom harming a sister—or could she?

"Hey."

Ari stood in the doorway, wearing grungy shorts and a dirty T-shirt. Biz guessed she'd been gardening, but despite her attire and her disheveled hair, she looked beautiful. She probably rolled out of bed looking amazing—a supposition Biz couldn't wait to test.

"This is a surprise. What are you doing here?"

"I need some help."

She slid into one of the client chairs, and Biz grabbed a notepad.

"Sure. What can I do for you?"

"Well, actually it's an out-of-town problem."

"How far out of town?"

"Laguna Beach. It's for a friend of Jane's. He's been accused of killing his girlfriend, but he says he's innocent and Jane believes him."

"Does she know him well?"

Ari rolled her eyes. "On Facebook."

She chuckled slightly. "Where everyone's your friend?"

"His name's Sam and he's willing to pay you for all of your expenses in addition to your time."

She scratched her head and pondered the predicament. She wanted to say yes, but if she left town without resolving the Wanda affair, she might return to find Big Jack Adams on her doorstep with handcuffs.

"How long do you think this will take?"

She shrugged. "I don't know. I can't be gone too long so we'd need to be back in a few days."

Her eyes widened. "You're going?"

"With Jane. She thinks I need to get away even if it is to investigate a murder. I guess the fates are on her side since a pipe burst in my kitchen this morning and flooded most of the rooms while I was at the nursery."

"Oh, I'm sorry. That sucks."

"Yeah," she said. "I just got rid of all the subcontractors and now the plumber's coming back."

Biz waited to see if Ari was going to comment on *who* the plumber would be. She knew Molly had gone to a rehab facility in Tucson to dry out and returned to work with her brother in the family plumbing business. Biz guessed she was sober since no one had seen her at Hideaway, her favorite bar, or anywhere else for that matter.

She found it surprising that Molly could turn away from the partying life she'd known for so long. No one could drink scotch like Molly Nelson, and before Ari came into her life, Biz and Molly regularly competed for women at Hideaway—and then for Ari. *And I've won.*

"I'd love to help you. I'll need a day or two to get a few things squared away, but I could fly over on Tuesday. Would that be okay?"

"That would be great," she said.

Biz stared into her green eyes, full of anxiety and a spark of interest. She knew it was there but if she pressed too hard and too fast, she'd get nothing. She used all of her willpower and refrained from kissing the gorgeous lips. She could be patient.

"Um, where are you staying now?"

"With Jane, of course. We leave in the morning."

"Okay, I'll see you in a couple of days. Tell Jane not to worry. We'll figure it out."

She touched Ari's shoulder, and they exchanged a brief glance before she headed down the hallway.

Yes, she could be patient and careful too. She'd eliminate Wanda and then go claim her prize.

CHAPTER FOUR

Jack had been disappointed when Ari called back and canceled, but he was glad she was getting out of town for a while. She needed a vacation and a break. He'd come to understand she lived on a bubble between happiness and sadness, never able to fully engage in life but unwilling to allow the misery of the past to consume her, a past he was partly responsible for constructing. When he looked at her, he felt pity and pride simultaneously.

Gradually they were getting to know each other again after four years. Eventually he would tell her everything she didn't know about her dead mother and her murdered brother, but it was far too soon.

He laced his fingers behind his head and faced the bulletin board covered in index cards and photographs. His way of solving crime was old-fashioned: create a timeline and stare at the clues until answers emerged. Andre Williams, Molly's former partner and the detective now assigned to him, initially had difficulty following the "chaos" as he referred to it. Apparently Molly's methodology was rooted in computer lists and endless circles on random sheets of paper, several of which he'd found stuffed in the drawers and cabinets of the office he'd inherited—her former office.

His gaze remained at the hole on the timeline, the place where a picture should be, the mystery woman who ruined Molly's life.

"Any new ideas?" Andre asked from the doorway.

He was still wearing his suit jacket. Jack had learned his unspoken agenda: break the stereotype associated with African-American men. His dress and grooming were impeccable and he was handsome, which explained why many of the female beat cops constantly gravitated to his desk. So far he seemed to be an up-and-comer. Molly had expressed a few concerns about his attention to detail, but she hadn't elaborated.

"We know most of it," he said. Jack picked up a dart, another one of his trademarks, and fired it into the blank space of corkboard. "But we need her."

Andre struggled to fit into one of the small visitor chairs, and Jack immediately decided to order some new ones just to piss off Captain Ruskin. He picked up a few skimpy notes from his previous meeting with Molly, who had been far less cooperative at the time than he would've liked, but he understood. She'd been betrayed in many ways.

"She was a blonde who was at Hideaway a few times prior to the night of the accident. The bartender confirms she was becoming a regular, but after that night, she's never appeared again. Molly's convinced the woman was a plant and part of Sol's setup."

"Damn right," Andre agreed. "Molly was a changed person after she met Ari. She quit running around with other women. She was totally devoted to her."

He held up a hand. "I get it, Andre. You don't have to defend her to me—"

"Yeah, I do," he said, his voice shaking. "Some of the rumors…"

He didn't bother to finish the statement, because Jack had heard all of the snarky comments made by the jealous detectives. Molly could be a hard-ass, and she hadn't bothered to make a lot of friends. Her downfall was a pleasure to many, including her former boss and Jack's old beat partner, David Ruskin.

"Just remember," Jack said, "that a lot of people respected her because she was a great cop. Those are the people you need to listen to now. The ones talking crap won't ever be half as good as Molly."

Andre took in his words before he said, "Thanks."

He held up the single page of notes. "Maybe you need to talk to her. She doesn't want to talk to me about this. I think she's terribly embarrassed about her behavior and the lesbian thing, which she knows I had a problem with—in the past," he added quickly. "Why don't you give it a try?"

"Will do," he said, rising.

"Really press her for details. It's been a few months since I spoke with her so maybe she'll remember something else. Time is running out. If we don't get a lead soon, they'll kill the investigation. It's going cold and the only reason the mayor has hung on this long is because he wants Vince Carnotti. We need this woman to connect Sol and Carnotti."

Andre nodded and left. Jack gazed at the stacks of files and boxes around the room. He was slowly making it his own, but he was having difficulty letting go of Molly's presence. He'd liked her as a cop and a girlfriend for his daughter, but Ari had made her love life a taboo topic. He guessed it was too painful to talk about. He had a hunch too that somewhere in the midst of the breakup was Biz Stone, a PI who had it bad for Ari. He couldn't decide if he liked her; there was a nagging feeling in his gut that something wasn't right about her. He just wasn't sure if it was his cop or dad instincts on alert.

Sol Gardener's last words played over and over in his head. He'd used his dying breath to warn Jack that Ari was still in danger, which meant there were still people who needed to be brought to justice.

Booming sounds like cannon fire echoed down the hallway. He went outside to check the source. A tall redhead had her arms wrapped around the soda machine and was rocking it back and forth.

"Son of a bitch," she muttered, giving up.

"Let me show you how this works," he said. He gave a quick pound right below the coin slot and the change dropped. "The quarters get stuck," he said, retrieving her Diet Coke. "Jack Adams."

"Dylan Phillips."

He cocked his head. "The new chief?"

She nodded. He decided she was beautiful, not exotic like Ari's mom Lucia, whose Mediterranean looks had turned heads, but in a wholesome and truthful way he imagined worked in her favor when she was interrogating suspects. She was in her forties, but she had a youthful face that hadn't aged. She wore designer jeans and a blue blazer over a tailored shirt, her black boots adding an extra inch to her formidable stature.

"I officially start on Monday. You seem surprised."

He looked away, embarrassed. "I thought you were a guy."

She popped the soda tab and stared at him cynically. "Don't you read the papers or at least the department email? They hired me two months ago."

"I've been busy. I'm running the task force on Vince Carnotti."

She winced and said, "Sorry, but my first act as chief will be to disband it. You've got nothing from what I hear." Her tone was flat, and he guessed she wasn't sorry at all.

"That's not true," he disagreed. "We're very close to making the connection. There's only one player missing, the key—"

"But you've still got to find him and break him—"

"Her."

"It's a her?"

"Yeah, she ruined Molly Nelson's career. Molly was getting too close."

She shook her head in disgust. "Don't talk to me about Molly Nelson, disgrace to the uniform."

He chewed on his tongue and held his temper. "Where are you getting your information?"

"Captain Ruskin, of course. I've spent a week with him. He's been quite helpful—"

"No doubt."

Her expression clouded, and he guessed she wasn't used to being interrupted. "And he's told me some stories about you, Big Jack Adams." She leaned closer, and her green eyes burned hot. "Let's be clear. I don't like rogue cops. I'm by-the-book, which is probably why they hired me to follow a corrupt chief after a major scandal. I'm a fix-it kind of person and I will rebuild the image of this department. People need to get in step with me or get gone, especially people who *might* be promoted."

"Hey, excuse me."

A woman in jeans and a denim work shirt stood behind them. The word "Hideaway" was embroidered above the breast pocket in neon pink. She held her purse tightly over her shoulder and looked uncomfortable.

"I don't mean to interrupt, but I'm looking for Jack Adams, Ari's dad?"

"That's me," he said.

"I'm Vicky, the head bartender at Hideaway, and I might have some more information."

He motioned to his office. "Please, come inside."

"Just a sec," she said, turning to Dylan. "I don't know who you are, but I heard you talking smack about Molly. She was one of the finest people I've ever met. Put her life on the line a lot. I'm just saying."

Before Dylan could respond, Vicky had walked past her. Jack followed, biting his lip to keep from laughing. They headed into his office, and when he offered her a chair, she declined.

"I won't be long," she said. "I'm not fond of police stations, but I'll make an exception if it helps Molly." She looked as if she was headed to work with her hair tied back to keep it out of the food and drinks.

"I appreciate you coming down. What did you remember since you were interviewed?"

"It's about the blonde who was all over her. I thought it was odd that she usually happened to show up right before Molly, but a few times she hung out."

"Did you share this with Detective Williams?"

She nodded. "Oh, yeah. But what I remembered wasn't about her drink order. It was about what happened when she paid. She paid with cash, and it was always this big clusterfuck because her wallet was buried at the bottom of her purse. She'd toss all her crap on the bar looking for it, including her key ring."

"What about it?"

"That's what I just remembered. It was filled with those little value cards, you know what I mean?"

"Yeah, like the ones for the grocery stores or the pharmacy?"

"Exactly. There was a gym membership card for Uptown Fitness. Is that helpful, do you think?"

Jack couldn't hide his smile. "More than you know."

CHAPTER FIVE

Stuck in bumper-to-bumper traffic on Highway One, Jane grilled Ari about her relationship with her father and her current mental state regarding the breakup with Molly. Ari periodically asked questions about Sam and Nina in an effort to refocus her on the purpose of the trip, but she had her own agenda.

"Did she ever reply to your emails?"

She pretended to read the map. "We're looking for Emerald Bay, an area just north of town. I imagine this is pricey real estate. You didn't tell me Sam was wealthy."

"He's not, but his family is, specifically his mother's family. She brought it with her to the marriage. His dad, Steve, is a city councilman with low public servant wages, but his mother, Georgie, owns a string of boutiques called The Bare Essentials that she operates in a lot of airports. They carry all kinds of things you might want for a trip, like travel toothbrushes and airline pillows." She swatted the map out of Ari's hand. "Now, answer my question. Did Molly ever reply to your emails? You must have sent twenty."

She knew if she didn't give her an answer she'd just keep asking the question. The truth was the only antidote for silence. "Yes. I wrote her several times and poured out my heart and I got a sentence back."

"What did it say?"

"Hmm. Let me see if I can remember the wording exactly. She said, 'I hate you and I never want to see you again. Delete my email address.'" She held up a hand. "My mistake. That was two sentences."

"Not even a *please*? Wow, she is pissed."

She picked up the map again to hide the tears. She re-read the email every day, and the words still took her breath away like a sucker punch. Of course, Molly believed *she* was the sucker.

"I'm sorry, honey," Jane said softly. "Let's forget about her for now."

Jane flicked on her iPod and the Carpenters began reminding them that rainy days and Mondays were the worst. She flowed into the singalong, the sight of the ocean an instant comfort.

They easily found the Garritson estate next to the highway, which headed inland near Laguna Beach, allowing developers to make millions on beachfront property along the coastline. The winding driveway burst with the oranges, purples, reds and yellows of jungle foliage flourishing in the mild California weather. As they turned in front of a majestic fountain, she realized the best view was on the other side of the house—the Pacific Ocean.

She was surprised when Sam Garritson greeted them. He shook her hand cordially but gave Jane a welcoming hug as if he'd known her his whole life. He was about thirty with hardly a line around his temples and not a strand of gray amid his chestnut-brown hair. He had a handsome face and sharp eyes, and she guessed in other circumstances his smile would be described as winning, although now he only could muster a slight look of gratefulness for their benefit. The chinos and blue button-down shirt he wore conjured an image of a young Republican in her mind.

"Please come out to the veranda," he said. They followed him through the impressive house, whose walls were mostly glass. They exited through a set of enormous French doors onto a deck worthy of the title "veranda." A tray of iced tea and cookies sat on a table surrounded by plush wicker furniture.

"Do you live with your parents?" Jane asked.

"Not usually," he said, munching on a cookie. "But since this hit the papers they're trying to protect me. It's all so unbelievable."

While he seemed upset, he wasn't distraught. He was either incredibly levelheaded as the son of a politician, thought Ari, or he was hiding something.

"Why don't you tell us what happened and what you know?" Ari asked.

He brushed the hair from his forehead and leaned back in the chair. "Apparently Nina was out for her evening run. She always liked to go up to the lookout at Crescent Point. You can see the ocean and the mountainside at the same time. A lot of people get married up there. I'm sure that was part of the attraction for her. The police said someone snuck up from behind and pushed her over the railing. They quickly ruled out accidental death because the railing was too high for her to fall over, but there's more evidence too."

Jane sipped her tea daintily. "Why do you say that?"

"One of the scene officers is a friend of mine from high school. He said they found something when they retrieved her body, but he didn't know what it was."

Ari nodded. As a former cop, she knew it was typical to withhold key evidence that might be needed later to identify the perpetrator. "And the police have you as the prime suspect?"

"I don't have an alibi. I was home alone that night working on my father's speech for his upcoming announcement. The governor is appointing him to a special commission overseeing child abuse law reform. It's a real coup to be selected."

"So, is there anything else?" Ari asked.

He stared at the sea and rubbed a hand across his five o'clock shadow. His eyes were glassy, and she realized he probably hadn't slept well in the last few nights.

"My breakup with Nina wasn't amicable. We'd been having trouble since summer, and when I finally broke it off a month ago I made the mistake of taking her to the Montage hoping she'd make less of a scene if we were in public."

Jane snorted. "You don't understand women, Sam. Hell hath no fury even in a room full of china. I guess she didn't take it very well?"

"No, she stormed out. I followed her and we fought in the parking lot. It got pretty heated. I finally grabbed my keys from the valet and left her there."

"That's not a very strong motive," Ari said. "Lots of couples fight."

He looked down, clearly embarrassed. "Yeah, but I said something I shouldn't have. She was very upset and said she'd publicly denounce my father's appointment to the governor's commission."

"What did you say in return?" Jane prodded.

"I told her if she said anything that could hurt my father's political career she'd be sorry. Of course, I didn't mean it, and she didn't mean what she'd said either. Even though she didn't agree with my father on the governor's position, she wouldn't have done something as rash as a public statement. Nina was too good for that."

"Someone must have heard you in the parking lot," Ari said.

Jane nibbled on a cookie, mindful of any crumbs landing on her lap. "Why didn't Nina agree with your dad? It isn't like the governor's advocating *in favor* of child abuse, is it?"

"No, of course not. He just wants the parents, usually mothers, to be held more accountable about their reporting even if they're also being abused."

Ari thought about the ramifications of an abused spouse being labeled as a criminal. "I imagine that was the point of their disagreement."

Sam nodded and swiped at his hair again. "Yes, she thought that would penalize the mother twice."

"She's right," Jane said.

Ari gazed at the sea, unsatisfied by the conversation. "Was there anything else? Did she know something that was embarrassing to your family?"

He shook his head. "My mom's company is on the level, we're not being investigated for anything and we pay our taxes. We're pretty boring actually."

An older woman wearing a red bandanna like a turban sailed through the French doors. She wore jeans and a man's crisp blue button-down, the breast pocket of which was missing. While the shirt looked new, her jeans were flecked with paint in every color of the rainbow.

"Hello, I'm Georgie, Sam's mother." Sam rose and introduced Ari and Jane. "You'll have to forgive me," she said, motioning to her attire. "I'm working on a piece right now, but I wanted to take a moment and meet you. Which one of you is the private investigator?"

"The investigator is actually a friend of ours who'll be joining us in a few days. We're here to get a head start," Ari said assuredly.

"I see," she said hesitantly and glanced at Sam.

"What do you paint?" Jane asked.

"Mainly glass right now. I decorate wine and martini glasses and sell them at my stores. Well, it was nice to meet you both. I hope you can help us pull Sam out of this terrible mess."

She glided back through the door and closed it behind her.

"My mother's a little abrupt," Sam explained.

"She doesn't seem very concerned," Ari observed.

"She's worried, but she's hopeful. I have a good attorney and the evidence is pretty flimsy. And then there's the truth. I didn't do it."

Jane looked at Ari. "Well, what do you think?"

She ruffled her hair. "I think the police have their suspicions for a reason and either they found something or, frankly, they know something you're not telling us."

He glanced from Jane to Ari. "I've got nothing to hide and I want her killer brought to justice." He choked up and his voice cracked. "I could never hurt her."

Jane reached over and squeezed his arm. "If you don't mind me asking, why did you break up?"

"Nina was high-strung in a lot of ways, but she was an amazing woman and I loved her."

Jane threw up her hands. "Then why break up with her, Sam? A lot of women—most women—are difficult. It's who we are. I don't understand."

He offered no explanation so Ari asked, "Was it your family? Did they not approve of her, particularly with your father's upcoming appointment?"

When he fidgeted in his chair and couldn't look at her anymore, she knew she was right. He'd sacrificed his girlfriend for his family, and from the look on his face, guilt and remorse were weights strapped to his back.

"Please help me. She didn't deserve this."

* * *

They headed to Nina's apartment, which was located a few blocks from Irvine Bowl Park. As Jane had spent part of her twenties in Laguna, the drive was a trip down memory lane.

She pointed at a small dive bar. "That's where I nearly got arrested."

"For what?"

She grinned proudly. "Public indecency. I tore off my top during an invigorating karaoke performance of 'I Love Rock and Roll.' Joan Jett would've been proud."

"When did you meet Nina?"

"When I was twenty and she was seventeen. She was my very first true love. I fell hard."

"But she wasn't interested?"

She shook her head. "No, she was as far from gay as you could get, but she was nice about it. We were friends after that."

Ari heard the wistfulness in her voice and imagined the memories were more difficult since everything about Nina was in the past tense. When they passed the Irvine Bowl, Jane laughed and slapped her knee.

"I can't tell you how many times we got chased out of that place. We'd jump the fence and see free concerts from the trees."

"You and Nina?"

"Yeah. We were great friends until I moved to Tucson to help my mom. When I think of my early twenties, I think of her. She was a hell-raiser. It's funny to think she became a social worker at a school, considering how often she ditched, but maybe that's why. She understood what it meant to be different."

"Why didn't she fit?"

"Her father was abusive. She hated going home. He hit her mom all the time."

"Was he abusive to her?"

Jane grew silent. "I'm not sure, and I'm not sure about sexual abuse either. I always wondered. I'm sure her own experience affected her feelings about abused children."

"Of course," Ari agreed, surprised by the revelation. "I wonder if she'd shared that information with Sam."

They pulled into an apartment complex, a series of rustic wooden cottages, each surrounded by dense foliage that easily grew with the help of the California rains. Nina's place was easy to find, the only door with yellow crime scene tape across the threshold.

"We won't break in," Jane said, pulling out a key that Sam had given to her. "We'll just slip between the tapes. That's probably legal, right?"

She decided a lecture on breaking and entering was inappropriate at the moment and chose not to answer as they made their way inside. Dust particles, caught in the sunlight, floated through the air, the remnants of the crime scene techs. She couldn't imagine what they might find following the police's search since the rooms had been ransacked and nothing returned to its usual place. More importantly, discarded cables and open credenza drawers suggested Nina's computer, phone and files had been removed.

Jane looked at her. "Any ideas?"

"Let's snoop," she said simply.

They opened cabinet doors, peered into the shower and studied the contents of the medicine cabinet. Nina seemed like a normal single woman without any peccadilloes or glaring secrets. She used white toilet paper, kept an ample supply of cosmetics on her vanity and apparently enjoyed covering her bed in bright throw pillows which were strewn across the floor after the police had searched her bed.

Her kitchen was in order, and the refrigerator contents of vegetables, hummus and various beans revealed Nina's penchant for healthy foods. A small wooden wine rack sat on the counter holding a single unopened bottle.

Jane grabbed it and read the label. "This is the pinot I recommended to her." She frowned at the empty rack. "That's a little odd. Nina loved good wine. Comparing wines was one of the topics that brought us back together on Facebook. I'm surprised she doesn't have a dozen bottles."

"Maybe she was due for a trip to the store," Ari said.

Across from the bed was a tall bookcase. What caught Ari's attention there was the common theme—Shakespeare. There were individual copies of the most famous plays, several enormous books that contained the complete works, books of selected sonnets and an entire shelf of critiques and essays.

"Did you know she was a fan?"

"Uh-huh. She loved Shakespeare ever since sophomore year when they had to read *Julius Caesar.*"

Around the room were several photos of her with her mother, who Jane said was now deceased. On her dresser sat a candid of her with Sam.

"For a woman who'd broken up she seemed to be hanging on," Ari noted, picking up another photo of him from the nightstand.

"I'm not sure they were really done," Jane said. She searched through the dresser drawers and the jumbled contents the crime lab hadn't bothered to refold. She burrowed through the lingerie drawer and murmured, "Maybe they found it."

"Found what?" Ari asked from the closet.

"Her journal. I know Nina had a journal. She's kept one since she was twelve after her parents started fighting. The school counselor told her it would help her cope with what was happening."

"Maybe she stopped."

She shook her head and rifled through the nightstand. "No, she mentioned it in an email not long ago. No two looked alike. Anytime she went to a bookstore she combed the journal section. I always joked that she had more empty books than completed ones."

"So where are they?"

She froze. "That's a good question. They've got to be here."

"Unless they were confiscated by the police."

"Nope, the police don't have them," a voice said.

They whirled to the doorway and faced a middle-aged woman with short, gray hair. Black shorts and a white tank top exposed a tanned runner's physique.

"You ladies want to tell me what you're doing here and why I shouldn't call the boys in blue?"

"I'm a friend of Nina's," Jane said. "We're just trying to help." She held up the key. "Sam asked us."

The woman remained suspicious. "I don't trust Sam. According to the papers he's the prime suspect and I'm not surprised."

"Are you one of Nina's neighbor's?" Ari asked.

"I live next door. I'm Rory and I'm Nina's friend, or I was," she added.

She was a handsome woman in her early forties who could've easily passed for thirty if she colored her hair, but the salt-and-pepper gray gave her a distinguished look suggesting intelligence and experience.

"I'm Ari and this is Jane."

Rory cracked a smile as she shook Jane's hand. "The notorious Jane from Facebook?"

"I wouldn't say notorious," she disagreed. "I don't remember friending you."

"You didn't. A few times I found Nina sitting in front of her computer laughing hysterically at your posts. You've got quite the reputation," she said with a disapproving tone.

"Hey," Jane replied, ready to argue.

Ari touched her arm and said, "Rory, you said Nina's diaries weren't here. Where are they?"

"She said they were safe, so I'm supposing she rented a safety deposit box or something like that. She was incredibly paranoid about anyone reading them because she reflected on a lot of confidential conversations she had with kids."

"But you don't *know* if she rented a box?" Jane asked pointedly. "She didn't really tell you anything. That's just your hunch."

Rory glowered and stepped beside her. "Yeah, that's my hunch."

"Um, Rory," Ari said politely, "wouldn't Nina keep her current journal here just for logistics' sake?"

She pulled her gaze away from Jane. "That would make sense, but it might not be in the house. She'd had a demoralizing experience with a past roommate who'd perused it and become so incensed by Nina's ruminations about the roommate's undiscovered sexuality that when Nina came home one night she found all of her things on the front lawn. After that she never kept it too close."

"Is there anywhere in the complex it might be?" Ari asked.

Rory nodded slowly. "Yes, there is. I'll show you."

They followed her down a path surrounded by plants and shrubs, which created a desirable privacy for each cottage.

"That's quite an advanced vocabulary you have," Jane said to Rory. "Not many people use words like 'ruminate' and 'perused.' Do you know what they mean or are you just trying to show off?"

Rory whirled around and Jane ran into her. She toppled to the left, but Rory gripped her waist. "I have a PhD in English Literature so words are my forte. Nina and I loved going to Shakespearean plays together. That was our connection." She narrowed her eyes. "So is your lack of adroitness a genetic flaw or can it be solely attributed to your idiotic choice of footwear? Jimmy Choos at a crime scene. Really?"

Jane leaned into her firm embrace. "A woman who knows fashion and is a master of words. You wouldn't happen to be a wine connoisseur as well? That would be a relationship trifecta in my book."

Rory shook her head. "Can't help you there, sorry. I'm a Franzia-in-a-box kinda girl."

"Ew," Jane scowled and stepped back. "That's a deal breaker."

Rory chuckled and led them to a clubhouse situated in the middle of a grassy area. She pulled out a key ring and opened the front door. "All the tenants use this space, but Nina had started a counseling service on Thursday nights, so the board of directors, of which I am one, gave her a little office."

They passed through the kitchen area, and Rory used a second key to open a corner door. In another life Ari imagined it had been a large storage closet, judging by the laundry sink and commercial-grade shelves. A worn floral loveseat and a matching chair faced a battered metal desk. Nina had left out several files and an open desk calendar.

Jane picked up a picture of Sam and Nina while Ari studied the calendar. Nina seemed to be available on Tuesday and Thursday nights. Most of the names were repeated several times and a few were couples.

"What kind of problems did she handle?" Ari asked.

"Most anything that kept people up at night. One tenant lost her husband a few months ago, another hasn't been able to adjust to a new job and still another has paranoia. The usual stuff."

Ari looked around at the makeshift office. "How did this happen? Is it legal for her to do this?"

Rory slid onto the couch with a subtle familiarity. "As a social worker, she's a licensed counselor in the state of California. She chose to work with children, but she was considering a job offer with a prestigious family practice group. They saw what we saw—an amazing listener and a very open person." She made a sweeping gesture. "How did this come to pass? She got tired of meeting in the laundry room," she laughed.

"What do you mean?" Jane asked.

"Nina had a very tight schedule in her life and she *always* did her laundry on Sunday morning. She said it was her version of church. She'd take a book with her, but inevitably someone would start chatting about their problems. She'd never get a single page read and eventually everyone knew her laundry time so they showed up if they needed help. We joked that her appointment times followed the wash and dry cycles. When the buzzer went off, your time was up. While she enjoyed helping people, she was very uncomfortable talking about confidential matters next to the dryers. That's when I suggested we let her have a spot for therapy sessions. She was all for it. Counseling isn't covered under a lot of insurance plans if it's covered at all. She was happy to do it if everyone agreed to let her have her laundry time in peace."

"Who's B. Cahill? That name is listed several times."

"That's Bonnie. She lives a few doors down from me. She and her husband are having problems," she said hesitantly.

Jane raised an eyebrow. "And how would you know this?"

Rory shot her a glance. "I'm observant. I can see through a person's facade."

"Oh, good word," Jane acknowledged mockingly.

"Ladies," Ari said, "let's stay focused on Nina. Bonnie Cahill's name is mentioned twice on every page of this calendar for the last three months. Whatever she was talking to Nina about must have been pretty heavy." She looked at Rory. "What about this job offer? Do you think Nina was going to take it?"

She shrugged. "I'm not sure. She'd made a few comments that suggested the pay was going to be a lot more than she made now, but I know money wasn't the most important thing to her."

"Do you think her journals are here?"

"I think it's highly likely. We're the only people with keys, and the police wouldn't have any reason to suspect this place exists. When they came by to interview me, I didn't tell them. I doubt anyone else did either. Who wants to admit they're seeing a therapist?"

"Were you seeing Nina?" Jane asked.

"That's irrelevant and none of your business. I was merely making a point."

"A sharp one," she murmured and received another caustic glare from Rory.

A quick check of the desk drawers revealed office supplies and snacks, except for the bottom right one, which was locked. She pulled at the handle several times but it wouldn't budge. "Do you have a key?"

Rory shook her head. "I never knew it was locked. The desk was donated by a neighbor who was closing his business. She probably got the desk key from him."

"So it's on her key ring with the cops," Jane concluded. "Fortunately I think I can handle this." She opened her purse and pulled out a nail file. "This has so many uses."

"So is burglar your day job?" Rory cracked.

"Only a talent, one of many," she replied seductively.

Rory turned red as Jane popped the lock. They found a single journal and a small manila envelope buried at the bottom. Inside was a key. Jane held it up and showed it to Rory. "Have you ever seen this before?"

"No, I don't imagine it fits anything around here."

"She just started a new journal," Ari said.

She flipped through the book which was completely blank except for the first page. The entry was dated a few days before she died.

"What does it say?" Jane asked, looking over her shoulder.

Ari closed it quickly, cognizant of Rory's piercing stare. "Nothing, really. Just about one of her kids."

"Then maybe the key unlocks the place where the other journals are hidden."

"Maybe," Ari said, holding it up, "but we need to go get ready for our dinner plans." She shut the desk drawer and said to Rory, "Thanks so much for your help."

"Sure."

"What kind of name is *Rory?*" Jane asked.

"It's short for Aurora, you know, the princess in *Sleeping Beauty?* When I was born my mama thought I was a little princess." Jane snorted, and she grinned broadly. "You think that's funny, do you? I don't strike you as the princess type?"

"Not really," Jane said. "I think that title suits me better."

"Jane, we need to go," Ari said impatiently.

Rory's gaze traveled the length of Jane's body. "I can think of several titles for you, sweetie, but princess isn't one of them. I'd say you're a termagant, a harridan, or a virago."

She frowned. She was quite competitive about vocabulary and was nearly unbeatable at Words with Friends.

Rory chuckled. "Look them up, sweetie."

They got into the car, and Jane quickly tapped on her iPhone. "I can't believe her!"

"Forget that for a second, Jane. You need to listen to this entry Nina made four days before she was killed."

"Is that why you wanted out of there so fast?"

She nodded and read from the page. "'The secret will be revealed—DANGER. Poor Benedick! Poor Horatio! And poor Orlando—a pawn?'"

"What the hell? Who are these people? Is she talking about Orlando Bloom?"

"I don't think so. Orlando, Benedick and Horatio were Shakespearean characters, but I think they were from different plays. I'm guessing Nina is using fictitious names to ensure confidentiality."

"It would make sense since she got burned in the past. Anyone finding a journal entry like that wouldn't have any idea what she's talking about. *I* don't have any idea what she's talking about." She tapped on her phone and gasped. "Well, she's a termagant, too!" When Ari looked at her quizzically, she added, "That bitch called me a bitch—using *better* vocabulary!"

CHAPTER SIX

The last hundred yards was the toughest. Brian made it look easy, adeptly positioning his feet on each of the sandstones, the well-developed muscles in his calves bulging. Molly stayed close behind, determined to make it to the top of Summit Trail, the most strenuous hike Camelback Mountain had to offer. He'd started her on the simple climb to Bobby's Rock, but she had challenged his choice, asserting she was in great shape. He laughed and then proved her wrong.

The next hike had been up Cholla Trail. It humbled her too, and she immediately realized she was an overweight, out-of-shape alcoholic. Every once in a while she also felt a twinge of pain in her left thigh, the place where she'd been shot nine months before. Yet, she'd complied with his personal training regimen, and in only six weeks she'd exchanged twenty pounds of gut flab for five pounds of toned muscles. She'd never felt better, thanks to his willingness to serve as her personal trainer.

She took a deep breath and pressed forward until they hit the summit and gazed at the valley below. She chugged from her water bottle and ignored her screaming legs.

"Not bad," Brian said, checking his watch. "Fifty minutes. You're getting better."

"How long should it take?"

"Our goal is thirty," he said with a grin.

"Slave driver."

Two women passed by and stared. They were serious hikers in boots, waterproof shorts and polyester shirts that offered sun protection. When Molly and Brian met their gaze, they smiled.

"They're flirting with you," he said.

She laughed and watched their backsides. "No, I'm certain they were checking out my brother's astounding physique."

"How do you know they weren't your type? I've seen the way women look at you lately."

She soaked up the compliment and felt her cheeks turn red. It was hard to imagine anyone staring at her so blatantly, although she knew Brian endured the flirtations and overt come-ons from dozens of women. He was beefcake with long blond hair and earrings. He'd done some modeling in his teens and hated everything but the money. He preferred to work with his hands, which was why he enjoyed plumbing and would inherit the family business, but he only had eyes for Lynne, his long-time girlfriend.

The women glanced again but Brian didn't notice. The extra attention was new to her, although Ari had maintained throughout their relationship that women regularly stared at her. She'd scoffed and assumed that Ari was trying to bolster her self-confidence, which was nonexistent. At least that's what her new therapist was helping her understand. She had no belief in herself except in her job, and now that was gone.

She sucked back a sob, something she'd frequently done during the last nine months. The women chatted and absorbed the view, but one caught her eye and smiled. She smiled back. She liked it. As her body morphed into a physique that matched her brother's, more women flirted with her at the gym, in the grocery store and now on the hiking trail. It was the fuel she needed even though she wasn't ready to date.

She was still getting over Ari, but every time a woman looked at her or spoke in a voice filled with laughter, she moved another step away from her pain and inched closer to a new life. She equated it to the childhood game of Chutes and Ladders. There were going to be gains and losses—such as any time she thought of Ari. She hated her and had told her as much in an email, but Ari still seemed to have a stranglehold on her heart. When she was reminded of her, she'd roll the hostility that evoked into a solid sphere as strong as a ball bearing and rechannel it into a mile run or an hour at the gym.

Lost in the past, she didn't notice one of the women had sidled up next to her until she cleared her throat.

"Oh, sorry," Molly said. Brian had wandered to another spot and she was alone with the cute stranger. "I'm in my own little world today."

"I'd offer you a penny for your thoughts, but that's so lame, something my grandmother would say."

The sun reflected off her white teeth, and Molly resisted the urge to shield her eyes. Now that they were only a few feet apart she guessed the other woman was probably in her early twenties. Molly's self-confidence took another step forward. Since she was thirty-seven, she must look good if a youngster found her attractive.

"Just taking in the view," she said. "I've only been up here a few times. I'm Molly."

"I'm Willow. It's nice to meet you, Molly."

Willow's hiking partner motioned that she wanted to head back down and Willow turned to go. "Maybe I'll see you up here again."

She nodded. "Sure."

"Maybe we could get a smoothie or something afterward."

"Okay," she said as Willow disappeared down trail. "Bye."

She glanced at Brian who was laughing and watching. "What?"

"A date," he said playfully.

"No," she disagreed. "It would just be a smoothie."

"You think you're ready for that?" he asked seriously. She scowled and started back down. "I mean, it's only been a few months since you've been home," he said, following behind. "Have you talked with Ari?"

She whirled around with a fierce expression. "I never want to see her again. I hate her. Biz can have her."

He stepped back and held up his hands as some hikers passed them. "Okay, sis. I got it."

"Good," she said and hustled down the trail.

They returned to the street in half the time it took to ascend the mountain. She gazed up and felt a sense of accomplishment.

"Thirty minutes," she whispered. "I can do that."

* * *

She found Andre seated poolside with some of her neighbors. He looked completely out of place in a three-piece suit next to two lily-white octogenarians in Hawaiian shirts and Bermuda shorts.

Dorothy Lyons, her favorite neighbor, waved. "Hi, Molly! Look who's here!"

Her companion, another tenant named Howard Birnbaum, glanced up from his copy of the *Arizona Republic*. "Why are you shoutin'? She's not blind. She can see him clear as day, at least for now. Blindness won't come for another forty years if she's lucky."

"Shut up, you old coot. I was being friendly and welcoming."

"What's to welcome? She lives here."

"Go back to reading the obituaries. Maybe you'll get some good ideas for yours. Then we'll know what to write."

He snorted and returned to his paper.

"Hey, Mol," Andre said, pulling her into a hug. When she tried to let go, he held her tighter. "I miss you so much. The department's just not the same without you."

She swallowed another sob and said, "Let's go inside." She turned to Dorothy and Howard. "Thanks for keeping him company."

Dorothy waved her off. "No problem, sweetie, and when you get a chance can you check out my disposal? It's making that funny whirring noise again."

Molly looked at her skeptically. "You weren't trying to stick corncobs down there again, were you?"

"Oh, no, I learned my lesson. What a mess that was! I've only used it for table scraps, just like you told me." She turned to Andre and said, "This is the first time in my life I've ever had a garbage disposal, not counting any of my ex-husbands. I had no idea there were rules."

"They're very handy," he replied. "It was nice seeing you again."

"Same here, handsome, and if that girlfriend of yours keeps giving you grief, let me talk to her."

They walked to her apartment and he asked, "What was that about the disposal?"

"I'm the property manager for now. It helps pay the bills."

She was grateful there wasn't laundry hanging from her piano. Since she'd left Ari, she'd allowed herself to slip back into habits Ari would never tolerate.

"Do you want some juice or water?"

He shook his head and stuffed his hands in his pockets. She knew he was nervous. He'd only been to her place twice. They had been work colleagues and rarely associated outside of the department. A twinge of jealousy stepped between them for a moment as she saw the difference. He was still a cop, not a great cop but a good one, but still, a *cop*. She was nobody except someone who fixed disposals and installed faucets.

"I came by because Jack thought you might have remembered something else that might help us catch Lola, a detail, anything."

She leaned against the counter. "No, I told him everything I could remember. Are they pressuring you guys to wrap up the task force?"

"Yeah. There's a new female chief coming in and she wants it done. If we don't have any leads she'll shut it down and Vince Carnotti will slip away again. Think, Mol. There's gotta be a clue, something she wore or a comment she let slip. People aren't that careful."

She cradled her chin in her palm and remembered Lola, the sexy blonde whose charms she'd finally succumbed to after Ari betrayed her. Lola had come on to her a few times when she'd snuck into Hideaway for a drink to escape Ari's suffocating love. She pictured each meeting separately—at the bar, in the back room and finally in the manager's office.

"What about her clothes?" he offered. "Talk it through with me."

"She typically wore a black dress with different accessories, but there's nothing unusual about that. Most women only have one or two outfits for bar-hopping."

"Jewelry, shoes?"

She shook her head. "Nope."

"What about her purse? Did you ever see inside or did she ever answer her cell phone?"

She hadn't thought about that. Once when they were sitting at the bar her phone had rung. Molly was half drunk and too focused on her own troubles to pay attention. She'd seen the display, though, and there had been something odd about it.

What was it? She closed her eyes and focused on the bag. Suddenly it came to her. "She got a call while we were at the bar...from a pay phone." She closed her eyes again and tried to see the little silver flip-phone. The blue digital numbers appeared on the screen...

"Mol, you couldn't have known it was a pay phone unless you *knew* the number."

She looked up and cracked a grin. "Good work, detective. That's right. I knew the number."

"There aren't a lot of pay phones left in Phoenix. Where do you go that has one?"

She sighed as the pieces came together. "Hideaway itself. That's why I knew it. Whoever was calling was probably watching us. Maybe she or he was coaching Lola, but I'm guessing it was a woman. Men stick out whenever they're there."

He sighed heavily. "Damn it. Most likely she has an accomplice. We're not looking for just one woman. We're looking for *two*."

CHAPTER SEVEN

How people spent their Sundays said a lot about their priorities. Biz remembered many stakeouts where the mark never got out of bed before noon, and she'd had trouble tailing others who were obsessed with getting twenty errands done before the weekend was officially over. So she had been somewhat impressed when Wanda strolled into Uptown Fitness at five o'clock for her kickboxing class. Anyone who made exercise a priority on the day of rest must have a few good qualities.

She checked her watch and extended the old Subaru's bucket seat. For stakeouts she'd acquired an old Impreza that few people noticed. Her customary Mustang would've stood out immediately, as well as her sleek Harley. She had an hour to kill before the gym closed and Wanda left.

She had met her in that same class and recognized her strong focus coupled with flimsy morals—exactly the kind of person who would do anything for the right price. She needed to learn more about Wanda's daily routines before she decided how to handle the situation. They'd always met in the locker room or the parking lot, so what Biz knew of the woman's life was limited to a few offhanded comments she'd made about her girlfriends and her love of cocaine. Biz found it supremely ironic that someone so committed to physical health would throw it away on drugs.

She scrolled through the photos on her phone and found one of her with Ari on the day she moved into her new house. They were standing at the front door, and while she wore a gigantic smile, Ari's expression was tentative and unsure. Biz constantly viewed the photo to remind herself of Ari's fragility. While she desperately wanted to fold her in her arms and carry her off to bed—a fantasy that occurred frequently in her dreams—Ari wasn't ready. Maybe solving the murder in Laguna would bring them a step closer to the fantasy. Until then there was always video chatting.

She pulled up Ari's contact and waited for her beautiful face to appear on the screen.

"Hey," Ari said in a loud voice.

They were apparently driving with Jane singing "My Sharona" in the background. Ari gave Jane a look and reached over from the passenger seat to silence the soundtrack.

"How's it going? Have you learned anything so far?"

"Quite a bit actually. We found Nina's journal and this." She shuffled through a bag and held up a key. "What do you think this fits?"

Biz studied it carefully, noting the teeth and size. "It's not a safety deposit box key and it's not small enough to fit a padlock. My best guess would be a locker."

"That's what I was thinking. The only question is where?"

"I'd start with the area around her house. People like security, but they don't like inconvenience if they need the items frequently. Look for a storage facility or if there's a bus depot in the vicinity, anything like that."

Ari nodded. "Good idea."

"So what are you ladies doing for the rest of the night?"

"Well, Sam's parents invited us to dinner at this swanky restaurant so we're heading back to the hotel to get ready."

Biz heard the trepidation in her voice. "You don't want to go?"

"No, I'm fine with going, but I didn't bring anything appropriate to wear."

"I did," Jane said from the driver's seat.

Biz laughed. "I assume she's prepared for all occasions."

Ari rolled her eyes. "Of course. She spent an extra two hundred dollars in baggage fees. In the event we're forced to attend a funeral, African safari or royal coronation, Jane will be ready."

"Hey," Jane chimed in, "you never know what could happen."

"So true," Ari agreed. "So we'll see you on Tuesday? Will you be done with your business by then?"

She glanced at the gym's front door. "Absolutely. Um, have fun with your shower...I mean *dinner*." She saw Ari squirm and she grinned. "Just a little flirting, Ari. I'm allowed to do that, right?"

"You're at the line," she said before she hung up.

She closed her eyes and pictured the contour of Ari's body outlined in the shower steam, rivulets cascading across her smooth skin toward her most delicious parts. She opened her eyes and groaned. She would give *anything* to join her in that shower, but first things first. She needed to delete Wanda from her life. The gym closed in another ten minutes and then she'd follow her home. Once she saw her neighborhood, she'd know what she needed to do. She tapped the steering wheel while she listed the goons who might be willing to help her if the price were right.

Her gaze focused on the exit door, she almost didn't notice the well-dressed man hurrying through the entrance—Andre Williams, Molly Nelson's former partner.

CHAPTER EIGHT

Ari knew Jane wouldn't tolerate a Budget Inn since the word budget wasn't in her vocabulary, but she had not expected a suite at the Montage, one of Laguna's finest resorts, which sat on a bluff overlooking the Pacific Ocean.

"I'm not particularly thrilled with our accommodations," Jane said as they unpacked, "but they will have to do."

"Are you crazy?" she asked.

The three-room suite was larger than Ari's old condo and could accommodate a family of five comfortably. She eyed the Jacuzzi tub longingly. The amenities were top shelf. She wondered if Jane would notice the extra charge on her credit card if one of the plush robes went missing.

Jane went to the balcony and stared at the hills in front of her. "I'd hoped for an ocean view, but I imagine it's impossible to get one of those rooms at the last minute."

"I think we'll live," Ari said. "Now, I hope you have a decent outfit I can wear."

She studied her critically. "Well, given the difference in our heights, the skirt is going to be short and sexy."

That proved an understatement. As they drove to the Watermarc Restaurant, Ari constantly crossed and uncrossed her legs, cognizant that the black leather skirt barely covered her mid-thigh region. Normally she was okay with just-above-the-knee. In fact, Molly had loved it when she wore her purple miniskirt, but she knew when she sat down her long legs would be almost completely uncovered.

"We must look fabulous," Jane said as she handed her keys to the valet, who leered at both of them.

They arrived before Sam and his parents and were seated at the premier table. Diners at the Watermarc were afforded stunning views of the high-tide waves surging onto the beach in the blue-black moonlight. She imagined the Garritsons' wealth and power guaranteed them the best table wherever they went. A middle-aged man continued to stare at them over his menu, but no one else seemed to care.

"See?" Jane said. "It's California. Everyone is expected to be beautiful. Here we're just normal."

Ari shook her head. She'd never thought of herself as beautiful. Her *mother* had been beautiful.

Before they could order drinks, the maitre d' approached with Sam, his parents and a man who looked almost exactly like Sam.

"You didn't tell me he had a twin," she whispered to Jane.

"I didn't know."

"Jane and Ari, I'd like you to meet my parents, Steve and Georgie, and my brother, Evan."

They finished the customary introductions and a debate ensued over the seating arrangement. Judging from the disconcerted expression on Georgie's face, Ari realized she and Jane had been given the best seats at the round table, the two facing the ocean. While Jane and Sam made small talk, Ari watched Evan and Steve cater to Georgie.

"Mom, why don't you sit here?" Evan asked. He pulled out a chair at the place Ari guessed was the second-best location, the side facing the dining room.

"All right," Georgie said with an accommodating smile. "Thank you, son." She adjusted the silk scarf draped around her neck and politely scratched her nose with a finely manicured finger. She wore multiple bracelets on each wrist and a variety of colored stone rings on her fingers. The gray-blond hair that had been scooped up by the red bandanna earlier now formed a halo around her well-maintained face. Her shimmering cocktail dress, a reward for what Ari imagined was a vicious exercise regimen or a lot of plastic surgery, clung to her curves.

Steve sat next to her, leaving the cheap seats, the ones facing the restaurant with no ocean view, for Sam and Evan. They were as identical as twins could be, she thought. Both possessed strong features and dark brown eyes. Ari wondered if she would be able to tell them apart if they were dressed alike.

She glanced at Steve. Brown eyes seemed to be his only contribution to their gene pool. He was short and portly with a receding hairline, and his doughy facial features conveyed kindness, not charm, which probably played well to his cynical constituents.

"You're going to love the food here," Sam said.

"What do you recommend?" Jane asked everyone.

"I always enjoy the veal," he replied.

"But the tri-tip is better," Evan disagreed.

"No, no," Steve interjected. "We all know the salmon is the best."

All three engaged in a lighthearted sparring match until Georgie looked up from her menu and said, "Boys, boys." She glanced at Jane and Ari. "Do you feel sorry for me yet?

One woman surrounded by all this testosterone for over three decades."

"You love it and you know it," Evan said. "You're the center of attention."

Georgie harrumphed. "If that's the case, then where's my martini?"

Steve motioned for the waiter, who took the drink orders and departed. Once everyone had set aside their menus, Steve faced Jane and Ari. "Ladies, I appreciate your help with our little problem. Sam has told me one of you is a licensed investigator?"

"Actually that's our friend," Ari clarified for the second time that day. "She's arriving on Tuesday. Jane and I are getting a head start doing some of the interviewing and laying the foundation."

"Ari's being modest," Jane said. "She's solved several cases herself even though she isn't a PI."

"Aren't you a realtor?" Sam asked.

"I am."

"But she used to be a police officer," Jane inserted, "until she became a born-again capitalist."

Everyone laughed and Georgie asked, "So how is it you solve murders?"

Ari didn't have an easy answer. "It tends to happen by accident. I'm just in the right or wrong place, depending how you look at it."

"All we ask is that you're discreet," Steve said seriously after the drinks arrived and the dinner order was placed. "So how can we help you?"

Ari pulled a small notebook and pen from her purse. "I hope you don't mind if I take notes, but I'll need to share this with the PI."

"Of course," Georgie said. "We'll help however we can. What's happened to Sam is such an injustice. Nina was a wonderful girl, but she was incredibly clingy. She couldn't understand when it was over."

Ari's gaze traveled to Sam, who'd grown tense, but he didn't disagree with her. She began to wonder about the relationship between mother and son.

"First, since I can't interview the police detectives assigned to the case, I'll need to ask you some review questions. I know Sam was home alone when Nina was killed, but where were the rest of you?"

"I was at a school music concert," Evan offered. "I'm the assistant principal where Nina worked."

"I was at my boutique at the John Wayne Airport, closing up," Georgie said.

Steve motioned for another drink and said, "And I was at a charity function for the fire department."

"And that's why they came after me," Sam summarized. "I have no alibi."

"Can any of you think of a reason why someone would want to harm Nina?" Jane asked.

"I'm certain it had something to do with her occupation," Georgie said. "She had some rather unseemly dealings with parents and students."

"Do you remember any specific examples?"

Steve pointed his fork at Evan. "What about that Michaela girl? She mentioned her a few times. Wasn't there a problem with the mother's boyfriend?"

Evan cleared his throat, and Ari sensed he was hesitant to discuss students with his family. "Well, Nina suspected there may have been some abuse by the mother's boyfriend—"

"That guy is nuts," Sam added.

"Sam, please," Evan said. "We're still talking about a family at my school."

Ari grabbed her pen. "What's the little girl's name?"

"Michaela Glass," Evan answered. "She was one of Nina's favorite kids. She's incredibly bright and optimistic, despite having a mother with a drug problem who chose an allegedly abusive boyfriend. Their names are Eden Glass and Bobby Arco," he added so she could write them down.

"So Bobby Arco didn't like Nina interfering?"

"He threatened Nina at one point," Sam said. "Told her to stay out of his business or she'd regret it."

"When did that happen?"

"About two weeks ago," Evan said.

"Was there anything else?"

Evan shrugged. "It's hard to say. They were constantly showing up at the school, and Nina had many conferences with Michaela. I imagine there was a lot Nina kept to herself."

Ari turned to Sam. "Did Nina ever talk about her journals?"

"Sure," Sam said with a nod. "She wrote in her journal constantly."

"You never told us that," Georgie interjected.

"It's not important. It was private."

Ari glanced up. "Do you know where she kept her recent journal or her old journals?"

He shook his head. "No, we didn't talk about it. I knew they were very private, so I didn't press."

The meals arrived and after sending her tri-tip back three times, Georgie was finally satisfied. Ari and Jane had both ordered the Catch of the Day, a roasted bass that was absolutely delicious. Ari couldn't imagine how Georgie's dinner could have been so sub-par that it needed to return to the kitchen repeatedly, but she noticed the men catered to her every whim, asking her continuously if she was all right or enjoying the meal. Ari sensed they weren't particularly worried about Sam's fate, and she imagined they'd hired an excellent attorney in case Sam was charged with the murder.

"Tell us about your boutique, Georgie," Jane asked. "You have several locations, don't you?"

She smiled as the conversation returned to her. "Yes, my store Bare Essentials is located in nearly every airport in California. We sell travel products for those who forgot their toothbrush or who want something unique like a neck pillow made from feathers."

"You do your own art?" Ari asked.

"Yes, it's a passion. Have you seen those painted wine and martini glasses?"

"Oh, yes," Ari said, though she was not sure she ever had. "They make great gifts."

"They certainly do," Georgie agreed. "You girls will need to stop by the store before you leave. I'll give you a special discount."

"That would be so nice," Jane said in her fake voice.

Ari could tell she didn't like Georgie, so she wasn't surprised when she turned and asked Evan, "Did you always want to be an educator or have you thought about a career in politics too?"

He laughed. "No, I think we've got enough politicians in the family. I always knew I wanted to be a teacher." He threw a glance at Sam. "And if it weren't for me, Sam and Nina never would've met."

"You introduced them?" Ari asked.

The men exchanged a grin, and Georgie said, "Yes, and I may never forgive my number two son," she joked, but her tone was laced with acid. "While I'm distraught over what happened, and I admire Sam for volunteering to plan Nina's funeral, I knew she wasn't right for him."

"Don't go there, Mother," Sam said sharply.

"Honey, I wasn't insinuating anything. I know you're still getting over Nina—"

"I was *never* over Nina, Mom. That's the part you couldn't understand. It's my duty to plan her service."

He threw his napkin on the table and stormed out of the restaurant. Evan and Steve stared at their plates while Georgie toyed with her olive. "Have you ladies heard about Steve's impending appointment?" she asked as if nothing had happened. "The governor is going to ask him to lead a special task force to investigate potential changes to the child abuse laws in California."

Ari chose her words carefully. "Are they insufficient?"

He cleared his throat before he spoke. "Well, they're rather antiquated. The governor is concerned that loopholes exist which allow many criminals to escape prosecution."

"And next year is an election year," Evan added. "The appointment could lead to something *bigger*."

"That's hardly the point, son," Steve said. "This would be a valuable examination at any time."

Evan said nothing but continued to look cynical.

"If I may ask, what did Nina think of the task force?"

"I think you just did, dear," Georgie said.

The two men ignored her snide retort, and Evan looked at his father. Neither commented, and Ari sensed it was a point of contention between them and Nina, a social worker who likely had clear opinions about child abuse laws, especially if domestic violence victims were criminalized. *Biz will hate this guy*, she thought.

"Let's just say," Steve said, "Nina didn't share my vision about reform. I'm sure she was a fine social worker, but her perspective was limited by her own experience in her own school."

"That's my school too, Dad," Evan added. "Nina and I were on the same page."

"About everything," Georgie snorted into her drink.

Ari sensed she was drunk and becoming less inhibited with her comments.

"Of course, the governor's interests are far more utilitarian," Steve said, ignoring his wife. "I'm just honored that he's considering me."

"We've earned it, honey," Georgie added, raising her drink. "After all that money I've contributed."

Steve seemed to bristle at his wife's comment. He dabbed his lips with his napkin and stared at his plate.

Attempting to lighten the mood, Evan asked, "Are you ladies interested in dessert or is that against your fitness regimen?"

Jane and Ari exchanged a glance, and each reached for her purse simultaneously. "We should get back," Ari said. "Traveling days are tiring."

"I couldn't agree more," Steve said.

The two men rose and shook their hands while Georgie's farewell was a dismissive nod with only a thin smile.

Once they were inside the rental car, Jane exclaimed, "Reality TV was never that good! What a bunch of suspects!"

Ari frowned, not sure she saw any of them as capable of murder. "I'd like to know more about Eden Glass and Bobby Arco."

"They're strong possibilities," Jane conceded, "but haven't you always said most murders are committed for personal reasons?"

"Yes, but since Nina was a social worker, she falls into a gray area. Her work was very personal and dealt with people's private lives. If she threatened to expose Bobby Arco as a child abuser, the family would be destroyed. People will do anything to protect their families."

"That makes sense," Jane agreed.

"It makes the boyfriend *and* the mother more likely suspects than any of the Garritsons," Ari continued. "Why would any of them want to kill Nina? I'm not sure disapproving of her marriage to Sam is enough of a reason, and their alibis seem solid."

They arrived back at the resort. Ari was dreaming of a hot bath and her plush robe when Jane said, "I arranged a little surprise for us." She wore a lascivious grin that scared Ari.

"It's not a surprise if you know about it," Ari said, "and I'm not up for that."

"It's not *that*." She checked her watch as a knock on the door sounded. "Right on time."

Ari dropped onto the bed, imagining Jane had invited total strangers over for an impromptu party. She couldn't fathom three more hours of small talk even it if was in the company of beautiful women—the standard guests at any of Jane's get-togethers. So she was slightly relieved when only *two* beautiful and buxom women in skimpy bikinis followed her into the suite carrying massage tables.

"Ari, this is Sage and Sunday, not their real names of course. I thought we, meaning more specifically *you*, could use some relaxation."

They were practically mirror images. Both wore their long bleach-blond-hair swept to the side and their matching pink bikinis revealed skin the color of copper. They clearly had read and revered the instruction manual for becoming a California girl.

She took a deep breath and opened the balcony's sliding glass door. "May I see you, please?" Jane bowed her head and followed her out.

"If you think—"

"Honey, they're real masseuses. I know you'd never agree to a professional, and you're not ready anyway."

They glanced into the room where both women were busily setting up their tables and pots of oil.

"C'mon, it'll be fun," Jane said, shedding her shoes and dress on the balcony and escorting Ari back inside.

Since all eyes were on her, she stripped and climbed on the table. It was luxurious. The knotted muscles in her back felt like stretched rubber bands about to break. She overheard Jane and Sage chatting continuously, but she preferred to listen to the quiet mood music from Sunday's boom box. She couldn't move when it was over.

"Just lie still for a few minutes," Sunday whispered. "Enjoy the after."

Only then in the absence of her touch did Ari's thoughts drift to Molly and the missing link in her life. She realized Sunday had massaged her broken heart as well as her body.

They exchanged a friendly hug as she left and Ari expressed her thanks. Jane's goodbye was completely R-rated. When she cupped Sage's breast, Sage scolded her.

"No, no. I don't mix business with pleasure. I really am a licensed masseuse, and I want to keep it that way."

"Sorry," she said, stepping back. "I was getting some signals."

Sage smiled. "Oh, there were signals. It's just that if you want some action, it'll have to be off the clock," she said, flashing a boob before she walked out.

CHAPTER NINE

Biz slammed her cup on the granite counter, sloshing coffee over its side. Time was running out, and she needed to end this herself. She couldn't wait for anyone else to do the dirty work. That was the most difficult part to accept since she couldn't imagine harming a sister. Her entire business was spent helping abused women. Maybe if she paid Wanda once more she'd really disappear.

"Not likely," she whispered to the beautiful kitchen.

She immediately grabbed a dishcloth, unable to leave a speck of mess. She'd paid handsomely for the condo, the remodel she'd commissioned before she moved in and the state-of-the-art furnishings she couldn't live without. She'd earned it, risking her freedom by working for Vince Carnotti. She had thought her slate was as clean as the new bamboo floors, but now she'd have to get her hands dirty again.

There was no way to thoroughly cleanse her soul. She'd harmed others and contributed to their delinquency, fed their addictions and ruined lives by stealing their possessions—in the case of Molly Nelson, she'd destroyed a good cop forever—but she believed that redemption was a decision. She could reclaim goodness with Ari, who would help her recover a part of the soul she'd lost or rather given away to Carnotti. She needed to get to Laguna as soon as possible.

Only Wanda stood in the way.

Her thoughts drifted back to the previous night. Andre Williams had left ninety seconds after he'd entered the gym. She'd timed him. He hadn't found Wanda, probably because Jordan, the front desk clerk, wouldn't recognize her as Lola. Not only did the description that the Hideaway patrons and employees had provided to the police fit half of the lesbian gym regulars, but no one at the gym had ever seen Wanda tarted up. Biz doubted they could picture it. Wanda the kick-boxing gym rat was a short, natural spiky-blond butch. It had taken some serious cash to get her to agree to transform into a lipstick lesbian wearing heels, colored contacts, a flowing blond wig, and thick makeup.

Andre had left with nothing, but Jack Adams wouldn't be satisfied. He would hold whatever clue had led them to the gym tightly in his hand and squeeze it until it produced results for the investigation. Biz would need to be faster than he was.

She studied the surveillance photos of Wanda's apartment and the nearby streets that she'd taken with her phone. She'd followed her from the gym to a liquor store where Wanda purchased two bottles of vodka before zipping into the parking lot of a large apartment complex just five blocks past the store.

It had been difficult to tail her after she'd entered the maze of identical, nondescript stucco buildings, but she'd kept her distance until Wanda finally climbed up four flights of stairs and ducked into a corner unit. She'd surveyed the area and deduced it was perfect for a stakeout. Wanda's building was isolated, away from the common areas such as the pool, laundry and parking lot. Across from her balcony at the edge of the property stood a workman's shed that Biz imagined housed all of the gardening and lawn maintenance equipment.

She'd stayed in the shadows of the shed, watching Wanda through the open blinds of her patio door. She'd thrown off her clothes and headed down a hallway, and when she'd emerged onto the balcony with wet hair and wearing a denim shirt and cargo shorts, Biz guessed she'd showered after her workout.

She watched as Wanda leaned over the balcony, a highball glass in hand, sipping the vodka she'd purchased. When the glass was drained, she set it on the thin railing and glanced toward her neighbor's patio. Apparently deciding she was alone, she'd pulled a joint and a lighter from her pocket. After a long toke, she glanced at her phone and scrolled through her messages. When she cursed and stormed back into the apartment, Biz wondered if she was upset because she hadn't received a message from Biz, agreeing to her blackmail terms.

Biz had surveyed the rest of the complex. A few scantily clad women offered long glances when she passed and she cracked a smile, pleased that she still attracted attention. She followed a couple into the pool area and determined the place was a meat market. Despite the darkness and the cool November weather, the couple wasted no time diving into the deep end and groping each other.

A quick surveillance of the parking area and entrances indicated management wanted enough security features to lure single women into signing a lease, features such as heavy-duty lights, but not enough to discourage an influx of visitors for the ongoing parties. Visitors were potential tenants. Security was lax by Biz's standards, and she had moved effortlessly throughout the complex. As she'd driven away, she had decided it was the perfect place to go unnoticed and the perfect place for Wanda to die.

The microwave's beeping interrupted her planning. After gobbling down some instant oatmeal, she took her coffee out to her patio and gazed at South Mountain in the distance, awash in morning color. Wanda could have an accident, but what kind? She wanted to keep it simple. Complicated plans led to mistakes, and she counted her keen judgment as one of her best qualities. She'd never been to jail nor faced questioning by the police except in her role as a private investigator. No one had ever linked her to Vince Carnotti and when she thought about what he'd do if he learned Wanda was blackmailing her, she shivered. They would both wind up buried in the desert.

Yet apartment complexes could be dangerous places. Drunks drowned in the pools all the time, and people constantly tumbled down the cement stairs when they lost their footing. Bathrooms were the most dangerous rooms in the home, the most likely place to slip and break a neck, but that would require her to face Wanda.

She leaned against her balcony, cradling her coffee cup, remembering that Wanda had adopted a similar pose the night before, the highball and joint in hand.

As Biz patted the heavy crossbeam that ensured she remained firmly planted on her patio, it occurred to her that she'd never trusted the poorly constructed balconies of her previous apartments. She'd worried that the bolts holding the railings in place on each side would eventually wear down the crumbling plaster and the metal frame would rip away and send her careening over the edge. It was another one of those apartment hazards. A smile crept across her face and she patted the railing again.

CHAPTER TEN

Jack had forgotten how much he hated Monday morning briefings, but sitting through one run by David Ruskin, who'd been promoted to chief of detectives, was dreadful. At least Sol Gardener had kept the jerk on a short leash. His broad swagger today suggested he was reveling in his newfound power.

Ruskin finally introduced Chief Dylan Phillips by reviewing a résumé that was admittedly impressive. She'd spent a respectable few years as a beat cop before being promoted to detective, where she jumped from narcotics to homicide as she climbed the food chain. Jack glanced at her tense expression.

Listening to her biography was obviously making her uncomfortable.

Ruskin ran out of gas and everyone applauded politely until Dylan quickly held up her hand. "I won't take up much of your time since we all need to get back to work. And that's all I care about, doing a good job. I say it like it is and expect the same. If you're questioning that right now, I'd expect it. You don't know me at all. For all you know, I'm full of crap."

A chuckle surged through the mostly male squad and Jack found himself joining in.

"Captain Ruskin will be my go-to person, and I'd ask that you go through him to get to me."

Doubtful eyes darted around the room. If she noticed it, she didn't say anything. Ruskin nodded and puffed out his chest. Jack pictured Molly standing in his place and what it would have meant. Two women running the show. It would've been quite the sight.

He guessed Dylan wouldn't have an easy time of it. Although Phoenix was the sixth largest city in the nation, it was still full of good old boys and traditional attitudes about subjects such as women, guns and gays. He knew Molly had faced constant harassment but never reported it. The job was far more important than the gossip swirling around her.

Ruskin absently patted his potbelly as he spoke, a result of more time behind a desk than in the field. No one had told him Brylcreem went out thirty years before; Jack could see the grease amid his silver-streaked dark hair.

"Adams and Williams, we're reassigning you," he announced.

Jack and Andre exchanged glances, and Andre opened his mouth to object until Dylan stepped forward, her arms crossed, daring him to talk.

"We want a fresh pair of eyes on Escolido," Ruskin said, and Jack saw the corners of his mouth turn up. They were being handed a case that was cold and most likely unsolvable.

"Great," Andre whispered. "A career killer."

Jack knew Andre had dreams of becoming a captain. Having his name stamped on a no-go case like Escolido could flush his future away.

Andre held up a finger, "Uh, Chief?"

Ruskin finished the briefing and Dylan approached them. "My office."

They followed her with Ruskin lagging behind. When the door shut they gathered in a semicircle, which suggested they wouldn't be there long enough to take a chair. Jack liked that.

"First, Captain Ruskin, in the future please do not announce changes in briefing. I know we're new at working together, so it's forgiven this time."

Ruskin offered a single nod and his ears turned red.

"Williams and Adams, this shouldn't be a surprise. We're out of time on the Carnotti investigation."

Andre raised his hand. "But Chief, we just got another lead. There were *two* women involved and we know where one of them works out."

Dylan considered this for a second. "So have you followed up?"

"Only with the front clerk. I didn't get there until closing and she didn't recognize her, but—"

"That's the problem, Andre," Ruskin said.

"But with a little more time…"

"There is no more time," he repeated.

Jack turned to Dylan. "Chief, why can't we work both for a few more days? Let Andre work the lead and I'll take a look at Escolido."

"There's no point, Chief," Ruskin disagreed, and Jack knew he was being an ass just because he could.

"There is if it pans out," Jack said plainly.

Dylan was deep in thought and Jack decided he liked her. She wanted to do what was right even if she didn't know Ruskin was an idiot.

"Two days," she said firmly and strode behind her desk as a way of dismissing them all.

Andre practically ran out of the room, but Ruskin remained rooted to his spot. "Chief, may I have a word?" he asked.

Dylan picked up a folder and put on her reading glasses. "Not if it involves this matter," she said. "I expect you to assist Adams while Williams is out."

He clenched his fist and stormed past Jack, who was still gazing at her. She peered over her specs and asked, "Something else you needed?"

He shook his head and gripped the knob on his way out. "Open or shut?"

* * *

In the time it had taken for the conference with Chief Phillips, the previous detectives assigned to it had filled Jack's office with the two boxes that comprised the Escolido case. He pursed his lips and held his temper. He'd worked a few dozen cases like this one. For Andre's sake, he hoped they would get lucky.

He grabbed the case file from the first box and propped his legs up. He knew the basic facts from the many watercooler discussions and morning briefings, but if there was any hope of catching the perp, he'd need to review every note Detectives Salt and Lawrence had collected.

Margarita Escolido was a twenty-two-year-old college junior who was last seen walking to her car on July twenty-first after her one a.m. shift ended at the posh Scottsdale resort, Bliss. A waiter had left with her, but they'd gone their separate ways since her vehicle was parked in a different lot. She never made it. The next morning her body was found in a ravine that bordered the resort's parking area. She'd been raped and strangled, and the vigilant security team at Bliss had already had the car towed before the body was discovered by one of the maintenance workers at the resort. Any traces of evidence surrounding the car had been destroyed. The perp had been smart and worn a condom and forensics had found nothing helpful.

Jack threw his head back and sighed. "Terrific."

He counted to three and pulled himself out of his chair. He went to the bulletin board and prepared to remove all of the notes and pictures from the Carnotti investigation, but he couldn't do it. Not yet.

Instead he pulled the vertical blinds shut and taped the five-by-seven photo of Margarita Escolido to the center. She was a beautiful girl, half Latina and half Caucasian. She had a winning smile and kind brown eyes. She was ready for the world. He imagined Ari had held much the same look at twenty-two, but unfortunately, he could only imagine, because he'd kicked her out by then. His gaze drifted to the floor as shame overtook him. When he looked back up at Margarita's face, it was with determination. He'd find the answers.

A soft knock got his attention. Andre stood in the door, almost fearful to enter.

"What do you need, kid? Don't worry. I'm not going to pull you into this mess yet. You've got your forty-eight hours."

He slid into a chair and pulled out his notebook. "I just wanted to run some ideas by you."

"Go on."

"Okay. So the front desk clerk at Uptown Fitness, who seemed to know everyone by name, couldn't match Lola's description.

"She wore a disguise."

"Exactly," Andre agreed, "but I was hoping her general physique might trigger a match."

"It does," he snorted, "for most of the women who go to a gym." Andre looked thoroughly dejected at the thought of losing the case. "So what should you do now?"

He threw up his hands. "I need help. I need someone who could picture her in a wig or a different outfit and say, 'That's her.'" He paused before he said, "I need Molly."

CHAPTER ELEVEN

Ari smacked the phone receiver down with force, angry that the wake-up call had robbed her of a wonderful dream. She had been playing in the waves with Molly, who had carried her into the surf and threatened to drop her into the icy water. They'd been laughing so hard she couldn't catch her breath. Then the phone rang.

She cried softly into the pillow, grateful they were in a suite and Jane was in the other room. The dream had been so real. It had been such a long time since she'd heard Molly's laugh, and she couldn't remember the last time she'd seen her smile. The weeks leading to the break-up had been so stressful. Perhaps it had been inevitable.

She heard rustling in the living room and pulled herself away from the luxurious bed to investigate. She found Jane ordering room service.

"Did you like your massage?" she asked when she hung up.

"Very much. Thank you."

She didn't want to mention the massage to her heart that she'd experienced. It was too difficult to explain, and Jane would probably spring for a year of massages if she knew the depth of Ari's pain.

Jane glanced at the journal sitting on the table. "Why can't Biz get here sooner?"

"She didn't say. The text was very short, but I sensed whatever she's working on is frustrating her."

"I'll bet," Jane snorted. "I'm sure she'd much rather be here with you."

She ignored the comment, unwilling to speculate about a future with Biz. She was attractive and they had chemistry but she wasn't ready, not when she was still dreaming about and crying over Molly.

They ate breakfast and hurried out the door, arriving at Brayberry Elementary School shortly before eleven. Evan had arranged for them to speak with Lark Tuppin, Nina's best friend and closest colleague at the school, who was also Michaela's teacher.

"As a school administrator, I can't discuss anything without breaking confidentiality, but the teachers have more latitude," he'd said, implying that Lark would be willing to bend the rules if it meant solving a murder.

A helpful office assistant took them to her room, an explosion of posters, charts and brightly colored bulletin boards displaying student work. Ari found the pint-sized furniture adorable, but she couldn't remember ever having a classroom so dedicated to learning.

Lark Tuppin was as cute as her room. She bounced over from her computer and greeted them. Ari and Jane towered over her by at least a foot, and her baby face suggested she was a recent college graduate. She wore a smock with pockets over her bright red-print shirt and chinos. She was one of those people whose appearance fit her job: she *looked* like an elementary school teacher.

"Hi, I'm Lark. Thanks for coming by." She might as well have been announcing the cruise activities for the day with her perky voice and bright smile. She gestured to a small kidney-shaped table and four pint-sized chairs.

"Sorry," she apologized.

"It's okay," Ari said. "It's been a while."

"Everybody says that. We forget how small everything was when we were little." She automatically glanced at the clock. "I only have about twenty minutes so how can I help?"

"We understand that Nina's work sometimes forced her to make unpleasant choices and we're wondering if anyone connected to her job might've wanted to her hurt her."

Lark gazed across the room and Ari guessed she was trying hard to hold it together.

"I can't imagine anyone wanting to hurt Nina. She was a dear person." She wiped a tear from her eye and sniffled. "But there was one family that had problems."

"You're Michaela's teacher, right?" Jane interjected, and Lark looked relieved that someone else had brought up the girl's name.

She nodded. "I was the one who originally suggested Nina start seeing her on a regular basis. I can't really discuss the details, but I suspected there was something going on. Initially Eden, that's her mom, agreed, but after about four sessions I found this very angry voice mail on my phone ordering the sessions to stop. Eden didn't sound anything like herself. It was almost like she was reading from a script. I guess Nina got the same message."

"So did the sessions stop?" Jane asked.

"Officially, yes, but we interact with the kids all the time. Nina made a point to show up in the lunchroom when Michaela was there or be out at recess with her. Since Michaela *adored* her, she was like a magnet stuck to Nina's side every time she saw her. I think she told Nina a lot, and a few weeks ago, Nina called the authorities."

Ari leaned forward. "So what happened then?"

She shook her head and sighed. "There was a big blow-up in the office lobby, right in front of other families. Bobby, Eden's boyfriend, stormed in and demanded to speak to the principal. Since she was out, Evan talked to him, and I heard it didn't go well. Bobby blew out of his office, yelling that the 'bitch social worker' was going to regret ever messing with his family." She raised her hand and added, "This is totally hearsay so I'm not breaking any confidentiality laws here. I have no idea if what I'm saying is true. It could be nothing more than gossip." She paused and added seriously, "But I doubt it."

"Have you met this boyfriend?" Jane asked.

Her eyes widened. "Oh, yes. He came to parent-teacher conferences and wasn't very pleasant. He made a lot of demands while Eden just sat there like a timid mouse. It was almost like *he* was the blood relative and Eden was the girlfriend who had no legal rights, not the other way around."

Jane couldn't hide her irritation. "Why does he have any say?"

"Because it's whatever the parent wants, and if Eden says he can be in Michaela's life, then he can. Even if he is abusing her," she added under her breath. "Did I say that out loud?" she asked with a sweet, primary teacher expression on her face.

Ari sensed she knew a lot more but was holding back to preserve her professionalism. "Where's Michaela's biological father?"

She shrugged. "I don't know. I doubt he's around."

"Do you think Bobby is capable of committing murder?"

"Definitely. I wasn't in the office when he came in that day and made a scene, but my source told me that Evan was lucky he didn't get punched in the face or stabbed in the heart with a pencil. She said that Bobby Arco was so mad, he looked like he could've murdered somebody."

* * *

They returned to the office and found a well-built man arguing with the school secretary. Dressed in dark workpants and a blue work shirt with the sleeves rolled up, he looked like an auto mechanic. The name patch that should've been over his pocket was gone, but Ari saw a name tattooed on his exposed bicep—Eden.

"That's Bobby Arco," she whispered to Jane.

"I need to see her now!" he bellowed. "I know she's on her break."

"Her preparation period is about to end," the diminutive secretary said evenly. "She needs to pick up her students from art, and she must be on time."

She guessed that he'd shown up to speak with Lark, but he was too late. He glared at the secretary; she held her ground, but Ari could see the woman was petrified.

"Then let me talk to Mr. Garritson. I want to file a complaint."

"I'm afraid he's busy," the secretary said. "You'll need—"

"That's just great!" he screamed. "I come down here on my break because I have serious problems and no one will help me. I have rights! I'm a parent."

"What's going on?" Evan asked, appearing from his office.

"We need to talk," Arco said, pointing his finger. "Those cops won't leave us alone and it's because your teacher can't keep her mouth shut."

Evan motioned to the hallway. "Why don't you come back—"

"I don't have time. My break's almost up. You just tell that teacher of yours that she needs to shut up."

He stormed past three parents, who quickly moved out of his path, and left in a huff. Evan whispered to the secretary, who explained what had happened. He patted her shoulder and noticed Ari and Jane. He offered a half-hearted smile and led them to his office.

"I'm sorry you had to see that. I'm sorry *everyone* had to see that."

"He's pretty scary," Jane said.

"I think he's more bluster than anything else, but we try not to push his buttons. Still, he has to follow the rules, and we don't give in to demands just because he raises his voice."

"Have you ever called the police?" Ari asked.

"No, he's always calmed down or left. It's the ones who won't calm down..."

He didn't bother to finish the thought, but Ari understood.

"I hope it was helpful to talk to Lark," he said, changing the subject.

"It was, and after what we just saw, I think Bobby Arco is a definite suspect. I'm guessing he was angry because the police are investigating him?"

"I believe so," he said, watching an email pop up on the screen as he spoke.

She imagined multitasking was a part of his day and few people got his undivided attention.

"The police asked me about Nina's relationships with people at work. They took several pages of notes about Eden, Michaela and Bobby, including the huge meltdown he had here in the office."

"*That* wasn't a meltdown?" Jane interjected.

"Hardly," he replied, "when compared to some of his past appearances."

Ari leaned forward in her chair. "And the big blowup happened about two weeks ago?"

Sticky notes and scraps of paper covered his calendar. He flipped back to October and pointed to a Wednesday morning. "October fourteenth. I remember because he made me late for a meeting with the superintendent."

"Did Nina ever mention Bobby calling her or confronting her after that incident?"

"No, she wasn't even aware that he'd threatened her until I said something. I think her mind was on other things."

"Like what?"

He rested his chin in his palm. "Probably Sam breaking up with her. I didn't understand why he did that. They were still in love."

"You didn't *understand* or you didn't *agree*?"

He looked up with a sheepish grin. "Good point. I understood why he felt it was necessary, but if she'd been my girlfriend, I never would've sacrificed her for Dad's career."

There was fervor in his voice, a strength Ari hadn't heard before. She was about to ask him about it when the principal knocked and entered.

"I'm sorry to interrupt," she said. An older woman with set hair and a conservative dress, she had an air about her that made Ari sit up straighter in her presence. She held out a massive key ring stuffed with keys of every color and shape imaginable. "Evan, which one is the master? We can't find the combination for one of the athletes who withdrew."

He flipped through them and held one up for her. It looked very familiar to Ari.

"Hey," Jane said. "Isn't that—"

Ari kicked her in the shin, shutting her up. It appeared the administrators hadn't noticed Jane's interjection, too busy studying the keys. After the principal had departed, Ari grabbed her bag.

"Well, we should be going, Evan. I know you're busy. Thanks so much for your time."

"No problem," he said. "Are you coming to the service?"

"When is it?" Jane asked.

"Tomorrow morning. Sam and I are arranging it since Nina didn't have any close family."

They glanced at each other and nodded. His phone rang and Ari said, "We'll show ourselves out."

They ducked into the women's restroom, and Jane leaned against the sink, rubbing her shin. "Thanks a lot. I'll have a nice bruise on my ankle."

"I'm sorry, sweetie, but I don't trust Evan."

"Why? You think he may be the killer?"

She pulled the key from her purse. "I don't know what to think, but I'm almost positive he had feelings for Nina."

"You think?" Jane asked sarcastically. "I thought he was going to cry."

"Exactly. I'm not sure where he fits into all of this. Maybe Nina knew he loved her and she refused him. That could certainly drive a person to murder."

Jane scowled. "I don't see it. Evan's too mild-mannered, like Steve."

"Perhaps," she replied, "but we need to find the locker that this key belongs to."

The restroom door swung open, and Jane and Ari dropped their conversation immediately and stared into the sink.

"Unbelievable." They turned to see Rory, shaking her head. "Are you two following me?"

CHAPTER TWELVE

The minute hand on Dr. Yee's bookshelf clock inched toward the nine, and Molly knew her hour was nearly over—finally. She'd only agreed to see a shrink once a week as part of her severance package. It was the department's way of showing they *cared*. At first she'd hated going, but after five sessions of facing the petite, older woman who kept her hands folded in her lap while she spoke in the calmest voice Molly had ever heard, Molly had decided to trust her. Maybe she could help her understand why Ari had cheated on Valentine's Day.

"So you were disappointed when you didn't find the photograph in the nightstand?" Dr. Yee asked after she recounted her reconnaissance through Ari's bedroom.

"Yeah."

"Where do you think it might be?"

"I don't know."

"No idea?"

She rubbed her forehead, sorry she'd mentioned it. She felt terribly guilty for snooping and foolish for caring. "It could be in one of the drawers I didn't search, or in a box in her closet, or it might be at her office. Maybe she threw it away," she said wistfully, praying it wasn't true.

"Was that the only picture of you two?"

She chuckled. "Yeah, I'm not big on photographs. We were up in Prescott with her friend Jane, who demanded that we pose inside the gazebo, you know, the one outside the courthouse?"

Dr. Yee nodded. "It's a lovely location for a picture."

"It turned out pretty good so Jane made us copies and put them in these nice wooden frames."

"Where's yours?"

She stared at the leather armrest. "In my nightstand drawer."

"I see." She paused and then said, "Molly, you're an incredibly bright woman and we both know that my role here is just to get you thinking, but I won't insult your intelligence. You don't need me to connect those dots for you, so I'm going to change the subject. After you left Ari's house, how long did it take you to quell the urge to drink?"

"About three frames," she joked, and Dr. Yee looked at her quizzically. "I went bowling."

It hadn't been easy. She'd actually driven to Hideaway and hopped out of the truck. She'd had every intention of marching through the front door, pushing whoever was on her stool onto the floor and demanding Vicky serve her a scotch. But fate had interceded. Biz had walked out of Hideaway as she'd taken a step away from the truck. She'd hurried in the opposite direction toward the closest business, a bowling alley.

"You weren't tempted to drink at the bar?"

"No, I know how bad the drinks are at places like that. It's all watered down."

"So you didn't drink because it wasn't appealing, not because you tempered the urge."

She fidgeted in the wingback chair. "Not exactly. If I'd been really thirsty I would've downed anything."

Dr. Yee stared at the ceiling. "What if the first business you'd seen had been a decent restaurant or another bar?"

"Rarely are there two bars in the same strip mall," Molly commented.

Dr. Yee's eyes narrowed. "You get my point."

She nodded glumly, watching the clock hand move closer to the twelve. Somehow they always circled back to the topic she hated the most. "What does this have to do with Ari? She's the one who—"

"Say it," Dr. Yee said, leaning forward, her hands resting on her knees.

It was their code phrase, the one she'd heard endlessly during the first two visits as she'd ranted and raved about Ari's indiscretion and her annoying perfectionist attitude, which she blamed as much for their break-up as the kiss.

"Say it."

Her anger retreated like a child who'd been threatened with a swat. She'd learned it couldn't survive against the truth.

"I'm an alcoholic."

A buzzer went off and she glanced at the clock's minute hand sitting perfectly on the twelve.

She stormed out of the office and drove to the bowling alley. Her accidental detour to avoid Hideaway might well be blossoming into a hobby. While she enjoyed hiking with her brother, she had found the feel of the ball flying from her hand and destroying the perfect array of pins completely satisfying. As a child she'd loved her family's monthly trips to the bowling alley, mainly because she regularly beat her older brother by twenty or thirty points. It was the only thing she could do better than Don, Jr.

Ari had turned her nose up at bowling the one time she'd tried to get her to go. They'd just left a birthday party at Hideaway and she'd spotted the enormous pin glowing in the darkness. She'd started in that direction and Ari had protested, saying it was too late and insisting she wouldn't be any good. She'd pulled Molly back toward the parking lot and they'd stumbled—or rather, Molly had stumbled—and they'd both fallen to the pavement. The bowling idea was abandoned when Ari cried out, having twisted her ankle. She'd been unable to stand and for some reason Molly couldn't help her. *Why was that?* Somehow Jane had appeared, found them sitting on the curb and taken them home.

She parked behind a '66 Mustang which she instantly recognized as Biz's car. She imagined Biz was in Hideaway, probably putting the moves on another woman while Ari vacationed in California with Jane. She resisted the urge to throw her truck back into drive. It would be horrible to rear-end such a beautiful classic, even if it did belong to Biz.

As she got out, Biz emerged from Hideaway and saw her. She slowly sauntered across the parking lot wearing a friendly expression. She'd won, after all. Molly guessed she wanted to gloat.

"Hey, Molly."

"Hey."

"You're looking great."

"Thanks."

Biz glanced at Hideaway. "I'm a little surprised to see you here. I thought you'd given it up."

She stiffened and her hands balled into fists. "I have, but it's none of your damn business."

"That's true, but I still care about you."

She laughed heartily and shook her head. "You care about *me*? What you cared about was stealing my girlfriend!"

"I didn't have to steal her," Biz said with a wicked smile. "She crawled right into my arms."

"You bitch!" she spat and took two steps toward her.

Standing toe-to-toe she towered over Biz, but the PI held her ground and said, "Besides, you'd already cheated."

The truth stunned Molly into silence. Biz climbed into the car and leaned out the window. "It was only a matter of time before everyone knew, Molly, including Ari. You and the blonde put on quite a show in the backroom that night. Are you still seeing her?"

Biz drove away and she leaned against the side of her truck, staring at Hideaway. Her body was too weak to pick up a bowling ball, but she wasn't too weak to lift a shot glass.

CHAPTER THIRTEEN

Biz edged the Mustang into a parking space at the other end of the strip mall to watch Molly, who was leaning against her truck and staring at her hands. It was clear she was on a precipice, debating whether or not to enter Hideaway, the place that had essentially ruined her career. She was hunched over almost as if she were praying.

Biz bit her lip. *Don't do it*, she thought, though in the next moment she realized if Molly fell off the wagon it would be one more piece of insurance. Ari would never reunite with her as long as she was drinking. But what if she stayed sober?

She'd never looked better. She looked nothing like the haggard and slightly overweight detective Biz had known for years. Of course, she had always been attractive. Long ago, in fact, they had spent a few wild nights together. Molly was an exceptional lover who'd had her pick of women every night she partied, despite the slight flaws in her appearance and character. Now, though, the woman was drop-dead gorgeous. Freed of a stressful job that most likely had been the primary reason she drank and the cause of her weight struggle, she seemed like a completely different person.

For the first few months, thinking of Molly's destroyed career and her role in its demise had sent Biz into a funk that usually lasted a few hours. She'd drop to the nearest couch or chair and wait for it to pass. Eventually she decided to focus her energies on winning Ari, erasing Molly from her mind, and forgetting all about Vince Carnotti and Sol Gardener. It had worked for five months—until Wanda's blackmail note arrived and she was yanked back into the past.

Molly remained in a trance, leaning against her truck. Biz sighed. As much as she wanted Ari, she couldn't wish any ill will toward Molly and her courageous fight against her alcoholism. "C'mon, don't do it. Go home."

Molly jumped and fumbled for her phone. She listened and gestured while she talked just like a cop. When she disconnected, she climbed back into the truck and pulled away quickly. Biz swallowed a knot in her throat, wondering if the phone call had anything to do with the past she was so desperately trying to erase.

* * *

Gaining access to Wanda's fourth-story balcony wasn't hard. Biz had picked locks since high school, and she had found it a necessary skill in her quest to incarcerate abusive boyfriends and husbands. Often she left illicit drugs or weapons in their homes, and when the cops searched the closets or under the bed after receiving an anonymous tip, the enraged batterer would usually take a swing at the cop, accusing him or her of planting the evidence. Then the scum had another charge to face, assaulting an officer.

The apartment complex was a virtual ghost town on a late Monday morning. Everyone was at their jobs, laboring for that next paycheck to support weekends of clubbing and partying. She'd checked Wanda's parking space, verifying that the old Honda was gone and Wanda was busy greeting customers at the bank where she worked.

Recognizing she was fairly conspicuous, she slipped through the complex carefully, avoiding the handful of groundskeepers who were busy trimming the hedges and cleaning the pool. She glanced up at the eight apartments that formed Wanda's building. Each floor held two units, the front doors facing each other. All of the blinds were closed and she saw no signs of life. She quickly circled the perimeter and checked the shed, finding its padlock still secured. She guessed it housed the riding lawnmower. Monday must not be mowing day. She certainly didn't want a groundskeeper to see her up on Wanda's balcony.

Seeing no one, she quickly ascended the steps to Wanda's door, her lock picking set in her hand and a tool belt over her shoulder. Dressed in gray coveralls and a cap, she looked like any other workperson who might fix a light socket or change a filter. That was going to be her story in the event a nosy neighbor stopped her.

She rang the bell for good measure, just in case Wanda had acquired an overnight guest. When no one answered, she jimmied the bottom lock, which gave in an instant. The deadbolt was trickier. She threw a glance toward the sidewalk, willing it to remain empty.

It took nearly a minute, but she managed finally to finagle the tumblers and slide the deadbolt free. She quickly entered the apartment and locked the door behind her. She didn't blink an eye at the clutter that covered most of the surfaces and the laundry that was strewn everywhere. Dozens of one-night stands had taught her women were just as slovenly as men; they just wouldn't admit it.

She went to the sliding glass door and found it unlocked. Clearly Wanda felt unthreatened by hovering four stories above everyone else. She studied the cheap metal railing that separated her from a fifty-foot drop onto the concrete sidewalk. The railing was like every other one she'd ever seen. Four cement screws held the top and bottom crossbars in place.

She went to work and unscrewed the railing. She'd reasoned that the murmur of the electric drill was worth the risk if it meant finishing the job in less than an hour. She prayed no tenants would jog past and the workmen wouldn't go to the shed.

Removing the screws consumed only a few minutes. It was harder to clean out the plaster holes that had held them in place. She went through three drill bits as she enlarged each one of the sixteen holes. By the time she finished the last one, sweat dripped down her face. She remounted the railing, satisfied. It looked exactly the same as when she'd arrived, but the first time Wanda leaned on it, as she had done the night before, the loose screws would pop out of their holes and she would career over the side and down onto the pavement.

Biz closed her eyes for a moment, sickened at the thought. But it was the only way.

She swept away the plaster dust and collected her tools. It was nearly one. If she hurried, she could make a late afternoon flight and be with Ari by nightfall. She didn't need to see Wanda fall to her death. In fact, she *couldn't* see her fall. It would be too hard. It would be bad enough to read about it in the paper.

She hustled out the door—and stopped two flights down. Standing in front of her was a huge man with bulging biceps. He stared at her with a thin smile.

"Ms. Stone, Mr. Carnotti would like a word with you, please."

* * *

She followed him out an employee gate and into a small parking lot. A black Escalade with tinted windows sat in the far stall, and she wasn't surprised when the wise guy opened the back door. She would be getting in but he would not.

She took a deep breath and realized she might crumple to the ground. She'd only met Vince Carnotti twice. Usually she had dealt with middlemen like Sol Gardener, a situation that suited her just fine. Vince was scary, freaky scary.

He was staring out the opposite window. He wore an expensive dark suit and his white hair curled over his collar. Her gaze reflexively dropped to his enormous hands. He was rumored to have killed a snitch by squeezing the guy's head between those hands.

"Join me," he said softly.

She climbed into the buttery leather seat, avoiding his stare.

"I like you, Elizabeth," he said. "You do good work."

"Thanks."

"No, I mean it," he said more emphatically. "You're one of the good guys, really. You take no-good sons of bitches like my daughter's ex and you make them pay. I like that. You're like me." She glanced at him, surprised by the compliment, as his black eyes bored into hers. "I know what's happening. I know why you're here. My people have been following Wanda ever since that night. More than once I thought about popping her myself, but…" His voice trailed off as he smoothed the crease of his pants. "She's not my problem, she's yours. Right?"

She nodded.

"Unfortunately, I've come to the same conclusion. My contacts in the department are telling me that Jack Adams's task force is being disbanded in a few days by the new hotshot chief. Wanda is the only lead they have. If she doesn't disappear before they discover her or before the task force dies, we'll all be in trouble. You understand that?"

She nodded again.

He checked his watch. "I have a busy schedule today, so I'll be blunt. Your little plan won't work." She gave a surprised look, and he squeezed her shoulder, offering a fatherly grin. "People only fall over railings in the movies, kiddo." His face hardened and her skin went cold. "She's going to need a push."

CHAPTER FOURTEEN

"What are you doing here?" Jane asked Rory. "I thought you taught college?"

She crossed her arms. "I do, but I also volunteer by working with some third-grade reading groups. I'm very *altruistic*," she said slowly.

"I know what that means," Jane hissed, "and altruistic people are usually not *ostentatious* about their activities."

"Enough," Ari barked. "A woman has died and you two are engaging in some sort of vocabulary foreplay, which I really don't need to see."

"This is *not* foreplay," Jane disagreed, shooting Rory a distasteful glance. "That woman is the last person in the world I'd want to sleep with."

"Right back at you, sister," Rory replied. "Now, what are you two doing here?"

Ari held up the key and said, "We've figured out where Nina kept her journals."

"Where?"

"Here at the school," Jane said. "In one of the lockers."

Rory stared at the key and slowly nodded. "That actually explains a lot. Once when I was here in the evening, I saw Nina coming out of the locker room. She said she'd been interviewing students, but I knew it was too late for any kids to be around. I wondered if maybe she wasn't having a walk on the wild side with the girls' P.E. teacher, but I never said anything. I've seen her going into the gym during the school day, but I didn't think anything of it."

"Isn't that pretty risky?" Jane asked. "I mean keeping your personal journals in a school locker?"

"Maybe Evan or the gym teacher knew about it," Rory offered.

"Can we get in there now?"

Rory looked doubtful. "I don't think I'd chance it during class. Coach Case is pretty tough."

Jane flicked some lint from her blouse. "She plays for our team?"

"Yeah," she said suspiciously. "What are you thinking? I don't want to get Coach in trouble. She's good people."

Jane waved her off. "I wouldn't dream of annihilating her career, but a little distraction wouldn't hurt. Where's the gym?"

They followed Rory to a tall building just behind the school. Instead of heading through the front entrance, they walked to the side, where the words "Girls Locker Room" were spray-painted on a gray door. Three bursts from a sharp, high-pitched whistle told them class was in session. Ari cracked open the door and they listened as the coach gave the girls directions and ordered them into the gym. When they were certain the students had filed out, the three of them moved inside.

"You two find the locker," Jane directed, "and I'll make sure the coach doesn't wander back here until you're done."

"What are you going to do?" Rory asked in an annoyed tone.

"Don't worry about it," she said with a smile.

She sauntered out and they studied the lockers. There were different styles and sizes, all with combination locks that had a keyhole in the center that gave the school the option of a combination or a key.

"Try one of those," Rory said, pointing to a large set of blue lockers. "Those are the ones for the athletes. There's always going to be one or two that's empty, so maybe Nina commandeered one of them."

The key slid into the first lock Ari tried, but it wouldn't turn. "You're right. It's one of these," she said, moving from locker to locker with little luck.

Ari heard Jane's cackle a few times amid all of the teenage girls' chatter. Rory peeked out a window and groaned. "Unbelievable. Your friend has absolutely no boundaries."

"That's Jane," she agreed. "What's she doing?"

"Well, she's not really *doing* anything except distracting Coach from supervising the students. They're standing off to the side laughing and carrying on. She keeps touching Coach's arm and flicking her hair back." She paused and added, "I don't think I've ever seen Coach Case laugh."

"Got it," Ari said, pushing up the handle. A gym bag filled with sports clothes and toiletries took up most of the space inside.

"She and Evan sometimes played racquetball together," Rory said.

Pulling the gym bag out, Ari discovered the locker was deeper than it appeared. A large metal box filled the rest of the space. She surmised the box would go unnoticed by most people. Inside it was a pile of journals and spiral notebooks. She grabbed the top journal, a beautiful leather-bound book, and flipped to the last page.

"This is her last journal," she said.

Rory grabbed one of the spirals. "This belonged to a kid named Devon, but it's from last year."

"I don't think these are in any particular order," Rory said.

"We'll need to take all of them."

"How are we going to get them out of here?"

Ari's gaze settled on the large duffel bag. "We need to make a swap."

They'd just finished the transfer when they heard the rush of students returning to the locker room. They scooted outside and waited for Jane.

"Did you find them?"

"Yes, and what did *you* learn?" Rory asked pointedly as they started back toward the parking lot.

"Well, your friend Melinda is quite a talker. I pretended I was from the district trust and I needed to examine her safety features."

Rory rolled her eyes. "She fell for that?"

"Hey, it's the best I could think of," Jane snapped. "Are you always so negative?"

"Are you always so slutty?"

Jane whirled and faced her. "How dare you call me that!" Her open palm flew toward Rory's cheek, but she deflected the blow. "Ow!" Jane cried. She rubbed her wrist and stared at Rory. "You hurt me."

"I barely touched you."

Ari dropped the heavy bag. "I can't deal with this. Rory, I could use your help, but this isn't going to work. You bring out Jane's inner child. Sorry." She picked up the bag and walked away. "Let's go, Jane."

* * *

Jane was still prattling about Rory's uncouth demeanor when they returned to the resort. "She's horrible!"

Ari hefted the duffel onto the dining table. "For god's sake," she shouted. "Just sleep with her!" Jane gasped. "This is what happens when you don't act upon your lust," Ari explained. "You can't bottle up your libido. It controls your personality and when it's not satisfied, we all suffer!"

Realizing she was shouting, she took a deep breath and fell into a chair. She rubbed her temples, wishing she were home in her garden—alone. She was tired of people and problems. Jane's optimistic attitude was what she loved about her, and she couldn't stand it when Jane was as negative as everyone else.

"My libido doesn't control my *entire* personality," Jane announced, "but I see your point. I am a very sexual being and my passion is at my center, literally. But there's no way in hell Rory's getting a key to the kingdom. I'll just have to stay away from her." She opened the duffel and picked up a handful of journals. "Let's focus on Nina."

They spread them out and created a timeline of three years, the length of Nina's tenure at Brayberry. The spiral notebooks were student journals, and after a quick glance at the contents and the old dates on the inside cover, Ari set all of them aside, except for the one written by Michaela.

Her pages were filled with crayon drawings, most of which depicted a little girl, who Ari assumed was Michaela, who was always happy in the school scenes, such as playing on the monkey bars, but who wore a frown in the drawings of her house. One picture in particular was very disturbing. Michaela was sitting on a sofa in a room with black walls. She'd drawn a picture on one of the walls—a fire-breathing dragon with teeth. A pool of yellow tears sat at her feet.

"That's a red flag," Jane said.

"Nina's concerns were probably justified. Let's focus on her journals. Happy reading," Ari said, handing Jane one with a bright pink cover. She took the leather-bound book, Nina's last completed journal. "This one should lead up to the first one we found."

It was quickly apparent that although Nina had kept the journals at school, she had interspersed entries about her adult clients from the apartment complex with the reflections about the schoolchildren she saw at work.

The content suggested Nina wrote to untangle her own thought processes. Many entries were strung together in stream of consciousness style and she consistently used the names of Shakespearean characters to disguise the identities of her clients, making it impossible to tell who was who.

Jane asked, "Who was Banquo?"

"Uh," Ari said as she searched her memory of senior English. "I think that was the villain who murdered Macbeth."

"So I guess whoever this guy is, he's probably scum."

She peered over Jane's shoulder. "I'd say so if he's pushing his wife's head through a wall."

"These are the people who live in her apartment complex?"

"I think so," Ari said, skimming ahead through several pages of the journal she was reading. "The names are odd, but the problems are definitely from the twenty-first century." She held up the book and said, "Listen to this. 'Adriana is at her wit's end. Needs to confront Frederick. Flaunting his indiscretions with Audrey is destroying her. Must have her list her strengths. Hotspur could help. Key: stop blaming herself for Cordelia's death. Bulimia is a disease.'"

"Wow," Jane said. "So we've got a wife with a cheating husband and a daughter who died from an eating disorder."

"Yes, and apparently a friend who could help. That would be Hotspur."

"And who was he?"

"I don't remember exactly, but I think he was in one of the Henry plays."

Jane raised an eyebrow and stared at her. "How do you know all this?"

"Unlike you, I actually went to class. I loved Ms. Amos's British literature class."

Jane snorted. "Sounds like a total snooze, if you ask me."

She offered a sly smile. "You never saw Ms. Amos."

They laughed and waded through Nina's difficult handwriting. After an hour Ari's head was throbbing. She'd read through the entire journal, encountering at least thirty different names of clients facing serious issues like domestic abuse, homophobia, schizophrenia and incest.

Two-thirds of the way through the last journal, she found some of the familiar names again—Horatio, Orlando, Cesario and Valeria—listed in five separate entries, each one more intriguing than the previous one.

May 4th
Horatio is closer. Benedick unaware. Cesario involved somehow? Ultimatums given. Where is Orlando's voice?

August 15th
Benedick growing distant. Orlando remains neutral—for now. Valeria knows Horatio is a hypocrite. Cesario is key!

September 5th
Valeria's undoing is Benedick's weakness. Horatio is silent ally. Orlando and Cesario—too strong.

October 6th
Horatio is a true friend to Valeria!

October 22nd
Valeria caught in secrets thanks to apothecary. Share with no one except H. Maybe Orlando? Must investigate! Can Benedick be trusted? Will it destroy? Cesario, oh, Cesario… It is Aguecheek.

She picked up Nina's last journal and reread its lone entry.

October 30th.
The secret will be revealed—DANGER. Poor Benedick! Poor Horatio! And poor Orlando—a pawn?

The secret would be revealed. Had Nina learned something so important that she was killed for it?

Ari flipped through the notes she'd taken and realized there were two other sets of characters that made multiple appearances. One was those involved in the drama over Frederick the cheating husband and the other involved a trio of characters—Edmund, Emilia and Caliban. The content was disturbing. All of the entries mentioned horrible things Edmund had done and Nina's grave concern for Caliban and Emilia, but the last one caught her attention.

Poor Caliban! Such a sweet soul with no voice. Emilia cannot protect from Edmund. She is in DANGER.

Could Emilia be Nina? She realized nowhere in the journal did Nina refer to herself in the first person. She pondered the fact as Jane snored quietly next to her, having given up her own reading after only twenty pages. She'd proclaimed exhaustion, but Ari suspected it had much more to do with a lack of interest in anyone who wasn't *her*. She nudged Jane's shoulder and one eye flew open.

"Have you learned anything?"

"Some of this is heavy-duty stuff. Who would have thought kids would have so many issues?"

"Well, you did," Jane said quietly, alluding to Ari's less than idyllic childhood.

"Yeah, but I had my mom for most of it. She was my rock. She made losing Richie and my dad's abandonment bearable."

Jane sat up and offered her a generous kiss on the cheek. "You are the most amazing person I know."

She smiled at her best friend with a love she'd never felt for any woman, including Molly. Lately she'd wondered if she and Jane had made a mistake in dismissing a romantic relationship after only an hour of dating years ago, but she'd always concluded it was a place they couldn't go. She wanted to protect their friendship at all cost, especially now when she felt so terribly alone.

Jane dropped the journal she'd barely read. "So, what do you think? Are the answers to Nina's murder somewhere in these tomes? That means books, by the way," she added.

"I know," she said, but the vocabulary lesson had given her an idea. "I think the murderer may be mentioned somewhere, but we'll need the help of someone who knows a lot more about Shakespeare than I do."

"Well, that won't be Biz..." Jane's face darkened. "Don't say it."

"Yes, I'm afraid I must. We need Rory's help."

CHAPTER FIFTEEN

When Molly saw Andre she threw her arms around him. "Thanks. You don't know why, but thanks."

He looked at her completely bewildered. "You're welcome."

They were standing outside Uptown Fitness, and Andre recounted his previous conversation with the front desk clerk. "I need a way to jog her memory."

She nodded. "What we need to do is give her a type so she can see one person and think of others who might fit the description."

He grinned. "Great idea. Let's go."

He flashed his badge at the front desk clerk and they strolled through the rows of elliptical and fitness machines, most of which were occupied by women.

"Her," Molly said, pointing to a short, wiry woman with incredible tone. "That's her body type."

"Wow, I wouldn't have guessed that. I would've thought it was someone taller and bulkier from the way the bartender and a few other patrons described her."

"Yeah, but appearances can be deceiving. She was wearing stilettos and big hair so she looked taller, and she definitely padded her bra. It made her seem more buxom. Whoever worked with her knew what she was doing. She understood how to create a disguise."

They watched a brunette at the lat pull-down machine. Her back muscles flexed each time the seventy-pound weights soared from the base. Molly dreamed of the day when she would look that fine. She knew she'd never be as skinny because of her bone structure, but she'd be grateful to shed the final ten pounds she needed to lose.

"I'll go get the desk clerk," Andre said.

"Excuse me, but could you tell me if my tag is showing?"

The brunette was moving through her circuit and had stopped in front of Molly, showing off a fabulous rear end covered in skintight workout pants.

"Um, no, you're fine," she squeaked.

The woman turned around, and Molly saw her front was just as appetizing as her backside. Her little white sports bra could barely keep her D-cups in place, and from the amount of makeup she wore, Molly knew she was here to troll, not exercise. She had worked out hard enough to generate a slight sheen of perspiration but nothing more. She was in her early fifties, but she wore it well.

She leaned closer and whispered, "When I wear this thong, I always worry that I'll embarrass myself. Do you think I look okay?"

"You look fine." Her throat was completely dry, and she decided she very much wanted to know what color thong was hiding under the black workout pants.

"Lime green," the woman said, reading her thoughts. "I'm Sienna. And you are?"

"Molly."

"Are you considering joining the gym, Molly? You and your friend?"

"Um, well I might."

"How fabulous. Will you be here for a while? I've got about twenty more minutes on my circuit and then I'm free for the rest of the afternoon. Do you have plans?"

Molly thought about the light switch in 3D and the bathtub caulking in 2B. Then she thought about the picture that *wasn't* in Ari's bedroom anymore.

"I don't have any plans at all."

Sienna's ruby lips curled into a smile. "Perfect. I drive a little red Miata that's parked outside. I'll see you in twenty."

Andre reappeared with a goth girl who looked slightly dazed and confused. "Molly, this is Jordan. She's the daytime desk clerk." Jordan nodded in her direction and followed his pointed finger to the buff woman Molly had identified.

"Well, there's a lot of people who look like that. It's a gym."

Molly rolled her eyes, remembering she was no longer a policeman and this wasn't her investigation.

"How many would you say?" he asked.

"Well, just among the regulars there's Heather and Jackie and Sykes and D.D. and Wanda and Curly and JuJu and well... probably a few more if I thought about it."

"So maybe ten or so?"

"Yeah, maybe a few more."

"Could I see their IDs in the computer? You guys have that on file, right?"

Suddenly Jordan looked much less confused. "Yeah, but you'd need a warrant for that, right?" She glanced at Molly, who shrugged her shoulders.

"Well, technically, yes," he hedged, "but that could take a long time and I could really use your help."

He flashed his most pathetic face, the one he always used on women to get his way, and for a brief moment Molly felt like she was back in the game and this was another case they were running together. But it wasn't. She couldn't wait to meet Sienna at her red Miata and see her lime green thong.

"I should probably call my manager and see if she can come over. She's over at the downtown location right now."

"Let's do that," he agreed. "Mol, are you sticking around?"

"No," she said flatly. "Call me when you've got something."

* * *

The Miata was far too small for her lanky frame; she felt like a folded sandwich as they cruised down Camelback Road.

"I live on the mountain," Sienna said, turning onto one of the few roads that actually led up Camelback Mountain. "But we're not superrich so we don't live up too high."

She chuckled at her own joke and made a few more turns until they reached a large electric gate. She punched a code into the keypad and the gate slowly opened. When it was just wide enough for the Miata to squeeze through, she gunned the engine and shot ahead.

"Don't want to waste time," she said, roaring up the driveway and into a garage whose door was already opened. She parked next to a new black Hummer that seemed to swallow the Miata in its shadow.

"Is that your *other* car?" Molly joked.

"Actually it is," she said. "C'mon."

They passed through a laundry room and a small storage area before they entered a pristine kitchen with a gorgeous mountain view. She tossed her gym bag onto a chair and headed for the bar, stripping off her clothes until all she was wearing was her thong, which was indeed lime green.

"What would you like to drink?" she asked. "I'm making a martini."

"Uh, I don't drink," Molly replied.

She looked up with a knowing look. "Took a second. How long have you been sober?"

"About six months."

"Good for you," she said. "Then I won't tempt you." She picked up two highballs and filled each with ice and seltzer. When she presented the drink she said, "The last thing I want you thinking about right now is booze. All I want you to picture is the body in front of you. Do you think I have a great figure?"

Molly coated her throat with the seltzer. "Beautiful," she mumbled.

Sienna playfully rubbed the sweating glass against her nipples until they were erect. "I just love that feeling."

She stared at her perfect breasts. They were a little larger than Ari's, and she was certain they weren't real, but she respected a woman who recognized that plastic surgery was about the whole body, not just making one part stand out.

"Follow me, Molly."

They wandered down a hallway and up a staircase lined with family photos. She stopped and gazed at Sienna's blatant heterosexual life, complete with a handsome husband and two adorable children. Some photos depicted the happy family skiing, hiking and celebrating Christmas while others were formal studio setups at various points in the children's lives.

"Surprised?" Sienna asked.

"Not really," she said. "I've known lots of curious straight women."

She threw her head back and laughed. "Oh, baby, I'm not straight. I have an amazing husband and two great kids, one's in college and the other's a senior in high school, but I'm completely bisexual with a lot of needs to be met. Thank God Louie gets that."

"He knows? Now I'm surprised."

"He's always known. He caught me with my maid of honor the day before our wedding and I gave him a choice: share or leave. He's been happily sharing me ever since."

She glanced back down the stairs. "Where are they now?"

She answered as if she'd been asked the question dozens of times before. "At this very moment? Well, I imagine my daughter's in the Harvard library studying, my son is at wrestling practice until seven and my husband, the amazing plastic surgeon," she said, gesturing at her body, "is at a conference in London. Satisfactory answers?"

She nodded and followed her upstairs into a beautiful guest room with a daybed. "What do you think of my boudoir?"

"It's lovely," she said.

A small white cabinet stocked with oils and candles sat against one wall and faced a much larger matching cabinet on the opposite wall. She worried it was stocked with bondage equipment and was relieved to see it housed a stereo and TV. Sienna opened the doors, grabbed the remote and filled the room with soft jazz.

"You don't look like the kind of woman who needs videos to get in the mood, do you?"

"Um, no," she said nervously.

Sienna faced her and stroked her arms, releasing a hunger she'd forgotten existed. Taking a new lover was sexy, and the anticipation of that first touch was like a plane seconds from touchdown, a combination of anxiety and exhilaration. As if she could read her mind, Sienna pressed her lips against Molly's ever so slightly, asking permission and previewing her skills.

Before she could pull her into a deep kiss, Sienna stepped to the bed. "You've been deprived, haven't you? Let's fix that."

Molly kicked off her black boots and stripped off her jeans, but when it came to unbuttoning the simple button-down shirt, she couldn't get her fingers to cooperate.

"Come here," Sienna cooed.

She joined her on the bed. "Sorry, I'm...sorry."

"You're fine."

Sienna slowly parted the fabric and caressed Molly's face and neck. "You have the most beautiful blue eyes."

She should have mumbled at least a thank you, but the wetness between her thighs easily destroyed nearly four decades of good manners. The remaining scraps of cloth dropped to the floor so kisses could be bestowed on the bare flesh. Sienna smelled flowery and fresh after her shower at the gym, and Molly longed to be swallowed up by something so clean and pure.

"I have a rule," Sienna whispered.

Lost in anticipation, Sienna's fingers burning heat inches from her center, Molly couldn't bring herself to inquire—or care—about rules.

"The first time it's only fingers. I want us to have something to look forward to."

"Yes," she moaned, rocking her hips forward, greeting Sienna.

The wait was over.

CHAPTER SIXTEEN

The whir of power tools reverberated against the steel walls of Lenny's Auto. Ari passed the service bays, noticing that Bobby Arco was standing under a car suspended on a lift, gazing upward, a tattoo in the shape of a serpent's tail poking his Adam's apple. She headed toward the office where Eden worked as the secretary/bookkeeper for her father Lenny. She'd rehearsed a story in the event that it wasn't possible to catch her alone, but her experience with auto shops had taught her usually only one person staffed the office since the money was in the bays.

She'd left Jane at the resort nursing her "burgeoning migraine" as she put it, which magically appeared after Rory agreed to stop by and analyze the Shakespearean references when her last class was over. She shook her head at the thought of Rory arriving without a chaperone or bodyguard, and she guessed she'd return to find them screaming at each other or nestled under the covers of Jane's bed.

Eden stood at the counter, squaring off with an elderly customer who was waving his bill at her.

"I'm not paying this! This isn't what we agreed to," he insisted. "Lenny said it would be three-fifty."

Eden nodded and replied, "That was for *one* drum. You needed two of them. I'm sorry, Mr. Rosen, but I think you misunderstood what my dad said."

He ranted about shoddy workmanship and false advertising while Eden listened politely. Only when he brought up the old days when honest businessmen ruled the world did she interrupt, her face turning red.

"My father is honest and I resent your comment. This is the cost of the work. You'll pay it if you want your car back."

He pulled out his wallet and threw his credit card on the counter. Not another word was spoken as she processed the transaction and he claimed his keys. Ari imagined he would never return to Lenny's, and she was completely unimpressed with Eden's customer service skills. Lenny probably lost a lot of customers if he relied on his daughter to smooth over the problems.

"May I help you?"

Eden wasn't smiling. Ari guessed the *last* thing she wanted to do was work for her dad. She was in her early twenties, which meant she'd become a mother while she was in high school since Michaela was seven. Despite the baggy sweatshirt she wore, her large bosom practically rested on the counter.

"Hi, are you Eden?"

"Yeah," she asked suspiciously. "Who are you?"

Ari held up a hand. "I'm not a cop. I'm a friend of Nina Hunter, and I'm just trying to get some answers to help her family." Eden stared at her keenly, and she added, "I know that Michaela loved Nina and I'm guessing she's heartbroken over losing her."

Eden's expression softened and she knew she'd found her weak spot.

"She's still crying about it. I keep telling her that Miss Hunter is in heaven and that seems to help her calm down for a little while."

Her voice started to crack and Ari thought she might cry herself. She couldn't imagine having a child during high school, and she guessed Michaela and Eden were growing up together.

"I heard that Michaela really enjoyed spending time with Nina."

"Yeah."

"Was Nina her counselor?"

She wiped a tear away and shook her head. "No, Bobby thought it was a waste of time. It's not like Michaela needs any help. She's just a kid who does kid things."

"How did you meet him?"

"He started working here for my dad about a year ago. We hooked up one night and it just kept going." She spoke with great pride, as if they'd been married for years. "I think my dad may give him the shop someday. He's really good with his hands."

Her grin widened and Ari's skin crawled. She paused before she asked, "Do you think Bobby didn't want Michaela visiting Nina because of the CPS calls?"

"Well, of course he was mad," she said, her temper flaring. "She had no right to accuse him of that stuff. He'd never hurt us. We're a family."

"I understand. Why do you think she got that idea in her head?"

"Because Michaela makes up stuff," she said emphatically. "She's a little liar, all kids are. They just say stuff that they see on TV. One time she got mad at Bobby because he made her eat green beans. The next day she told Miss Hunter that Bobby was abusing her."

"Is it true he threatened Nina?"

She gasped and said, "Not really. I mean, he said some things he shouldn't have said, but he wouldn't hurt anyone."

"But did those things make him a suspect?"

"I guess," Eden said, slouching. "He was here working late that night, but he was by himself."

"Is there anything that can prove he didn't leave? Did he make a phone call from the landline or did anyone come by?"

She shook her head and looked at Ari warily. "Who are you again?"

A volley of cursing erupted from the bays. Through the glass they watched Mr. Rosen confront Bobby. He was still waving his bill and pointing at Bobby's chest, screaming that he'd done a piss-poor job on the brakes. Bobby took it for about thirty seconds, looking somewhat amused by the confrontation, and then he suddenly grabbed the old man's arm.

"You're hurting me!" the man cried as Bobby led him back to his car in the parking lot.

Bobby leaned over and whispered in his ear, after which Mr. Rosen nodded slowly and got into his car, like a dog beaten into submission. When Bobby returned to the service bay, the two other technicians high-fived him. Ari noticed Lenny was nowhere to be seen.

"Where's your father?"

"He only comes in part-time now. He's semiretired and trusts Bobby. Like I said, he's starting to take over."

"Does your dad approve of him grabbing customers like that?"

The question surprised Eden, and she sputtered, "Of course not. That was just a one-time deal."

"So Bobby's never grabbed you?"

Her left hand automatically reached for her right bicep, and Ari stared at the heavy sweatshirt. Despite the mild temperatures, Eden was dressed for a California winter.

She stared at Ari and said, "I think you need to go now."

"Eden, I—"

She crossed her arms, her eyes narrow slits. "I don't know who you are or what you want, but you need to get the hell out of here. You *don't* want me to call Bobby."

Behind the hard words Ari saw the glint of fear in her eyes. She left quickly, glancing over her shoulder several times until she was safely in the confines of the rental car.

She gazed toward the sea and spotted Crescent Point, the place where Nina was killed. Since arriving in Laguna, Ari had seen several brochures advertising it as a premier wedding spot, and now she wanted to see for herself.

She pulled into the small parking lot and headed up the cement sidewalk, stopping every five or ten feet to admire the beautiful foliage that lined the path. She couldn't identify most of the plants. They would never survive the Phoenix heat. Still she was jealous of the gorgeous scenery and vowed her garden would someday be worthy of a photo spread.

A four-foot railing kept pedestrians out of the plants and away from the dangerous cliffs. Leaning over, she realized that no one could survive the fall. Huge jagged rock formations jutted from the ocean floor along the shoreline.

She reached the point and a lovely semicircular cement bench that faced west, a perfect vantage point for a sunset. Huddled in a corner was a couple accompanied by a well-dressed woman who was scribbling on her iPad with a stylus, taking notes about everything the woman, obviously a future bride, had to say. The groom remained quiet with his hands in his pockets, staring at the ocean. Ari felt a twinge of jealousy. In one of her recurring dreams she'd imagined marrying Molly in a place like this, but she'd never told her about it. Just exchanging "I love yous" had increased her drinking. Ari guessed the idea of a wedding would've pushed her over the edge.

Remembering why she'd made the climb, she gazed into the surf, the waves crashing over the rocks directly below. Sam had said emergency workers rappelled over the edge to retrieve Nina's body since access from the shore was impossible.

Crescent Point was absolutely beautiful and treacherous at the same time.

Using the few cop instincts she still had left, she studied the immediate area carefully. The four-foot railing posed a greater danger to her at five-eleven, but Nina had been only five-five. There was no way she could have accidentally fallen over it. She put her back against the railing and realized the killer would have needed several feet to gain momentum and propel himself—or herself—into Nina. Would it be enough force to throw her body over the railing?

She pulled out her cell phone and made a video call to Biz, who was sitting in her office behind her desk. Ari immediately sensed something was wrong when Biz didn't crack a grin. She usually loved having FaceTime.

"Hey, I'm sorry to bother you, but I have a question about the case."

"Um, sure. I'm just really busy."

"I know. I'll be really quick. How hard is it to throw someone over a railing?"

"What?"

Her jaw dropped and Ari was momentarily speechless. "I'm sorry. Did I say something wrong? That was how Nina was murdered and I'm trying to determine how strong the killer would need to be to get a five-foot-five woman over a four-foot railing."

Biz took a deep breath and said, "I'm sorry for my reaction. I'm really distracted right now. Uh, well, yeah, if you had a running start, you could throw someone over. The risky part is their reaction."

"What do you mean?"

"If the victim has excellent reflexes he or she might pull the killer over as well."

"Because the tendency would be to reach out, to try to grab something to hang on to," she concluded.

"Exactly," Biz said in a flat tone.

"Are you okay? Is the case you're working on that bad?"

She nodded and seemed on the verge of tears. "I have to go. I'm not sure when or if I'll get to Laguna. I'll let you know. I'm sorry if I'm letting you down." With that she hung up.

Ari stared at the black screen. Something was going on, but Biz clearly didn't want to discuss it. It had to be horrible because she knew Jane was right: Biz would do anything to spend time with her, and if she didn't show up, they were on their own.

She scanned the area near the railing. Nina was an accomplished athlete, an endurance runner in great shape. Her reflexes would've taken over when she realized what was happening.

She stared over the edge again. Sam had mentioned the police had originally thought it might be an accident, but something had changed their mind. They must have found something. Perhaps in her last moments Nina had grabbed something from the killer—maybe a piece of jewelry or a patch of hair—before she went over. Maybe she'd been holding it when they found her.

"Solved it yet?" a voice asked.

She turned to a short, bald man with a goatee, wearing a Mexican wedding shirt over his dress pants. He was sitting on the bench, his arms stretched along its back like a tourist enjoying the view.

"I don't know what you mean," she said dumbly.

"You're the PI the family hired, right?"

"No," she said honestly. "I'm just a friend of a friend."

"Ah," he said with a nod. "But you didn't answer my question. Got any ideas? I could use some."

"Who are you?"

He rose and extended his hand. "Clay Justice, and yes, that's my real name. Great for a police detective, don't you think?"

She chuckled and met his firm handshake. "I'm Ari Adams. Is the Nina Hunter murder your case?"

"It is. What did your friend on the phone say?"

"How long have you been here?"

"Long enough to hear your theory about Nina grabbing for something."

"Is that true, Clay?" she asked, turning on her feminine charms. If it worked on Kip Harper at the nursery, then maybe she could charm him. "Did the police find something in her hand?"

"Maybe," he said coyly.

"How did you know about the PI?"

"It's a small town, Miss Adams. There are no secrets." He started to walk away but quickly swung around. "That's not really true. There are secrets." He paused before he added, "I can't believe Nina didn't keep some kind of record about her sessions, like a journal or a log. What do you think?"

She shrugged. "Not a clue."

"Yeah," he said with a sly smile, and she knew that *he* knew she was lying.

* * *

Ari could hear them fighting before she reached the suite's door. She half expected the room to be trashed when she entered. What she didn't expect was to find them in the middle of a Bananagrams game.

"I'm supposed to believe that 'dixit' is a word?" Jane argued, pointing at Rory's tiles. "You made that up just to get rid of your x."

"Look it up," she said. "But remember, if it's a real word…" She pointed to the box of Franzia chardonnay sitting next to her.

Ari noticed a half-filled wineglass in front of Rory and an empty one in front of Jane, who was still debating whether to consult her smartphone.

"I don't believe you," she snarled and tapped in the letters.

"Let me just get this ready for you," she said, putting Jane's glass under the plastic tap and filling it with the cheap wine. "'Dixit' is dogma. From the Latin phrase 'Ipse dixit,' it refers to a statement that must be accepted on the faith of the speaker." She held the glass out. "You have a problem accepting what I'm telling you."

"Aagh!" she gasped. "I can't believe it." She stared at the wine, her expression like that of a child faced with eating liver, and chugged it quickly.

Ari glanced at her watch. "How did you get here so soon?" she asked Rory.

"Oh, I let my TA teach my two thirty class. This sounded much more interesting." She grinned broadly. Ari imagined her smile charmed most any woman she wanted. She'd certainly done something to Jane, but Ari wasn't sure if it was good or bad.

"So what happens if you question one of her words and it's real?"

"That hasn't happened yet."

"Yet!" Jane yelled, pointing a finger. "And when it *does* happen, she has to take me out to dinner at a fine restaurant that serves very expensive wine. For each word, the price of the bottle goes up by fifty bucks."

Rory looked at Ari. "So far I'm paying for a carafe of Yellow Tail."

"How about we look at the journals?"

"We already did that," Jane slurred. "Tell her what you think."

Rory went to the couch and the stacks of journals. Colorful sticky notes protruded from many of the pages, and corners were turned down throughout.

"I coded these with pink, green and yellow because they are the most prominent names, and if the killer is mentioned, I'm guessing it's in one of these strands. But let's back up and I'll tell you why I've come to that conclusion. First, I am truly impressed by Nina's knowledge of Shakespeare. The Folger Library in D.C. could've hired her. I had to look up several of the characters she referenced because I couldn't remember them, and I've read everything multiple times."

She opened a journal to a dog-eared page and pointed to an entry. "For example, 'Hecate's shoplifting is driving Dromio crazy. Must stop enabling—allow for tough love.' Hecate was the leader of the witches in *Macbeth*, but Dromio is actually two characters, twin servants in *Comedy of Errors.*"

"So there doesn't seem to be any reason she picked these characters from these plays. It's totally random just to keep confidentiality," Ari surmised.

"Sometimes," she agreed, "but in other entries I think there's some reasoning behind it." She flipped to another page with a turned down corner. "'Portia continues to believe Angelo despite his behavior. Cheated with Audrey. Paulina: listen and hold temper.' Portia was a lawyer, which may or may not be important, but Audrey was a loose woman in *As You Like It* and Angelo was a womanizer in *Measure for Measure*. So it fits that time."

"Who's Paulina?" Jane asked.

Rory grinned and wagged a finger. "I think you were on to something, Ari. I think Nina has cast herself in these entries, at least some of the time."

"Is she always Paulina?"

"No, but Shakespeare created many roles for strong women, including Paulina, Valeria, Portia, Bianca, Katherine and Cordelia, just to name a few. And all of them are mentioned."

"So," Jane summarized, "the characters could be either symbols of Nina or other females involved in these problems."

"Or they could be men," she said. "In some of the comedies like *Twelfth Night*, characters changed form so a woman was a man disguised as a woman or vice versa."

"And wasn't one a donkey?" Jane asked.

She nodded. "You're thinking of *Midsummer Night's Dream* where Bottom is changed by Puck to have the head of a jackass."

"Was George Bush in that play?"

Ari sighed. "Okay, so how do we make sense of this?"

"That's where the color coding comes in. I see three main strands involving three sets of characters, the same ones you found in Nina's next-to-last journal. First, there's the plot with Frederick, the treacherous husband, his wife, Adriana, Hotspur, Cerimon and the dead daughter, Cordelia."

"The girl who died from bulimia," Ari clarified.

"Right." She opened to a purple tab and read the entry. "'Adriana is growing paranoid. Frederick is constantly gone. Hotspur suspects Cerimon is the problem. Dangerous?'"

"That's so cryptic," Jane said.

"It is," she agreed. "But Nina rarely mentioned danger in her entries and only within these three strands."

Ari grabbed a notepad and wrote down the four Shakespearean characters before she flipped to the second page. "What was the next one?"

"The plot with Edmund, Emilia, Katherine and Caliban."

"Who was Caliban again?" Jane asked.

"Caliban was a deformed servant, a monster."

"Sounds like a great description of someone who might commit murder," Ari said softly.

"Or abuse a child," Rory said. "Listen to this. 'Emilia equals pathetic girl. Supporting Edmund at any cost. Katherine and Caliban are the strength!'"

"It's almost like she's siding with two people and against two others," Ari suggested.

"Maybe Edmund is Steve Garritson and Emilia is actually Sam," Jane said. "She underlined 'girl,' so maybe that's a clue that Emilia isn't a girl at all. Maybe Caliban and Katherine are Georgie and Nina?"

Ari shrugged. "That's as good a theory as any at this point."

"Finally, there's the third plot line," Rory said, picking up Nina's last journal. "It involves Orlando, Cesario, Benedick, Valeria, Horatio and finally, Aguecheek. Something was about to be uncovered and danger is implied for someone. That last entry before she died was very important. 'The secret will be revealed—DANGER. Poor Benedick! Poor Horatio! And poor Orlando—a pawn?'" She looked up at both of them. "It's interesting to me that only three characters are mentioned here. What happened to Cesario, Valeria and Aguecheek?"

She tapped the book and said, "I think this is the most important storyline, and I'm guessing this secret is the reason she was killed."

"We don't even know who these people are," Jane said. "We've got five men and one woman."

"Or that character could be a little girl in danger," Ari suggested.

"Or it could be Nina," Jane said. "But who are all the guys?"

"Well, remember that sometimes men and women were confused. Cesario is one of those characters. She's actually a character named Viola who's posing as a man."

Ari looked at Rory. "How do you suggest we organize this?"

"I think we write out all the entries on these three sets of people and see if we can figure out who they are. That way we can watch all of our suspects at Nina's funeral tomorrow."

"*I* think this is impossible," Jane said.

"It'll be a little tricky, that's for sure, but I'm rather certain I've got one story figured out already."

"How so?" Ari asked, pouring herself a glass of wine from the box.

Rory chuckled. "Because I'm in it."

CHAPTER SEVENTEEN

Jack wiped his eyes, which were starting to cross from reading so many files. Pictures, index cards and sticky notes filled the makeshift collage he'd created against his closed vertical blinds. Margarita Escolido's smiling face hung at the center.

He was starting to understand why Molly drew circles to nudge her thinking. This was a complicated case with many possible suspects, all of whom had been ruled out. Margarita had a large family, several close friends and dozens of co-workers, all of whom were investigated, but everyone had said the same thing—she was loved by all and had no enemies. No one had emerged as a viable suspect.

One fact bothered him: David Ruskin had supervised the detectives assigned to the case, and Jack had already caught a few minor procedural errors that would've spelled trouble for the prosecutor in the event a suspect was ever arrested, nothing huge, but he worried he'd find more mistakes the deeper he dug. As much as he hated Ruskin, he was past the point in his life where he desired confrontation. Or was he? If he was offered the promotion and accepted, he'd be working closely with Ruskin. He sighed. It would be worth it because he'd be in the same city as Ari.

He looked from the blinds to the corkboard that housed all of the notes on the Carnotti case and chuckled.

"Something funny, Adams?"

He looked up at Dylan Phillips, standing in the doorway with her purse and jacket over her shoulder. She was on her way out and she looked tired.

"I was thinking about life," he said honestly.

She raised a sculpted eyebrow. "Oh? Reconsidering your choices?"

He shook his head. "You don't understand my humor."

"Perhaps you'll have the opportunity to explain it to me some time. Your promotion is going through."

He was marveling at the dimple that appeared on her chin when his phone rang. "Adams."

"Jack, you gotta get over here right now!" Andre cried.

"Whoa, slow down. What happened? Is Ari okay?"

He glanced at Dylan, watching her smile and dimple morph into concern.

"I'm sure Ari's fine, but you know our lead from the gym? She's dead."

* * *

The Arroyo apartment complex was well known by law enforcement. The beat cops fielded endless noise complaints, arrested drug dealers routinely and constantly fined minors for underage drinking at the legendary parties there. It was a meat market for the under-thirty crowd. As he passed the pool at nine forty-five, Jack wasn't surprised to see two dozen men and women splashing in the water while a boom box blasted a rap backbeat that drowned out their laughter and playful screams.

He found Andre interviewing the neighbor who'd discovered the body. Andre motioned to his left, and he wandered down a sidewalk crowded with techs and uniformed officers. Her body laid on the concrete in a twisted sleep. He glanced up at the balconies filled with tenants and partiers staring down at the corpse until he found the one with a CSI officer working on it.

Andre joined him, pulling a folded paper from his pocket. It was a printout from Uptown Fitness that included her bio and a picture. "Her real name was Wanda Sells, a bank teller with Saguaro Credit Union. She was the one, Jack. After I sweet-talked the gym manager into pulling the possibles for me, I took them to Molly tonight and she ID'd Wanda."

"I'm surprised she's not with you now. How'd you keep her from tagging along?"

Andre shrugged. "It was weird. *She* was weird. It was almost like she was happy. Didn't care about Wanda at all. Anyway, I came right over, and the uniforms had just gotten here to answer a call about a jumper."

"Did anyone *see* her jump?"

"No, I think they just assumed, though apparently more than a few drunks have fallen over these balconies, if you can believe it."

"I can. Do we know if she was drinking?"

"Yeah."

They walked several feet past the body to a spray of glass shards glistening in the moonlight. Jack found a larger chunk and surmised it was a highball glass. He sniffed it.

"Vodka."

"Yup. According to the neighbors Wanda had a reputation for guzzling vodka on her balcony every night. She's lived here for more than a year and nearly every tenant in her building knows her habits. The guy who discovered the body was out power walking, making his laps around the complex. He says he does it three times every night. Second time he came by everything was normal, but on the third lap, which was about ten minutes later, she was on the ground. Whipped out his cell phone and called nine-one-one."

"So she wasn't dead very long before she was discovered. That's good," he said. He glanced up at the balcony. "That's a hell of a fall. Let's go upstairs and check out her apartment."

"So I guess this is our case, huh?" Andre asked eagerly. "Do you think the chief will give us more time since our best lead is dead?"

"Hard to say."

A uniformed officer guarded the door; they passed him with a nod. The place was a mess, but there was no sign of foul play. They went to the balcony, where a crime tech was just finishing up.

"Just her prints," he said as he left.

Jack took a deep breath. "Do you smell it?"

Andre shook his head. "No."

"Pot. Just faint traces, so either her neighbor is toking up or she was." He leaned on the railing and was surprised when it jiggled. "What the hell? Check the other side," he told Andre.

He squatted and examined the screws. The plaster around each one was worn down and they floated in the holes.

"Same thing over here," Andre said, wiping his hands on his handkerchief. "That railing was about to go."

"Or went," he muttered.

He peered over the railing and noticed fresh-looking drag marks moving toward the edge of the building, as if the railing had come out and been pulled back into place.

"What do you think?"

"I'm thinking this is fishy. How tall was she?"

"Five-five."

"And this railing is four feet tall. For her to fall over the railing and not catch herself is somewhat implausible. And look at this." He pointed to the drag marks. "At some point the screws popped out, probably as her body went over."

"That makes sense," Andre agreed.

"So why are they back in the holes? She was flying through the air. How did the screws go back?"

"Maybe they popped back in?"

He pushed the railing and the screws popped out again, but when he let go, the railing didn't move.

"So you're suggesting that somebody pulled the railing back?"

He nodded. "Maybe it was one of the techs. We'll need to check." He pointed to the ground where the broken glass glistened in the moonlight. "That makes me uncomfortable too. If you're falling over a railing accidentally, you're going to fall straight down. You don't project out, and the fact that her drink is so far away from her body suggests she was still holding it when she fell—or flew—over the railing."

"So somebody pushed her."

"It would make sense. Let's see what else there is to find."

They wandered through the bedroom and noticed the unmade bed and clothes strewn everywhere. Wanda's life seemed to revolve around work and the gym. Silk blouses were heaped in piles with running shorts and exercise bras.

Foraging through the medicine cabinet yielded prescriptions for Vicodin and Zoloft amid the typical over-the-counter drugs for colds and allergies. "It's gotta be somewhere," he said.

He went to the corner of her living room she used for a home office and studied the small bookshelf above the desk. He opened a few trinket containers and found the usual mementos—movie ticket stubs, change and discarded keys. He pulled out each of the books while Andre went to the kitchen.

In the middle of the second row he found an old dictionary. Most young people didn't bother with them anymore because of smartphones. He opened the book and chuckled. The center of the pages had been carved out, creating a great hiding place—for her pot, cocaine and Ecstasy.

He carried three baggies into the kitchen and waved them at Andre. "Oh, my," Andre said, pulling his head from the refrigerator. "Apparently Wanda enjoyed many recreational activities." He opened the cabinet under the sink and revealed an empty vodka bottle in the trash can. "I'd say Wanda loved to drink."

"Let's look at the rest of the trash," Jack said.

He pulled out the liner and inspected the contents of the partially filled bag. In addition to the vodka bottle, he found the recent edition of *People*, a Lean Cuisine TV dinner box and several pieces of junk mail.

"There's only trash from a single meal in the can, suggesting that she was rather particular about removing garbage. I'd say this is from today, meaning that unless she spent the entire day getting snockered, it's highly unlikely she drank the whole bottle by herself."

"She might've been finishing it," Andre said.

"True," he conceded, "but did we find another glass?"

Andre went to the cabinet where glassware was stored. "It looks like she bought a standard set with highballs, tumblers and fruit juice glasses."

"How many tumblers do you see?"

"Eight."

"How many juice glasses?"

"Five, but…" He opened the nearly empty dishwasher and found three more. "There's eight total."

Jack felt a familiar rush of energy. "How many highball glasses?"

Andre paused and looked around the kitchen before he answered. "Six."

"Let's go through the house again," he said.

They scanned all the rooms but found no additional glasses and nothing to suggest Wanda had entertained anyone.

"So if she was pushed off, then the killer took the extra glass. Six plus the shattered one on the concrete equals seven. But she could've broken one before today."

"That's certainly possible. People do it all the time."

"But you don't think so."

"Those glasses look pretty new. They don't have any dishwasher stains or filmy bottoms, you know, the stuff that happens eventually to your glasses after you've sent them through the dishwasher a hundred times."

"Yeah, so it's a little less likely that she broke a new one."

"Possibly."

He went to the coffee table. A single glass coaster with a visible ring confirmed it had been recently used. It rested near the edge, suggesting Wanda and her guest—if she'd had one—had sat on the couch, talking and sipping drinks. He glanced at the coaster stand on the nearby end table. Each coaster had its own little compartment, and one was empty, which accounted for Wanda's. He pulled the rest of them out and set them on the table. All of them were dry except one. Droplets of moisture remained on it, even after someone had hastily wiped it off.

"Here's our evidence."

He motioned to a tech with a camera. The guy took pictures of the coasters while he pulled out his cell phone. "You asked if Chief Phillips might give us some more time. Since our only lead in the investigation of Vince Carnotti was just murdered, I'd say she might."

CHAPTER EIGHTEEN

Biz glanced at her watch under the hazy glow of the fluorescent lights illuminating the ten gas pumps. Although it was two in the morning, the Quik Mart was busy, filled with night owls who needed smokes or alcohol. She was still an hour outside of Laguna Beach, and although the Harley had a half tank of gas, she'd stopped to acquire some insurance, carefully scoping out the Quik Mart as her best option.

She casually picked through one of the nearby trash cans. Not finding what she needed, she headed to another one and resumed her search. Still nothing. She shook her head. It should be easier than this. She noticed a can over by the bathrooms outside the front door of the shop. A young Hispanic man pushed through the door, discarded his receipt in the trash and headed for his car.

She smiled.

She walked around the building so no one from the store would see her pass directly in front of the windows and quickly thumbed through the trash, knowing she'd need to burrow toward the bottom.

"Excuse me. Are you okay?" a voice said.

The woman had clearly been clubbing all night, judging from the alcohol on her breath and her glassy eyes. She wore tight jeans and a black jacket with a tank top on underneath, but what Biz noticed was her sparkling turquoise lipstick. Definitely L.A.

"I'm fine. I walked out of the store and accidentally threw away my receipt *and* I dropped my bike keys in here too."

"I could help you look?" the clubber asked in a very friendly tone.

"No, I got it. Thanks."

The woman shrugged at the dismissal and walked into the store. Biz searched faster. The idea was to be invisible, not have conversations with people. *Yes!* Nestled against some used paper towels and an empty cigarette pack was a white slip of paper. She grabbed it and searched some more, until she found two more slips.

She quickly pocketed them, jumped on the Harley and zoomed away. She turned into the next gas station and pulled up next to the air and water station. She pulled out the receipts, praying one of them would serve her purpose. She grinned when she scanned the second one. It had been generated at ten eighteen p.m., just a few hours ago. The customer had bought ten gallons of gas, a Diet Coke and a bag of Doritos—and paid with cash.

"I love Doritos," she murmured.

If anyone ever asked, she could now prove that she'd been in California, that there was no way she could have been pushing a woman off a balcony in Phoenix at nine p.m. It was physically impossible for her to be in two cities at the same time, and by the time anyone would think to question her, the store videotapes would probably be erased.

She carefully slid the receipt in her wallet, noticing for the first time in six hours that her heart had stopped pounding. She'd thrown up twice already and nearly toppled the Harley outside Quartzite when she started to cry, but she'd regained more and more control as the mile markers descended and she'd ridden closer to the California border.

She hopped on the bike and blasted Springsteen through her earbuds for the last part of the ride, refusing to think about anything except making love to Ari. It was easy to forget the darkness of the last six hours when she pictured the two of them in Ari's new Jacuzzi tub, the jets massaging their bodies while they kissed and cuddled.

She went out of her way to Costa Mesa and found an all-night motel. She doubted the sleepy-eyed clerk would ever remember her or the fake name she used in the event anyone ever investigated the story she planned to tell Ari—that she'd spent the night on the beach.

The place looked relatively clean. She fell onto the bed, her last ounce of energy depleted. It had been the most emotional day of her life. She could still hear the three tiny gasps that had slipped from Wanda's lips. She was too inebriated and too surprised to scream, but in a cruel twist of fate Biz deserved, she'd spiraled and stared at her for the four-story drop. She doubted she'd ever forget the look of confused terror on her face.

She'd made three mistakes and she couldn't stop beating herself up for them. She'd staged crime scenes before. She'd lost track of the number of deadbeat dads she'd set up, and she knew how the police operated. She'd never been questioned because she was *good*.

But she'd never killed anyone.

She'd been so careful with the setup. She'd run into Wanda at the gym and they'd spoken for less than thirty seconds. She'd agreed to her terms and told her she would bring the money to her apartment at eight thirty, when the weeknight parties would be in full swing and darkness would disguise her as she moved through the complex.

Wanda had answered the door carrying a highball. When she saw Biz in tight jeans, her black leather jacket over a white Western shirt with no sleeves and her black bra peeking through, she immediately asked her to stay for a little party, pouring vodka tonics for herself and Biz and willingly shared her coke stash. After a drink and a line, Biz found the courage to do what needed to be done. They made out for a while, and she was careful about what DNA she transferred. After Wanda downed four vodkas and was ready to head to the bedroom, she suggested they go to the patio and toke up first.

Marijuana had never affected her, but by the time they finished the joint, Wanda was lightheaded and off guard. When they stood to go inside, Biz moved behind her and caressed her breasts. For a split second she lost her nerve—until she noticed a black Escalade parked in the deserted alley behind the apartments. She had no choice. Her hands slid to the center of Wanda's back and she planted her feet in a football stance. Then Wanda was gone, hurtling over the balcony, drink still in her hand, wearing an expression of complete surprise and betrayal. Biz had gazed at her lifeless body on the pavement and nearly vomited.

Then she'd made the mistakes. She put on her leather gloves and pulled the railing back into place. Mistake one.

Then she'd rushed into the living room determined to erase the evidence of her visit in the fastest way possible, worried that the Escalade might be waiting for *her*. She'd grabbed her empty highball glass and stuffed it in the pocket of her jacket. Mistake number two. The police could count, and if someone like Jack Adams were assigned to the case, she imagined a missing glass would bother him endlessly.

The last mistake was the dumbest. She'd rubbed the wet coaster across her leather sleeve and put it back in the coaster holder without completely drying it. Hopefully no one would notice and by the time someone thought of it the tiny droplets of moisture would be gone. But a smart tech or a detective like Jack...

She rubbed her eyes. She was crashing but she wasn't tired. She needed sleep but the adrenaline rush from committing murder, the cocaine high and the long bike ride made it impossible. She'd need a little help as usual. She reached into her knapsack and found the familiar pill bottle. Dr. Nasab understood. She'd been abused for years by her tyrannical Iraqi husband—who was now being deported thanks to Biz. In return Dr. Nasab freely prescribed pills to help her through long stakeouts or gain the needed rest that often eluded her. She popped a few of the red and blue pills into her mouth and closed her eyes. She would be with Ari in a few hours and everything would be better. They were about to start their life together, and Ari would save her soul.

CHAPTER NINETEEN

During Nina's funeral at the Shepherd by the Sea Church, Ari, Jane and Rory each sat by a different set of suspects, having spent most of the past evening matching characters with real people. They'd analyzed and cross-referenced Nina's journal entries until they were rather certain who was who, but they were still no closer to finding the killer or killers since there seemed to be plenty of people with motives.

At one point in the evening Biz had texted that she might get to Laguna by morning, much to Ari's disappointment. She could've used some help with Rory and Jane, who had endlessly volleyed barbs and vocabulary puns. When she had finally retreated to her bedroom, they were starting another Bananagrams game with a bottle of Boone's Farm next to Rory.

She looked around the full sanctuary. Still no sign of Biz. Nina's neighbors, Bonnie and Fred Cahill, sat directly in front of her. Last night they had concluded that Adriana, the spurned wife, was in fact Bonnie and that her cheating husband Fred wore the accurate moniker of Frederick. They had indeed lost a daughter, although Rory had never known the exact cause until Nina mentioned bulimia in her journal. Rory recalled a few weeks before Nina died, she had asked her about Fred, a man who freely shared his extramarital exploits around the pool house. Since Rory had heard about the cheating, she became Hotspur in the journal entries. Jane had thought it was such a wonderful nickname she'd addressed her as such for the rest of the night.

Ari doubted infidelity would lead to murder unless there were some other facts still waiting to be uncovered. Nina had mentioned in one of the final entries that "Frederick's inheritance was vulnerable," and she knew that a sizeable inheritance split in half during a divorce proceeding could be a motive if a prenuptial agreement wasn't in place.

She craned her neck and noticed Jane sitting between Evan and Sam, who was having a difficult time holding his emotions together. He was supposed to read a scripture, and she wondered if he'd be able to make it through without breaking down. Both Steve and Georgie looked perfectly stoic and somber in deference to the occasion. Next to Steve was a handsome gentleman who whispered to him several times; she wondered if he was a relative.

Rory had surmised the Garritsons were portrayed in the journals as Orlando, Cesario, Benedick, Valeria and Horatio. If, in fact, Nina was one of the characters, then the other four Garritsons completed the list, one of whom could be a murderer. Something had happened in the summer that triggered Nina's entries in the journal, followed by a secret that may have led to her murder. Someone was hiding something in the Garritson family, although Sam had maintained they were boring and free of scandal.

She gazed at the row of Garritsons again. The character Aguecheek only appeared in the last entry of the completed journal. She pulled it from her large bag and reread it again. "Valeria caught in secrets thanks to apothecary. Share with no one except H. Maybe Orlando? Must investigate! Can Benedick be trusted? Will it destroy? Cesario, oh, Cesario… It is Aguecheek."

She realized that if the handsome man next to Steve Garritson were added to the character count, there were enough people to create the scenario in Nina's journal, assuming she was either Valeria or, as Rory had mentioned, Cesario. Whoever the man was, he was close enough to warrant a seat in the Garritson pew at the funeral, so perhaps he was important enough to be a character in the journal.

Rory had planted herself behind Michaela and her mother Eden. Bobby Arco was nowhere to be seen. She wasn't surprised, considering the threats he'd leveled against Nina at the school. Ari had tried to stay out of Eden's line of sight, knowing she would be suspicious after their confrontation at the auto shop. Eden and Michaela's attention, though, was focused on the altar and the portrait of Nina that stared at the crowd. Michaela looked terribly forlorn and her mother whispered in her ear and squeezed her shoulder. *Poor kid*, she thought.

More than likely the Edmund in Nina's journal was Bobby Arco and Emilia was Eden. In a cruel twist of symbolism, Rory deduced that Caliban, the pathetic creature from *The Tempest*, was in fact Michaela and that Nina had cast herself as Katherine, a strong Shakespearean female who protected Caliban.

"I've got my money on Bobby Arco," Rory had said the night before. "He's got a horrible temper, he works near Crescent Point and it's obvious Nina is afraid of him."

It was true that the strongest wordings in Nina's journal were reserved for the Edmund, Emilia and Caliban story. Perhaps Bobby Arco's absence from the funeral was motivated by guilt, not anger.

The first row, traditionally for family members, held only Nina's aunt and a distant cousin. Both of her parents were dead and she'd been an only child. Ari understood that pain.

Standing in the back was Detective Clay Justice. He caught her eye and nodded. She nodded in return and leaned forward in the pew, in the hopes of overhearing the Cahills, who were already sniping at each other in whispered tones. Their facial expressions and body language suggested they couldn't stand each other, and when Fred Cahill checked his watch and sighed, she guessed he was present only because his wife had forced him to go or because his absence would be noticed.

The ceremony lasted an hour as several colleagues and friends offered remembrances, sang songs and read poems in Nina's honor. When Sam approached the lectern, his hands shook and he started to sob. Evan ran to his aid, but his voice quivered throughout the Psalms scripture. Ari's gaze darted among the suspects. Eden wiped tears from her face, Bonnie Cahill dabbed at her eyes with a tissue and Steve Garritson stared at the floor while Georgie put a hand to her mouth, obviously channeling the pain of her children. Only Fred Cahill showed no reaction.

After the pastor offered a prayer, the recessional began. As the rows of guests snaked outside, Eden and Michaela quickly headed toward the street, holding hands. They were evidently walking home without saying a word to anyone. Ari motioned Rory to join her.

"Did you notice anything?"

Rory shook her head. "No, the little girl was terribly upset and her mom just kept talking about how the angels would take care of Miss Hunter in heaven. It made me cry. I don't think she had anything to do with this, but I think the boyfriend is guilty as hell," she quickly added.

"Come with me," Ari said. "I want you to introduce me to the Cahills."

Bonnie and Fred Cahill apparently had rushed to the buffet luncheon. While dozens of people milled about, they were two of only a few people who actually held a plate full of food.

"It's such a shame," Bonnie said between bites. "I can't believe they haven't found her killer. Maybe he's actually here," she whispered.

Fred harrumphed and rolled his eyes. "You watch way too much *Law and Order*. Besides I heard they're getting close to arresting Sam Garritson."

"Where did you hear that?" Ari asked.

Fred licked potato salad off two fingers before he said, "Friend of mine in the department. Apparently when she went over the railing, Nina ripped off part of a shirt."

Rory crossed her arms. "What kind of fabric was it?"

"Don't know, but you can get DNA off stuff."

"And you think *I* watch too much *Law and Order*?" Bonnie snorted. "You're full of crap, Fred."

"It's true, B," he insisted. "If she ripped off part of his shirt, she might've grabbed some chest hair too."

"Did you speak with Detective Justice?" Ari asked. The Cahills stopped bantering and stared at her. "I mean, did all of the neighbors get questioned?"

"Not everyone, just the people in her list of contacts. Since I've been visiting with her each week, they asked us where we were on the night of the murder. It was just like on TV."

"And where were you?" Rory laughed, as if the inquiry were nothing more than a joke.

"Well, I was working late, and Fred was out at the bar with his friends." She patted his shoulder playfully. "Since he wasn't one of Nina's favorite people, I'm grateful he's got an alibi."

"You're the one who was in cahoots with her. She was trying to get you to leave me. Damn cunt," he said quietly.

"Excuse me?" Rory asked, stepping into his personal space.

"I don't have to talk to any of you," he growled and stomped off.

Looking quite embarrassed, Bonnie said, "I'm so sorry," and left too.

Jane joined them and watched the Cahills' shouting match escalate as they got into their car.

Rory glared in their direction. "Okay, I'm going to add Fred Cahill to the prick category. I wish he and Bobby Arco had done it together. I'd love to see 'em both fry."

"Don't you mean be lethally injected?" Jane corrected. "I thought California didn't use the electric chair."

"How unfortunate," Rory murmured. "Whoever killed Nina deserves to suffer."

"I agree."

Rory faced her. "So we actually *agree* on something?"

Jane's eyes smoldered. She was a few inches shorter than Rory, and when she tipped her chin up to meet her gaze, Ari thought for sure they'd wind up in a torrid kiss, one that was entirely inappropriate for a funeral. She broke the spell and asked, "Is Sam okay?"

Jane blinked and shook her head. "He's not okay at all. He really loved her and there's no way he could've hurt her. The fact that the police suspect him is only adding to his pain."

They looked over at the family clustered together with Nina's aunt and her cousin as mourners continued to wander by and offer condolences. The man who'd sat by Steve at the service remained at his side.

Ari pointed at him. "Who's that?"

"That's Scott Kramer. He's an old family friend and Steve's closest political advisor."

She studied the tall, handsome man. He was younger than Georgie and Steve by several years, but if he was that close to the family, she imagined he might know all of their secrets. He flashed a smile at something Evan said. *He should be the politician,* she thought. That smile was worth a lot of votes.

Evan waved them over and introduced Scott. "He started cleaning our pools when he was a teenager. Dad was so impressed by his drive for success that he helped him start his company."

Scott looked appropriately humble, although she felt his eyes all over her as Evan detailed his climb from pool cleaning service to landscaping business.

"He recently landed the Montage account," he added. "Excuse me." He moved to another group that she assumed were schoolteachers.

Scott flashed a winning smile. "How do you all know Nina?"

"She was one of my best friends a long time ago," Jane said.

"It couldn't have been *that* long ago," he said playfully.

"What are your thoughts about Nina's murder?" Ari asked.

The question seemed to surprise him. "Well, it's horrible. I can't imagine why anyone would want to hurt her."

Rory stared at him and crossed her arms. "Do you think Sam and Nina were still in love?"

He nodded. "Yeah, I don't think they were done. It was only a matter of time before they got back together. Love's like that, you know? Even if it's not what's good for you or what other people think is right, it's there."

She guessed he was talking from his own experience. She wanted to ask more questions, but Georgie appeared and looped her arm through Scott's. "Well, we need to officially start the food line, although some people rudely jumped ahead," she chided. "Excuse us."

"She's a piece of work," Jane said after they left.

Rory looked at her. "We agree on *two* things. I think Georgie Garritson is the most narcissistic person I've ever met."

"Ooh, good word," Jane cooed. Ari sensed the icy wall between them was melting.

Steve and Sam joined Georgie and Scott in line while Evan lagged behind, talking to a short Hispanic man in a dark three-piece suit. They followed and Evan introduced them to Juan Bojorquez.

"I guess Juan and I were rivals, vying for Nina's employment."

"Really?" Jane said, surprised. "I thought Nina loved working at the school."

"She did," he agreed, "but we couldn't pay her what she was worth, and frankly, I think having to deal with people like Bobby Arco was wearing her down."

"Was she really that afraid of him?" Ari pressed.

Evan nodded. "Oh, yes. We'd actually talked about a restraining order. If she decided to stay at Brayberry I promised I'd go to the judge."

"How did you meet Nina?" Rory asked the other man.

Juan's face turned stony. "She helped me with my daughter. She saved her life."

She guessed Juan would do anything to help Nina. "When was she going to make the decision?"

The men exchanged a glance. "Two days after she died," Juan said quietly. "I think she was going to take the job. She'd completed all of the paperwork, taken the drug test. She just wanted to be sure, especially considering the situation."

Ari eyed him carefully. "What situation?"

Juan glanced at Evan, who turned red. Apparently he'd revealed a secret. "Nina was pregnant."

CHAPTER TWENTY

"That's her," Molly said, staring at the black-and-white head shot of Wanda Sells lying on the morgue slab. Even without her Lola makeup or wig and wearing the pallor of death, she recognized her talented lips and turned up nose. "How did she die?"

"Pushed off her balcony," Andre said.

She dropped her legs into the shimmering blue water. They were poolside, Andre showing up just as she was finishing her daily routine with the chemicals and filter. The news of Lola's death seemed anticlimactic, but she still felt vindicated and slightly pleased, or perhaps that was just a holdover from her previous afternoon with Sienna.

"Whoever did this wasn't a pro," he said. "Too sloppy, too many mistakes."

"Like what?"

He told her about the moved railing, the missing glass and the wet coaster. "A pro wouldn't have moved that railing, and he *or she* probably would've just shot her."

"Not if it was supposed to look like an accident," she disagreed. "I think your killer was trying to end the little drama with Lola." He took out his notepad and started to jot down her thoughts. "I'm going to guess that this second woman was controlling her, but maybe she started to get greedy. Maybe she wanted more money or maybe she was threatening to go to the cops."

He cocked his head. "Why would she do that?"

"Think about it. I don't know what else she was into, but she didn't break any laws with me, except giving me Ecstasy. She didn't kidnap me, and she certainly didn't drive drunk or destroy private property." Realizing her voice was rising, she took a deep breath. "I did all that," she said softly.

"So the killer needed her out of the way."

She nodded and stood up. "She was a loose end and potentially very dangerous. Do you have any suspects other than Carnotti?"

"He could still be involved," he said as they strolled to his Caprice in the parking lot. "Maybe he controls her handler and maybe it was the handler who killed her."

She smiled proudly. "Those are distinct possibilities."

He grinned. "Thanks, Mol. I still like bouncing ideas off you. I mean, Jack's a great guy, but he gets all quiet and moody when he's thinking."

"Reminds me of someone else," she said with a snort, thinking of Ari's aloofness. "Any leads on who the handler might be?"

"We're going through Wanda's life right now. So far it seems she lived to work out. She went to her job at the bank and the gym. As far as we can tell, she wasn't involved in any community groups and didn't have any family in the area. We're interviewing her co-workers and people at the gym, so hopefully a name will surface."

He got into the car and leaned out the window. "You look better today, happier," he said slowly, as if he wasn't sure he should mention it.

She knew she was blushing. "I am."

* * *

Sienna's tub was just big enough for Molly's long frame. An old claw-foot, it cocooned their bodies, Sienna nestled between her thighs, surrounded by thousands of bubbles. When she rubbed the bath sponge over Sienna's breasts, Sienna laughed.

"I don't think those are dirty."

"That's for me to decide."

The purpose of the bath was to remove the scented body oil they'd massaged over their limbs during foreplay. She had never known anyone as attuned to complete satisfaction as Sienna, who truly believed that great sex involved all of the senses.

When she'd arrived, she'd found a note on the door. "Come upstairs." She'd followed the strong smell of incense into the boudoir, where Sienna waited on the bed, wearing a lacy black camisole and panties. After she undressed, Sienna ordered her to lie on her stomach and take deep breaths. She'd felt the warm oil drizzle down her back, and within minutes Sienna's hands had commanded every nerve in her body, smoothing the oil over her skin like a sculptor. When she'd turned over, she was completely aroused.

Sienna had enjoyed her front as much as her back, and once she was slick and glistening, Sienna had pulled off her camisole, kissed her stomach and slid between her legs. It had been heaven.

"You're still thinking about it, aren't you?" she chuckled.

"Well, when you haven't had sex for nine months and then you get laid twice in two days, it's momentous."

She laughed and nuzzled against her cheek. "I'm glad I'm *momentous*, or would you have said that about anyone?"

She kissed her. "No, I've never met anyone who is as skillful a lover as you are."

Sienna lifted a perfectly pedicured foot from the bubbles and caressed Molly's calf. "Even your ex? What was her name?"

"Ari, and no, she wasn't like you."

"Hmm. Interesting answer. So I'm skillful. How so?"

"I can't explain it. It's not just that you're great in bed, a lot of women are. It's like the difference between someone who's a good cook and someone who's a chef."

"Well, that's quite a compliment. I guess all my studying paid off."

She gazed into her deep blue eyes. "You *studied* love making?"

"Of course. Making love takes practice. Anyone can smash their lips together or jab a few orifices until somebody comes—"

"That's a great image," she groaned.

"Was Ari a chef or was she just a good cook?"

She glanced at her inquisitive face and sensed her sincerity. "Neither," she said. "It was beautiful even if it always wasn't skillful," she added with a laugh, an image of the two of them falling into the back of Ari's SUV during a camping trip because they couldn't wait until they got to a motel.

"But to be a lover of lovers, you have to know what you're doing," Sienna said. She turned to face her and caressed her shoulder. "Did you know that touching the skin releases oxytocin, the cuddle hormone? The more oxytocin we generate during foreplay, the greater the orgasm, or at least that's what I think."

"Makes sense," she mumbled, as Sienna's fingers crept down her chest and circled her left areola.

"Now, yesterday was a little bit of an experiment. I wanted to know what you like. Some women don't like their breasts touched because the nerve endings are so sensitive. You're not one of those."

Proving her point, Molly's nipple grew erect and she moaned when Sienna's tongue flicked against it. "What else do you know?" she gasped.

"Many things, but we don't have time for another lesson today. I have a kickboxing class at six."

Remembering Sienna went to the same gym as Wanda, she asked, "Did you know Wanda Sells? She was a regular."

"Oh, yeah. Wanda's in the class. That woman is strong." When her expression shifted, she asked, "Did something happen?"

She stroked her cheek and broke the news as gently as she could. "She was murdered last night. My former partner has the case. He says that she was pushed over her balcony."

Shock covered her face. "Murdered? I can't believe it. Everyone liked her, and I don't know how anyone could throw her over a balcony. She'd put up a good fight if she was ever attacked."

"They think it was someone she knew, so she probably wasn't expecting it. She had her guard down. You said everyone liked her. Can you remember any arguments or disagreements with anyone?"

She shook her head. "No, we all got along great. That gym is like my second home. It's just so unbelievable." She climbed out of the tub and wrapped herself in a robe.

Molly followed her and found her sitting on the edge of the bed in the master suite. Feeling like an intruder in the room Sienna shared with her husband, Molly said, "I'm gonna go. I'm really sorry to end our afternoon on such a downer. The police will probably want to question you about your relationship with Wanda. Did you and she...?"

"No," she said sharply. "Wanda wouldn't dream of hooking up with a bisexual. She'd made that very clear. It was the one fight we had," she added absently.

Molly kissed the top of her head. "She didn't know what she was missing."

Sienna mustered a slight smile. "Thanks." She reached for her phone. "I should probably call a few people and prepare them for this. Jesse and Sheila, and I should start with Biz."

Molly whirled around. "What? Biz goes to that gym?"

Sienna looked surprised. "You know Biz?"

"Yeah, you could say that. Is she in your kickboxing class?"

"Uh-huh. All three of us."

CHAPTER TWENTY-ONE

Ari, Jane and Rory pored over the journals scattered on the coffee table. Biz had finally shown up at the resort in mid-afternoon looking haggard and troubled. When Ari asked her what was wrong, she shook her head and walked straight to the minibar. After downing two tiny bottles of tequila, she had dropped onto the love seat. She hadn't moved or spoken since.

The news of Nina's pregnancy was a game-changer in Ari's mind. While Bobby Arco was still a primary suspect, the chance that Nina's murder was motivated by personal reasons seemed far more likely.

Evan had admitted that he and Juan were the only two people who had known Nina was seven weeks pregnant. Even Sam didn't. Evan was struggling with whether or not to tell him, since Nina was dead.

"Why didn't the police confront him about this?" Jane asked. "Wouldn't they want to see the expression on his face when they announced it?"

Ari shook her head. "You're right about that. Something isn't right. They're keeping it a secret for a reason."

"Maybe Nina had another lover?" Rory suggested.

"I doubt it," she disagreed. "She still had pictures of Sam everywhere."

"I still think it's Bobby," Jane said.

"Why?" Rory asked, always ready to poke at Jane.

"His work shirt gave him away. Ari never notices these things, but when we saw him at the school, his work shirt was missing the name patch, like it had been ripped off. I'll bet Nina grabbed it as she fell."

Rory rolled her eyes. "If it were that simple, don't you think he'd already be in custody? If they'd found Nina clutching a patch with the name of a parent who threatened her, I'm pretty sure they'd call that a smoking gun, wouldn't they, Biz?"

They all looked at her draped over the love seat, her eyes closed. "Probably," she mumbled.

"What's wrong with you?" Jane spat. "You're the PI and you're not doing anything!"

She sat up on her elbows and scowled. "Jane, I had a horrible night sleeping on the beach after a terrible case. So cut me a little slack." She rolled off the couch and disappeared onto the patio.

"You need to talk to her," Jane said to Ari. "Something's terribly wrong. Rory and I will keep looking through the journals."

"And we'll focus on the Garritsons," Rory said sharply.

"No," Jane argued. "I'm telling you it's Bobby."

Ari slipped out to the patio and shut the door behind her. Biz was gazing at the perfectly manicured interior courtyard that surrounded the suites. The view wasn't as dramatic as the ocean, but it was beautiful and her thoughts drifted to her garden. Biz's gaze dropped to the ground and her shoulders fell forward. She was crying.

"Hey," she said, pulling her into an embrace. "It's okay." Biz cried on her shoulder, hugging her tightly. "I don't know what's wrong, but I want to help."

"You are," she said softly. "This helps. Holding you gives me strength."

The top of her head was seven inches shorter than Ari's and fit under her chin. "Tell me what happened," Ari whispered, stroking her back.

"It's too horrible," she whimpered. "Someone died."

"Oh, God. I'm so sorry."

She imagined one of Biz's battered wives had lost her life to an abusive husband or boyfriend after she'd returned despite her pleas to stay away. It wasn't the first—or second time—she'd seen her cry over a dead client. Her work was so important, and she poured her soul into helping all the women who struggled to break the cycle, many of whom couldn't. When Biz's brown eyes gazed up into her own, all she saw was her goodness and the sadness that surrounded her.

The kiss was tentative, and Biz trembled, her vulnerability revealed. Ari hoped her lips offered reassurance and her embrace security. Biz seemed to need both. She pressed against her to silence her quaking body—and released her hunger.

The next kiss was bold and passionate. She flashed back to their tryst on the couch, when Molly caught them. *Molly...*

She tried to pull away, but Biz held her tight, reclaiming the moment, *their* moment, demanding she submit to her feelings and acknowledge her loneliness. So when Biz's fingers grazed her breast, she moaned softly.

"Please," Biz begged. "I've wanted you for so long."

The shadows made it difficult to read her expression. She couldn't tell if Biz was angry or upset, but the frustration was apparent. And why shouldn't she be frustrated? She'd led Biz on for months now, unable to let go of a lover who hated her, but unwilling to dismiss Biz because of the heat she felt whenever they were together.

Shouts came from the suite; Jane and Rory were arguing again. She glanced through the sheer curtains and saw they were facing off. She cupped Biz's face and kissed her completely.

"Soon," she said, her voice filled with desire.

A wicked smile crept across Biz's face and her hands slid down Ari's buttocks. "Promise?"

She grinned and led her back inside. The fact that they were holding hands wasn't lost on Jane, who immediately abandoned her confrontation with Rory. "All better, Biz?"

"Much." Biz pecked Ari on the cheek and dropped into a chair. "Now, why are you ladies arguing?"

Rory picked up Nina's last completed journal and positioned her reading glasses. "Jane and I have a difference of opinion regarding the interpretation of this entry. I think it makes a lot of sense if you keep in mind Nina was pregnant." She flipped to the next to last page. "'Valeria caught in secrets thanks to apothecary. Share with no one except H. Maybe Orlando? Must investigate! Can Benedick be trusted? Will it destroy? Cesario, oh, Cesario… It is Aguecheek.'

"An apothecary was another term for pharmacist, but perhaps in this case it's a doctor, meaning Valeria is Nina." Rory glanced at Ari and Biz, who nodded their agreement. She continued to read. "'Share with no one except H.' Horatio is Evan since he's the only one who learned of the pregnancy."

"Makes sense," Biz said. "And I don't think she ever would've told him if he hadn't seen her running to the bathroom all the time."

"Here's where Jane and I differ. I think Orlando is Sam and Benedick is Steve. That would leave Georgie to be Cesario."

"And I think Cesario is Sam," Jane said. "Look at the way she keeps saying Cesario. It's like she's sad. I can't imagine Nina ever being sad about Georgie."

Ari stared at the journal entry. "She says she needs to investigate. Why? My guess is she learned something after she found out she was pregnant, something about the family, something that could damage their reputation."

Biz touched her hand. "The part where she asks if Benedick can be trusted could indicate that he's Steve because it sounds like she trusts Orlando more than Benedick, which would be Sam. Nina would've trusted Sam before she trusted Steve."

"*If* you're reading the context correctly and that's why this is difficult," Rory stated. "And the last part is also important. She says, 'It is Aguecheek.' There's no doubt in her mind. She's learned something about him and she's absolutely positive—"

"But she needs proof, so she'll investigate," Jane said, finishing her thought.

Rory looked at her with admiration. "Whatever she discovered and investigated was the cause of her death. Excellent postulation, Jane."

The sexual energy had increased in the room again. Ari wasn't sure if it was the sparks between Jane and Rory or between her and Biz, who had taken her hand again.

Jane looked at Biz and scowled. "Hey, PI! Quit making googly eyes at my best friend and tell us what to do. Where do we go from here?"

Biz pulled her gaze from Ari and cleared her throat. "Well, I think we need to divide and conquer. There are still too many damn suspects, especially if you count Bobby Arco, and I think we should. We need to split up and watch them before they arrest Sam for murder."

CHAPTER TWENTY-TWO

The full moon bathed the employee parking lot outside the Bliss resort, making it easy for Jack to review the files he'd brought with him. The Honda that Margarita Escolido had driven to work on the night she was murdered had been parked one spot over. It wasn't her regular car, which might have been a reason the security guard had had it towed so quickly. He hadn't recognized it.

She'd parked underneath one of the enormous lights, which suggested she might have been security conscious. The lot sat on the edge of a ravine forming a natural property line. There was only one way in or out, meaning that her attacker had passed through the main gate half a mile away, under the watchful gaze of the security cameras. However, the detectives had reviewed hours of footage and found nothing useful. He glanced up at the lone camera that scanned the hundred spaces, installed two weeks *after* Margarita's murder. Apparently she regularly parked in this small overflow lot, most likely because it was only a short walk up a hill from there to the restaurant where she worked as a waitress.

He reread the statement made by Ian Patton, the waiter who'd escorted her to the main path. Although her purse had not been found with her body, Patton clearly remembered her holding a key ring that included a can of pepper spray. Jack pictured a cautious woman advancing to her car in the wee hours of the morning without the benefit of a full moon, her finger poised on the trigger of the spray. The killer would've been waiting in the lot or he might have followed her out. Still more likely, her attacker was someone she knew and she didn't feel threatened. A note had been attached to Patton's statement, verifying his dozen sessions with a therapist after the murder when he was consumed by guilt for letting Margarita go to her car alone. He'd been ruled out as a suspect when a mini-mart security camera showed him buying a six-pack of beer just ten minutes after he'd left Margarita.

Jack shone his flashlight into the ravine, picturing Margarita tumbling through the desert brush to the bottom. The killer had followed her down and attacked her under the cover of darkness, leaving after he raped and strangled her. He'd had the sense to wear gloves and a condom, and he'd dusted his footprints away when he climbed out of the ravine.

He grabbed the scattered files from the hood of his Prius and walked up the sidewalk to the major path that circled the resort. It was here that Ian Patton had said goodnight and headed west toward the larger employee lot, leaving Margarita to make the short walk to her car by herself. It was later than usual, about one thirty, since Ian and Margarita had stayed to help restock the bar.

He gazed at the restaurant's patio as a few employees hurriedly stacked the patio furniture, clearly motivated to go home after the one a.m. closing. He followed the path another hundred yards to a set of steps that led down to the west lot, which was much bigger and more secure than the tiny overflow lot Margarita used. He frowned, sorry that she had sacrificed safety for convenience.

He checked the file notes again. Dozens of people had been questioned. Jack noted several places where follow-up interviews should've been conducted, but the two detectives assigned to the case weren't that experienced so it hadn't occurred. *David Ruskin wasn't known for his thoroughness*, he thought. Jack doubted he'd even read most of his detectives' reports.

He chuckled, remembering Ruskin's response when he'd asked him to come along for his one a.m. field trip. Although Chief Phillips had ordered him to help, Ruskin had quickly declined, stating it wouldn't do any good to see the crime scene in the middle of the night. Jack thought otherwise. It was important to observe the surroundings through the eyes of the killer.

"May I help you?" a voice called.

He looked over his shoulder and saw a lanky security guard strolling down the path.

He pulled out his badge and showed it to the young man, who couldn't have been more than twenty-two. "Sergeant Jack Adams. I'm investigating the Margarita Escolido murder. Do you know about that?"

The guard's eyes widened and he swallowed hard. "Yes, sir. Terrible tragedy. I was on duty that night."

He raised an eyebrow and opened the case file. "What's your name, son?"

"Dean Horn, sir."

"Did you speak to the police, Dean?"

"Yes, sir, I did."

He found a copy of Horn's statement. "Tell me what you remember."

He cleared his throat before he said, "Well, I'm assigned to Area Three, which includes the restaurant and the lot where Margarita was…well, killed." His voice trailed off and he stared at the ground guiltily.

"Go on, son. What happened?"

"Well, at approximately one thirty I was patrolling near the restaurant since my orders are to be nearby when the employees get off work. You know, to help them feel safe as they go to their vehicles."

The last words trailed off into a whisper, and he guessed Horn felt responsible for Margarita's death.

"Um, I really didn't see anything specific. Most of the employees were already gone. I saw a few people leave, but I didn't know Margarita so I'm not sure if she was one of them. I heard she left with a waiter. I might've seen that."

"So how long did you stay near the restaurant?"

He looked puzzled. "Pardon, sir?"

"I assume your job is to patrol an entire area and make rounds so I'm wondering when you moved out of the restaurant's vicinity."

"Ah, gotcha." He bit his lip in thought. "Probably five minutes. I probably moved on around one thirty-five. Sometimes I come over this way, you know, to check on the big lot."

Jack looked down at the rows of cars in the subterranean lot, which included a guard shack at the front.

"Is there someone on duty?" he asked, throwing a nod toward the small building.

"Uh, yeah, that's Lisa inside. Great lady."

Even in the darkness he noticed Horn's blush. "Was she on duty that night?"

His gaze shot up, and he looked worried, as if Jack might be accusing her of wrongdoing. "Yeah, but she didn't have anything to do with what happened."

He held up a hand. "I know, son. I wasn't suggesting she did, but I'd like to ask her a few questions anyway."

"Oh," he said, relieved.

They crossed to the shack, and a voluptuous woman, her black hair tied up in a bun, emerged from inside. *Definitely one of the few people who look good in tan polyester*, thought Jack. He glanced at Horn, whose tongue was practically wagging.

"Hello," she said.

He again flashed his badge. "Sergeant Jack Adams with Phoenix PD. I've been assigned to the Margarita Escolido murder, and I'd like to ask you a few questions."

"Sure," she said, her brown eyes curious. "Lisa Moore. But I don't really know anything."

Horn hovered over them like a protective lover. Jack turned his stare on the kid and said, "Why don't you go patrol for a few minutes so I can speak with Lisa alone?"

His face fell at the dismissal. "Oh, okay."

He hurried away and Lisa shook her head. "He's a nice guy, but he tries too hard."

"He seems very concerned about you."

She shrugged. "Like I said he's a nice guy, but I've been telling him for months that I'm not interested."

"Is he harassing you?"

"No, no," she said quickly, "nothing like that. He's like a puppy dog, totally harmless, but definitely persistent," she laughed.

"So why would anyone park in the other employee lot? This one seems much more secure."

"It is," she agreed. "But there are times during the day when there are too many employees on the premises at once. The other one is for overflow. Some people just go there anyway, because it's easier to find a space. And for people who are traditionally late for work, it's faster."

"Did you know Margarita Escolido?"

Her face grew somber. "Not really. Just a hi or hello. She was one of the people who usually parked in the other lot because it was closer to the restaurant."

She pointed up to the patio, and he realized the guard shack had a clear view of the patio area and the surrounding grounds leading to the path that led to the small lot where Margarita was killed.

"So did you see anything that night?"

She shook her head. "No. I remember the initial wave of people leaving about one fifteen and then it was like it is now. We're in a lull until about five a.m. We make our rounds and hang out. I'm sure that night we were doing the same thing."

"*We?*"

"Me and Dean."

He raised an eyebrow. "Dean was down here with you? Wasn't he out of his area?"

She looked embarrassed. "He comes down here a few times each night just to say hi, no big deal. He can see most everything from here."

He scribbled on his notepad. "Was he down here that night around one thirty?"

She stumbled for an answer. "Probably. It's his usual routine. He waits until the crowd of employees makes it to their cars and then he hangs out for half an hour or so. He's not in any trouble, is he?"

He sighed. "He told me he was up at the restaurant at one thirty that night." He flipped to Horn's witness statement and tapped the page. "He gave an official statement swearing he was up near the restaurant at the time Margarita left. Is that the truth, Lisa?"

She obviously heard the sternness of his tone, and her gaze flicked from the statement to the forlorn young man wandering between the cars in the lot.

"You weren't asked these questions before so you haven't violated the law, but I'm asking you now—officially. Was he with you that night at one thirty?"

She nodded. "He's always down here by one thirty."

He couldn't hide his frustration. "Were you ever questioned by the police?"

She shook her head. "I only heard that people were being questioned. The day after Margarita was killed was my first day of vacation. I was out of town for two weeks. When I got back, the whole thing seemed to have blown over."

He took a deep breath and held his temper. "May I?" he asked, motioning to the small desk inside the shack.

"Of course," she said.

A rush of adrenaline surged through him as he readjusted the small desk lamp and located Ian Patton's statement. Patton had said a security guard was standing near the restaurant as he and Margarita walked down the main path, which was one of the reasons he hadn't thought it necessary to walk her all the way to her car. He'd assumed she'd be safe.

He gazed toward the restaurant, now completely dark. If it wasn't Dean Horn who Ian Patton had seen, who was it?

CHAPTER TWENTY-THREE

Molly nervously tapped her coffee stirrer on the marble tabletop while she waited for Andre on the patio at Copper State Coffee. She'd spent the entire night drawing circles and hypothesizing about connections between Biz Stone, Wanda "aka Lola" Sells, Sol Gardener and Vince Carnotti. As she reviewed the doodles on the two sheets of paper that remained—after discarding dozens of others—she saw the connection. It was plausible, and if she could convince Andre then she *might* go to Jack.

The commuters on Seventh Avenue raced past her, headed for their mundane jobs, unable to enjoy the magic of the crisp fall morning. She took a deep breath, working to temper her excitement. She hadn't felt this happy in ages. It was like being on a case again, and if her theory resulted in the arrest of Biz Stone, her year would be made. She would find vengeance against the person who set her up, and Ari would be completely humiliated and embarrassed. Falling in love with a *criminal*? She laughed out loud, but it faded away against the roar of the passing engines when she thought about the potential charges against Biz, including murder.

What if Ari was in danger? What if she learned the truth? Would Biz kill the woman she loved to save herself?

Molly glanced at the stirrer in her shaking hand. She dropped it on the table and pulled a worn and folded sheet of paper from her bag. It was one of the emails Ari had sent to her after their breakup. She'd apologized endlessly for five paragraphs, professing her love for Molly and trying to explain what had happened.

Molly had shown it to Dr. Yee, and much to her chagrin, Dr. Yee's first question had been, "Do you notice that she never once mentions your drinking or bouts of anger? Do you see how she takes complete responsibility for her behavior?"

She'd roared in reply, "Well, isn't she a fucking saint!" and Dr. Yee had stared at her.

She didn't realize she was crying until a teardrop trickled to the tip of her nose. She quickly wiped it away and shoved the email back in her bag when she heard the clip of dress shoes approaching.

"Hey, Mol," Andre said, dropping into the chair across from her. "What's so urgent?"

She stared at him. "You may think I'm crazy," she said calmly, "and you'll probably accuse me of retaliation, but I think the second woman working with Wanda is Biz."

He leaned forward. "What?"

"Hear me out," she said quickly. "It all makes sense." She pointed to the four circles that surrounded the interior circle she'd labeled "Wanda." "We know that her handler knows about disguises, is probably a regular at Hideaway and is a member of her gym, since she lived to work and work out." She tapped the fourth circle. "And we know whoever set me up had a reason, which means that woman had a connection to Vince Carnotti."

He shook his head. "That's where you lose me, Mol. We don't have any proof that Biz works with the mob."

She held up a finger and showed him the other set of circles with Biz at the center. "We can't prove it directly, but think about it. First, how does a PI who does a ton of pro bono work afford two cars, a motorcycle *and* a seven-figure condo that she remodeled before she moved in? Do you know how expensive a condo is at Trombetta Dwellings?"

"Maybe she has other income or a grateful client," he suggested.

"Doubtful. Have you seen the women who hire her? And what if I told you that one of my connections knows for a fact that Carnotti's former son-in-law was hauled in on three domestic violence charges? And then he was magically arrested for drug possession, although drugs were never on his record previously. Now he's out of the picture doing time in Florence for the next ten years. And did I mention that one of the witnesses who offered testimony on behalf of the daughter was none other than Biz Stone?"

Andre was silent, processing. "How do you know all this?" he finally asked.

"I still have a few friends who'll talk to me," she said coldly.

"Hey! I'm one of those friends!"

"I know, I know," she said softly.

She'd thought about it all night, but he was hearing it for the first time, questioning the plausibility without the added bias of hating Biz Stone.

He picked up the two sheets of paper and said, "I suppose it would've been easy for her to keep tabs on you since she was Ari's client during that whole mess. She bought her condo around the time the two of you broke up." He glanced at her and added, "Maybe she was using Ari to get to you."

"Ari was a willing victim," she replied acidly.

"She could be in danger if this is true. We should tell Jack."

She took the papers from him. "Not just yet. I want to do a little digging of my own first. I'd like to have something more than a few hunches to show him so I don't just sound like a scorned girlfriend."

He took her hand. "You need to be fast, Mol. If you're right, and Biz is involved with Carnotti, he won't hesitate to eliminate anyone who's in his way, and she might be desperate enough to hurt Ari too."

* * *

Her first stop was Hideaway. She hesitated before she opened the familiar door. Was she craving a drink? No. That gave her the confidence to wander through the maze of tables and across the small dance floor to the bar where Vicky was restocking the shelves. It also helped that the harsh work lights destroyed the ambience she usually enjoyed with her scotch.

When Vicky saw her approach, she nearly dropped the bottle of rum she held in her hand. "Well, I'll be damned."

She slid onto a stool in front of her. "Hey, Vic."

She shook the bottle at her. "Don't you be askin' me for a drink or I'll knock you upside the head!"

"No, I'm sober and I intend to stay that way. You have my permission to throw me out if I ever ask you for a scotch."

"I'll remember that."

They exchanged knowing smiles. After years of pouring her drinks and threatening to call her a cab dozens of times when she shouldn't have driven—and actually doing it twice—their relationship was shifting.

"I need your help, Vic, but I'll understand if you refuse after I tell you why I'm here."

She shrugged. "What's going on?"

She pulled out a copy of Wanda's gym picture. "This is the woman you saw coming on to me, right?"

"Yeah, that's her," she said, peering at her face, realizing the discovery was old news. "Who is she?"

"She's somebody who's friends with Biz," Molly said, excluding the detail that Wanda was dead. "What I need to know is if you remember ever seeing them together here at Hideaway when she was dressed up as Lola."

She looked at her suspiciously. "What's up, Molly? Bad blood between you two now that she's after Ari?"

"She's already *got* Ari," she said.

"Not what I hear. Biz has it bad and Ari's shutting her down. She's not over you."

"Whatever," she mumbled as a tingle went down her spine. "I need to know if Wanda, that's this woman," she said pointing to the picture, "ever met Biz here or if they hooked up in the back."

She pulled a case of beer onto the bar. "Why do you want to know?"

"That's the part you might not like, seeing as you're a friend of Biz's."

"Biz ain't my friend," she said, clanking the bottles together as she pushed them into a refrigerator. "She's good for business and she always pays her tab, but I've seen the way she treats women. She was eyeballin' Ari before you were ever out of the picture. Only one that didn't seem to notice was Ari. Or you," she said with a little grin.

Molly scowled. "Do you remember anything?"

She studied the picture and glanced toward the back room. "That's hard to say. Biz is *always* here, kinda like Jane. You should ask Jane if she ever saw them together."

She nodded. It was a good idea.

"For some reason I've got this memory of coming out of Karis's office and seeing Biz in an argument with someone while she was on the pay phone. I thought it was odd that she was using it in the first place since she has a fancy smartphone." Karis was the owner and Vicky's ex.

"She might not have wanted her name or number to pop up," Molly guessed.

"Maybe. I remember it because after I saw her arguing, I came behind the bar and saw that woman you showed me,

Wanda, arguing with someone on her cell phone. I don't know what she was talking about or who she was arguing with, but for some reason I connected the two conversations. Weird, huh?"

Molly shrugged. "Not necessarily. Do you remember anything else?"

"Not really. Just what I told Ari's dad about the keychain and the gym membership. That helped, didn't it?"

She grinned. "Yeah."

Vicky looked at her seriously. "Any chance you and Ari will get back together? She loved you so much, Mol. I've never said anything, but what the hell? She put up with a lot of your shit, like the night you tumbled on top of her and twisted her ankle. You were so wasted and kept talking about going bowling. Ari knew you'd wind up in jail if she didn't take you home. You were just in one of your moods."

The night in front of the bowling alley. She'd hurt Ari and Jane had shown up and driven them home. She gazed at the bar and swallowed the truth. How many other nights had been like that one?

Vicky touched her shoulder. "Hey, I'm sorry. That was out of line. I love you both and I just want what's best for you."

She nodded and slid off the stool, unsure if she could find the exit through the tears that were blinding her.

* * *

It had been easy to slip into Wanda's apartment complex. She simply waited by the gate in her pool attire until a handsome twenty-something guy strolled out. After giving her the once-over, he was more than happy to hold the gate open for her. The complex was quiet since it was the middle of the work week. She found an empty chaise lounge in the pool area and pulled out a mystery novel she'd been reading forever. Tucked in the pages was the only photo of Biz she could find, a group shot taken at Ari's birthday party. Molly and Ari were at the center, wrapped in each other's arms, while Biz stood at the periphery her gaze caught between the camera and the couple. *Even then she wanted Ari*, Molly thought.

She hoped to find someone who had seen Biz at the apartments the night Wanda was killed. She gazed at her building in the distance, able to make out the crime scene tape that covered the front door. She doubted that anyone saw Biz actually enter the apartment. However, to get there she would've had to pass by the pool area and Biz cut a memorable figure, particularly to gay women.

She watched the pool-goers, looking for a regular who was also a lesbian. Half an hour passed as multiple straight couples wandered in and out, engaging in various displays of affection. She pretended to read her book while she soaked up the rays, all the while staring at the birthday party picture.

They'd been completely in love. She knew that now. Why had it been impossible for her to accept that when they were together? Why did she run away? Maybe she was blaming Ari too much for the breakup. Even Vicky saw how much Biz had wanted Ari. She rolled her eyes. Dr. Yee would remind her that a breakup takes two people. She stared at the photo again. It couldn't have been easy for Ari.

But Ari *chose* to cheat, she reminded herself, her heart brimming with pain.

The gate screeched and a woman entered, running from another woman who was attempting to snap her with a towel. The first woman was clearly a femme, dressed in a revealing yellow bikini. The towel snapper was a butch wearing men's swim trunks and a white T-shirt over a sports bra.

"You left a mark," the femme pouted, pointing at her lower back.

"Ah, let me kiss it," the butch said, grabbing her playmate by the waist and smacking her on the rear end, which caused the femme to squeal in delight.

Judging by their tans and the casual way they claimed one of the square tables, Molly guessed they spent a lot of time poolside. Within seconds the butch shed the T-shirt and dove into the pool. When she surfaced, she was inches from Molly's feet.

"Hey there," she said. "Just move in?"

Molly offered a mysterious smile. "No, I'm sorta subleasing from a friend for a couple of weeks, but the manager doesn't know." She put a finger to her lips and the butch nodded.

"Don't worry, I won't tell. There's a *lot* that happens around here that management doesn't know about. I'm Tony," she said with a wave.

"Molly."

"You two look way too friendly," the femme said playfully, stepping carefully into the water. She floated next to her girlfriend and asked Molly, "Is she hitting on you?"

"Yes, and it's making me uncomfortable."

They all laughed, and the femme smiled at her. "I'm Chanda, like chandelier?"

"And I'm Molly, like...Molly."

"She's an unauthorized guest," Tony whispered loudly, "but I told her we wouldn't tell."

Chanda laughed. "There's plenty of unauthorized guests here all the time."

"Yeah, I can tell this place sees a lot of action," Molly said. "Didn't somebody die here the other day?"

Chanda's smile faded, and Tony wrapped her in a hug. "It was awful. I knew Wanda. She was really cool. She showed me some kickboxing moves one time while we were stuck waiting for our clothes to dry."

"How'd she die?" she asked innocently.

"She threw herself off the balcony, I think," Tony said. "I couldn't believe it. She didn't act suicidal. She was all about the party."

"Yeah, I think there's more to it," Chanda said. "The police were here questioning everybody who lives on this side of the complex, asking if they'd seen anything suspicious."

"What'd they find out?" She hoped she sounded like a curious busybody and nothing more.

Tony shrugged. "Nobody knows anything. Our neighbor Joseph was the jogger who found her and called nine-one-one."

She pulled out the picture. "Did he happen to see anyone?"

"No, except for some of the usuals, you know, the evening crowd."

She held out the photo and pointed to Biz. "Have you ever seen this woman around here?"

A slow smile crossed Tony's face. "Why do you want to know?"

She sighed and settled on the truth. "Okay, look, here's the thing. I'm not really subletting and I don't live here, but I knew Wanda and this person in the picture. I used to be a cop and I'm helping with the investigation."

"Really?" Tony asked skeptically. "I didn't think the cops liked help."

She shrugged and said sincerely, "I've got a lot of friends, and we want to know what happened to Wanda. I'm thinking this person might know."

They both stared at Biz's face and Chanda said, "I can't swear to it, but I think I saw her here a couple days ago."

"You mean Monday night?"

"No, it was Monday morning. I do the graveyard shift at Five and Diner, but I stayed an extra few hours to cover for somebody who hadn't shown up. It was probably after noon. I came home, changed and went to get the mail before I crashed, and I saw this woman and a really scary dude going around Wanda's building. She only glanced at me for a second, so I could be totally wrong, but I think that was her."

Molly's adrenaline kicked into overdrive. "Where were they going?"

"Out the back gate, which is weird because that area is only for the workers. I didn't think anything of it because she was dressed like a service person in coveralls, like she'd been fixing the plumbing or something."

"How was the other guy dressed? Was he in coveralls?"

"Oh, no, he was in slacks, a dress shirt and a blazer. They looked odd together."

"Did you see her again?"

"Nope. She just went out the gate with him. End of story." She held up her hands and added, "But like I said, I'm not positive. I'd just worked a fifteen-hour shift, I was a complete zombie. I could never be certain." She looked again at the picture. "But her face is really memorable."

"How memorable?" Tony asked with a hint of jealousy.

Chanda slid into her arms and kissed her passionately. "Not nearly as memorable as yours, honey."

Sensing their kiss had the potential to rapidly turn pornographic, Molly tossed out a thank you and headed for the gate. Chanda was right. Biz's face was very memorable. If James Dean had been a woman, she thought, she would've looked like her. She was absolutely certain now that Chanda had seen Biz setting up Wanda's murder.

CHAPTER TWENTY-FOUR

After breakfast the group at the Montage decided to split up and dig deeper into possible motives for Evan, Steve, Georgie and Bobby Arco. Biz declared she agreed with Jane that he was the most likely suspect, as well as the most dangerous, and demanded the attention of the licensed PI.

"I think she's just showing off for you," Jane mumbled to Ari as Biz handed out the assignments.

Biz didn't hear her comment or chose to ignore it. "Jane, I want you to cozy up to someone in Steve Garritson's office. See what you can find out about him and check out his alibi. He says he was at a charity function, but was he with anyone the whole time? Where was it located? Could he have slipped out for a while unnoticed?"

Rory raised an eyebrow at Jane. "Cozy up, huh? Sounds like that won't be too much of a stretch."

Jane scowled. "Quit being so epigrammatic."

Rory wagged a finger at her. "Actually, sweetie, that doesn't work. You're looking more for pithy or witty. Epigrammatic implies conciseness, and while I am concise, I know that's not what you meant."

Jane growled and slowly turned toward Biz. "And what will Rory be doing? Playing in traffic on the 101?"

Biz, having been absent for most of Jane and Rory's sparring, sputtered a response. "Uh, no, I was going to put her on Evan." She glanced at Rory, who was nodding in agreement. "I mean, you already have an in with the school. Find out what he did at the music concert and when it ended. Since we're guessing he had a thing for Nina, maybe it went south when he realized his brother wasn't going to give her up."

"There are a few teachers who are his confidantes," she said. "I'll see what I can find out during lunch. That's when all the tongues seem to wag."

Biz turned to Ari with a little grin on her face. "Baby, I want you to check out Georgie. Go to her boutique and see what you can dig up. Her alibi could be a sham, and from what you and Jane have said, it's obvious she didn't want Sam and Nina together."

They headed for the parking lot together. Biz kept her arm around Ari's waist until they reached the rental car. Rory had offered Jane a lift so Ari could use it to make the trek to Georgie's boutique at the John Wayne Airport, her flagship location and where she'd claimed to be when Nina was killed.

"Be careful," Biz said, pulling her into a hug.

"I will," she said. "You too since you're the one following the abusive boyfriend."

"Just another day at the office for me," she scoffed.

She caressed Ari's cheek before she kissed her passionately. Ari enjoyed it—mostly—but she could've done without Biz's hand sliding down her front and copping a quick feel before she released her. She stepped away and quickly climbed into the rental, but before she could start the car Biz knocked on the window. She lowered it, a pleasant expression on her face.

"Hey, I'm sorry if that was out of line, but your body does things to me."

She willed herself not to roll her eyes. "I just think there should be boundaries in public. I'm all for affection, but I like it private, okay?"

She grinned. "I can respect that. I guess we have a lot to learn about each other, but just so you know, when we're alone, there are no boundaries."

Before she could answer, Biz sauntered off, looking especially pleased with herself. Ari doubted she was sincerely sorry about the groping, and she spent much of the drive to the airport slightly annoyed with her—and missing Molly, whose public and private personas were completely different. She had relished the idea that most people knew nothing of her private life, specifically her devotion to family, her gift as a pianist and her commitment as a friend. They had been excellent friends and very compatible lovers. Ari had felt privy to huge secrets unknown to the rest of the world, which added to the specialness of their relationship.

She blinked away some fresh tears. *I need to move on*, she thought.

The John Wayne Airport was crowded, but California airports were, as a rule, and there wouldn't be a lull in the traffic or the congestion until after midnight. Midday was as good a time as any to go there. She parked in one of the adjoining lots and headed for the departure level, already grateful that she wasn't at LAX.

She found Georgie's shop, The Bare Essentials, sandwiched between Hudson News and a local candy confectioner. She grabbed an iced coffee from a vendor and planted herself across the concourse on a comfortable sofa. A handful of people wandered through the shop under the watchful eye of a mid-thirties woman, who floated between the displays, rearranging items and answering questions. Shoplifting wasn't a problem with her on duty.

She scanned the store but didn't see Georgie anywhere, surmising perhaps she was visiting a different location. She noticed the Hudson News did a brisk business as travelers whisked through to purchase snacks or reading material for their flights. The candy company wasn't so lucky. Perhaps it was the morning downturn, but the young girl standing behind the counter looked bored enough to stack the truffles to the ceiling.

She ditched her coffee cup and sauntered up to the display case, eyeballing her favorites, the chocolate-covered cherries.

"It all looks so good," she said.

The girl offered an affirming mumble but made no effort to rise from her stool until Ari pointed and asked for something specific. She surveyed the entire display and returned to the cherries.

"I'll take four of those, please."

The girl finally slid from the stool with great effort and reached for a treat box. Ari realized conversation wouldn't come easy and that discussing sweets wasn't an engaging topic for her. She was searching for something to say when the girl's necklace freed itself from her blouse as she scooped up the last cherry.

"I love your cross," she said, pointing to the ivory symbol visible now against her chest.

The girl finally smiled. "Thanks. It was my mom's, but she's gone."

"Oh, I know how that goes," she said sincerely. "I lost my mom when I was young too."

"I'm sorry."

She rung up the chocolates, and Ari said, "It's funny that we're talking about this. Today's the anniversary of her death."

She hadn't meant to say it, but it was the truth, a truth she'd been avoiding discussing with her father for the past month.

"Wow, I'm sorry," the girl gushed. "What a bummer."

"It's okay. I'm taking a trip to see my sister in San Francisco so that'll be great." She pointed at the Bare Essentials. "What's that store like? I just realized I left my neck pillow on my bed."

"It's okay. A little overpriced, but hey, you're paying to have something you forgot, right?"

She nodded at her intuition. "Do you know the owner?"

The girl turned up her nose and handed her the cherries. "She's a snob. I've worked here a year and she's never once said hello when she's walked by. She acts like I'm invisible. Her husband is some big politician in Laguna."

"Is that her, the one there now?"

She checked her watch. "No, it's too early. She's only here later in the day until closing. That's the manager, Paisley."

"Paisley?"

She chuckled. "Yeah, it's an odd name, but she's cool. The owner's the weird one. Sees herself as an artist making these ceramic gifts and those painted wineglasses. It's pretty tacky."

"Is she here every night?"

"No, I know she's got several stores, but sometimes I close on Mondays, Wednesdays and Fridays, and I've seen her a lot. Why are you asking all these questions? Are you a cop?"

An arguing mother and daughter stepped up to the display case just then, distracting the clerk, and Ari left quickly. She wandered into the Bare Essentials and scanned the displays.

Not much of a traveler herself, she had no idea there were bags that kept clothes from wrinkling or tubes that kept toothbrushes sanitary, and she wouldn't know what to do with the female urination device. It reminded her how much of a homebody she really was. Molly had been the same; they'd never really planned a formal vacation, both of them content with their surroundings as long as they were together.

Toward the back of the store two painted privacy screens separated Georgie's gift items from the travel supplies. She'd acquired some chic and shabby cabinets to showcase her painted glasses, ceramic bowls and trinkets. Ari studied a martini glass covered with small diamonds and swirls. She couldn't imagine actually using it, but she'd heard of others doing so.

She liked the ceramic keychains, which were various animals like pandas and giraffes. She imagined younger pre-teens needing their first house key would be drawn to such things. She fingered a few of the bowls, noting everything was expensive.

"Can I help you find anything particular?" a pleasant voice asked.

She beamed at Paisley. "There's so many great gifts. I'm a little overwhelmed." She offered a sweeping gaze and said, "When I've been in the airport, I've never had time to actually stop by, but I'm early today."

"Where are you headed?"

"Seattle. I'm from Phoenix," she said, knowing that it was preferable to always tell as much of the truth as possible when crafting a lie.

"Oh," she replied, and Ari imagined she asked that same question twenty times a day. "Are you interested in something for yourself, or are you looking for a gift, or both?"

She smiled and shrugged. "Either, I suppose. I don't need anything for my flight, but I love ceramics. Who's the artist?"

"Oh, that would be the owner, Georgie Garritson. Don't you love her stuff?" she asked excitedly. She held up a wineglass painted with a baby theme and a cute quote about a little wine keeping a future mother sane. "I just love these."

"Is she local?"

She nodded proudly. "Born and raised in Laguna Beach. Her husband sits on the city council and her father was in real estate. She has a home studio, but sometimes she dabbles here at the shop in the back room. She's carved out a corner for herself."

Ari affected a troubled look. "Oh, I think I read about her family. Isn't her son in some kind of trouble?"

"It's absolutely ridiculous," she said, exasperated. "Sam couldn't hurt anyone, although if he'd listened to his mother, none of this probably would've happened."

"What do you mean?"

She glanced toward the empty store before she said, "Georgie knew Nina wasn't right for Sam. She was too clingy and demanding, but I suppose that became a moot point."

"Why do you say that?"

She leaned closer and said, "I heard Nina was pregnant."

Ari feigned surprise. "Wow, that wasn't in the papers. Are you sure?"

She nodded, clearly unworried about airing her boss's dirty laundry to a commuter stranger she'd never see again. "I overheard Georgie talking to Nina. It was a rather heated argument."

"What were they arguing about?"

"I wasn't paying too close attention since it was a private conversation, but it sounded like Georgie was trying to convince Nina to go to a doctor, which makes sense if you're pregnant. She's full of good advice," she added proudly. "There was something about getting a second opinion."

"When was this conversation?"

"A few weeks ago, not too long before she was killed."

"Did the police ask you about this?"

"Uh-huh. There's this interesting detective, kinda cute for an older guy. I'm pretty sure he'll solve it. He told me not to say anything to *anyone* about the pregnancy, but I doubt you're included," she said dismissively.

"You don't think they suspect your boss, do you?"

"No, of course not. Besides she was closing that night."

"Wow, it sounds pretty interesting around here." She glanced at her watch. "Oops! I gotta go."

"What about your gift?" Paisley asked, holding up the wineglass.

"It'll have to wait. My plane leaves in ten minutes and I've got to get through security," she said, hustling out the door.

She wandered down the concourse a little further and processed what she'd learned. Georgie knew about the baby. She hadn't liked Nina, but, still, Ari couldn't imagine a would-be grandmother killing her grandchild. In any case, it seemed as if Georgie had an airtight alibi.

She'd wanted Nina to get a second opinion, which suggested there might've been something wrong. She wondered if Evan knew the specifics. Her stomach rumbled. She debated whether to eat one of the chocolate-covered cherries, but she decided to settle for a healthier smoothie instead. When she and Jane had flown in on Sunday, they'd passed a yogurt store and she was rather certain it wasn't much further down the concourse. She saw the lit sign but noticed an employee lowering the steel gate over the front.

"Excuse me, but are you closing?"

The twenty-something surfer, whose nameplate read "Shane, Manager," shook his head. "Only for ten minutes. I just need to take my break and I'm the only one here." She noticed he held a little sign with a clock on it. "We don't have any bathrooms."

She looked up and down the concourse and noticed a second shuttered business with a sign. "I guess everyone's in the same boat," she said, pointing to the closed shop, which sold Western wear.

"Yeah," he said. "It's pretty common around here. We either help each other out and cover or we explain to customers why our neighbors are closed."

The wheels in her mind were turning. She smiled conspiratorially. "So, is it really *just* for ten minutes?"

He grinned. "Around that. It depends if my girlfriend's on break too. She works over at the Starbucks."

"But nobody really keeps track, right? Nobody would know if you closed early and just never came back."

He grinned and pointed at his nameplate. "I'm the manager, so who would?"

CHAPTER TWENTY-FIVE

After an hour on the computer and phone, Biz confirmed that Bobby Arco was indeed the scumbag everyone suspected him to be. She wasn't sure he was a murderer, but he definitely belonged in jail based on the information provided by her friends in various departments of law enforcement. Most damaging was his arrest record for drugs, according to a clerk at the FBI, a woman who'd made the mistake of hooking up with the wrong guy and owed Biz her life—literally.

Arco had already done time in Wyoming for heroin distribution and, as a California resident, had managed to rack up two domestic violence charges, later dropped, with two different women, neither of whom was Eden. He'd never held a steady job until he went to work at Lenny's. Biz imagined he owed his current employment entirely to Eden. Ari had recounted her visit to the shop and his manhandling of an elderly customer. Biz knew the adage about leopards not changing spots was totally accurate in regard to abusive assholes.

She plotted her course of action and headed to the Laguna Police Department. It only took an hour of schmoozing and charm to get the information she needed. Then it was off to Lenny's Auto Shop. She wanted to get a look at Eden and Bobby Arco, so she posed as a salesperson. Not surprising, Eden dismissed her immediately, but she finagled a visit to the employee bathroom and on her way there gazed out into the bays and spotted Bobby Arco. Confident they were both remaining at work for the day, she made two quick stops—a grocery store and the Macy's at the Laguna Hills Mall—before she headed to their home, a condo in the middle of town. Either Lenny had paid for it—it was far too upscale for a mechanic and a secretary to own—or, as she suspected, Arco had other business ventures that kept the cash flowing.

She was relieved to see the complex was older and lacked a security gate. She parked in one of the visitor stalls near their patio entry. The gate latch was secured with a padlock, unlike those of their neighbors, suggesting that Arco felt he had something worth protecting. Grabbing her duffel bag, she fished an enormous ring of keys from its side pocket. She'd learned from a locksmith that companies only make a set number of masters, and during her career she'd acquired many, with the help of a locksmith who understood her need for breaking into various businesses and homes. The sixth key did the trick.

The patio was filled with children's toys and boxes stacked against the high block wall fence. A security camera perched in a far corner. She adjusted her baseball cap and kept her head down. A basic home model, the image it was capturing was probably going straight to Arco's computer, not a reputable company that would send out a guard or call the police. She seriously doubted Arco would want to draw attention to himself.

On the other side of the patio door sat a homely brown mutt who seemed to be a cross between an Australian and German shepherd. He barked twice, but she could see the slight wag of his tail, suggesting he was friendly but on guard. She was prepared for this. She'd been bitten several times by animals that were treated as poorly as the women and children in the home. She pulled out a beef marrow bone she'd purchased at the grocery store and showed it to the pooch. He instantly fell silent while she manipulated the tumblers and popped the lock.

She opened the door slightly and dropped the bone at his feet. He scooped it up and ran off. She knew he'd be busy for at least thirty minutes trying to lick the marrow from the middle.

She zipped through the house, assessing the layout and confirming there wasn't a security keypad anywhere. She assumed Arco was dealing again because of the security camera, but she wasn't here to look for drugs.

The bottom floor was a typical living space with a small office nook in the corner of the den, complete with a laptop and a two-drawer filing cabinet. She rifled through the files and found nothing but bill statements, information on the auto shop and, ironically, a thick folder containing Arco's prison paperwork.

She went upstairs and immediately found what she was looking for—a locked door. The master bedroom, guest bath and child's bedroom doors were wide open, as if everyone had left in a hurry on their way to school or work. The third bedroom door was closed and had a sophisticated lock installed on it.

She shook her head at the common sight. How many times had she encountered abusive men who flaunted their secrets in front of the women in their lives? She thought the women to be just as responsible for ignoring what existed behind the locked doors rather than demanding to see.

It took nearly six minutes to pick it, but she'd found Arco's lair. A desk sat under the window with a bookcase beside it that held a few gaming manuals. The far wall was painted black and a dingy leather couch sat against it. Posters advertising various computer games were tacked on the walls, depicting buff men and women in very little clothes, as well as the monsters they would slay. There was nothing that suggested Eden's presence. She had her own office downstairs.

Biz turned on the computer and heard the hard drive whir. While it was booting up, she donned her black gloves and searched the desk. Besides the usual office supplies she found some interesting treasures, including a crack pipe, a box of condoms and two *Playboys*. Her gaze settled on the closed closet door.

She opened it, flipped the light switch and was greeted by stacks of book boxes. Most of them were very heavy, but she moved them out in five minutes and surveyed the empty closet. The carpet was tacked down securely and there were no holes in the walls. She scratched her head. Her gut was telling her there was something wrong, but she couldn't see it.

She opened a box filled with hardbound books. She pulled out an old copy of poetry by W.H. Auden, not a poet she imagined was a favorite of Arco or Eden. On the inside cover was a penciled number two in the right-hand corner. Someone had bought the book at a used book sale or a Goodwill. She thumbed through the pages and found nothing except poetry.

She shook her head and pulled out the second book, *The Yearling*. She searched it and six more books but found nothing. She was halfway through the box and growing frustrated. While they were all hardbound, there were no similarities. Some were literary classics, while others were technical books, biographies or self-help. She couldn't imagine Arco or Eden reading any of them and her suspicion fueled her search.

She was at the bottom of the first box, and only four books remained. She opened a copy of *The Butterfly Book* from the forties and sighed. She checked the covers and fanned the pages. Suddenly she stopped. She'd missed something. She thumbed through the book slowly, scanning the endless paragraphs of words interspersed with diagrams and pictures of butterflies.

On page twenty-four she found the first one. In place of a butterfly image was the picture of a naked child. Her jaw dropped, and she continued to flip the pages, realizing that many of the book's original butterfly pictures had been replaced with child pornography. Some of the pictures were completely disgusting, obviously printed from the Internet. Her heart nearly broke when she reached page 212. Staring at her was a black-and-white picture of Michaela in a completely inappropriate pose, sitting on the leather couch just a few feet from where Biz stood now. Ari had shown her the drawing from Michaela's journal—of a room with black walls and a dragon. Above the couch was a poster of a dragon from an anime game.

She thought she was going to be sick. She took a deep breath and searched through the books again. She determined Arco had a system. He kept the pornography buried under several books that had not been changed, at least not yet. She searched a second box and confirmed her theory. She imagined pornographic books existed in every box, but she didn't have the time or the stomach to check. She put everything back into the closet and checked her watch. Twenty minutes.

She returned to the computer and faced a password screen. *Of course*, she thought. She typed in the obvious ones and a few other ideas based on the info from her FBI friend, but she couldn't crack it. She realized Arco would be smart enough to know the best passwords were long and included a variety of letters, numbers and symbols, but he probably wasn't smart enough to remember it. So where would he put it? The obvious place would be on a cryptic file on his smartphone or it would need to be someplace close...

She flipped over the keyboard, checked the bottom of the desk lamp and scrounged through the desk again hoping to find a scrap of paper. She shoved the desk drawer closed and wanted to scream. Where was it?

She stared at the posters again. One advertised a game called Hellions Revenge and featured a brunette bombshell in a leather jumpsuit, her cleavage bursting. In the poster's background was a computer screen with what appeared to be some sort of code on it. Biz grinned. *Hiding in plain sight*, she thought.

She typed in the random letters and numbers and the password screen disappeared.

"Excellent," she said. "First things first."

A series of clicks took her to his security files. Fortunately, it was one she'd conquered before. Within three minutes, she'd erased the footage of her entering the condo, after which she went ahead and disabled the camera.

"Now let's see what you're up to."

She opened his Internet history and wasn't surprised to see a list of sex chat rooms, sites that she assumed contained child pornography, as well as inmate support groups. It occurred to her that parolees as well as current inmates who were pedophiles would be paranoid about using the Internet for pornography. They would appreciate the *library* Bobby had accumulated.

His documents folder included a list of names and addresses from around the United States. All were men, save one. About half were in prison, a fact which gave her confidence that her theory was correct.

She found another file of disturbing messages and journal entries where he claimed that the government was conspiring against the people. She quickly closed it, unwilling to spend her last few minutes reading his rants. The other folders contained gaming information, none of which was useful.

She clicked on his picture folder and scrolled through rows of folders with disgusting names such as Naked Tweens and Tubby Photos. She didn't open any of them since she was certain what she'd find. The last one was titled simply "HER." She took a deep breath, supposing that he had devoted an entire file to Michaela but uncertain enough to know she needed to check.

Images of Nina appeared. He'd obviously followed her during her evening run on multiple occasions. Judging from the people in the background, it was summer and Laguna was filled with tourists. Nina wore her cute jogging attire and he'd made a point of taking photos when she bent over to stretch. It was evident she had no idea she was being photographed. Biz's heart skipped a beat when she saw that the last photos were taken at the murder site.

At the end of the pictures was another subfolder—untitled. Her eyes grew wide at the images she found. Nina's head from the previous candid pictures had been PhotoShopped onto the bodies of several naked women in pornographic poses.

She closed the screens and inserted her thumb drive into the computer to begin the copying process. As the files transferred she pulled the Macy's bag from her duffel.

"You're going down," she whispered.

CHAPTER TWENTY-SIX

Ari unclenched her teeth as she chugged up the Garritsons' long driveway. It was after three and she'd lost nearly an hour to an accident on the freeway that closed two lanes of traffic. Sam was home alone, and she'd decided to confront him about the baby and ask him about the journal entry.

He answered the door wearing his familiar button-down shirt and khakis, as well as a pained expression. "Let's go out to the veranda. Lately it's the only place I like to be."

"Could I ask a favor? I was wondering if you'd give me a little tour of this amazing house."

"Sure," he said, unenthused.

He wasn't in the mood to be much of a tour guide, but she learned the general floor plan, making mental notes of where she wanted to snoop while he pointed and stated the obvious like, "Kitchen."

He also off-handedly mentioned they were alone, as it was the housekeeper's day off.

"Where's your mother?" she asked, wondering if there was any possibility Paisley would meet up with Georgie.

"She's making her bi-monthly trip to San Diego today. She won't be home until tomorrow." He pointed down a hallway to a door in a glass atrium. "That leads to Mom's studio." He turned and faced her. "That's it."

She nodded and they returned to the veranda. After he served them both a glass of lemonade, she took a deep breath. "Sam, I came here today to tell you something that I think you have a right to know. Nina was pregnant when she was killed."

"What?" he asked, as if he hadn't heard her correctly. "Say that again?"

"Nina was pregnant," she said gently.

He shook his head in disbelief. "That can't be. She would've told me. She *should've* told me."

"I don't think she knew for very long before she died, and you two had broken up. She might have been waiting for the right time."

"How do you know about this?"

"The detective assigned to the case told me," she lied. "I happened to meet him and we were comparing notes."

"Does anyone else know?"

"I'm not sure. Nina may have told someone in confidence just because she needed a friend," she said slowly.

He closed his eyes. "Evan. I'll bet she told him."

"Why would you say that?"

His shoulders sagged, and she sensed his growing anger. "Because she told him *everything*. He wanted her, but she only wanted to be friends. *Best* friends." He licked his lips and stared at her. "If I find out that son of a bitch knew about my child before me..."

"Sam, you need to calm down—"

"Calm? You expect me to be calm?"

He jumped up and accidentally knocked over his glass, which shattered on the Mexican tile. He stomped through the gate that led to the beach. She watched him trudge along the shoreline, his head hung low and his hands stuffed in his pockets. When he was merely a dot on the sand, she darted into the house, determined to search Steve's office and Georgie's studio while she had the chance.

Steve's large office included a wet bar and a fifty-five-inch TV mounted on a wall facing a leather sofa that smelled expensive. All of the cabinetry was a rich, dark oak, and most of his awards were clustered together on a display shelf near the door. Visitors would be instantly greeted by his accomplishments, particularly his large framed diploma from Yale. *It's almost like he's got something to prove*, she thought.

She grinned when she saw the PEZ dispenser collection arrayed along a window frame. It included some cartoon characters like Mickey Mouse and some vintage designs such as a green Easter bunny without much form or definition. She'd never seen a PEZ dispenser with feet.

Rows of books about history, business and public speaking lined the wall behind his desk, which also included a large bay window that faced the ocean. She imagined him working on a speech and turning his chair to face the sea for inspiration.

Two of the drawers were locked, and a key was nowhere to be found. The other four drawers contained knickknacks and office supplies and a few files of projects and notes for his work on the city council. On his desk was a file labeled "Child Abuse Prevention Task Force." She flipped through the pages, which included an overview of the child abuse problem as well as recommendations from experts. He'd made notes in the margins and underlined key facts and statistics. He'd also circled the summary at the end.

As they'd discussed at dinner, if the governor were successful, there would be stiffer penalties for spouses who didn't report domestic abuse in homes where children were present. In other words, women who were victims of continued domestic abuse could be guilty of child abuse if their children continually witnessed acts of violence. Ari could only imagine how Nina would have felt about turning abused women into criminals. What if Steve had been threatened by her potential vocal opposition? Once the baby came she'd be part of the family. Would he be forced to step aside?

She looked for a day planner and realized it was probably with him or he kept it on his laptop, which was also missing, the cords abandoned on the desk. She picked up a family photo taken when the boys were teenagers. She was struck anew by the twins' handsomeness as they smiled at the camera in matching red sweaters.

She glanced out the window at the empty veranda. Sam was apparently still walking. She went to the hallway, momentarily lost in the maze of square footage. She made two wrong turns before she found the atrium. Through a window she could see the inside of Georgie's studio, a glass room overlooking the sea. An easel with a canvas sat in a corner, and art supplies were stacked haphazardly everywhere.

Finding the door unlocked, she entered. The studio reminded her of the solarium at home. It was well organized with wall-to-wall shelving and drawers, all of which were labeled. She opened several cabinet doors and found more canvases, some lighting equipment and photography supplies, suggesting that Georgie had dabbled as a photographer and given it up.

A sliding glass door led to a balcony. It was easy to picture Georgie sitting on a stool there, sketching ideas while she listened to the ocean beneath her. She went back inside and checked the hallway. Still no Sam.

Behind a naked mannequin in the corner sat a small closet: it was filled with aprons, smocks and a few of what appeared to be Steve's old dress shirts that Georgie had claimed as painter's smocks. She searched the room, unsure of what she expected to find. Nina had written in her journal about exposing a

Garritson secret. Ari was certain it had something to do with her pregnancy. It was just too coincidental.

The desk was a cluttered mess. She sifted through the bills, receipts and notes that covered the desktop, but none of it seemed personal. Frustrated, she gazed about the room and pulled open all the drawers and cabinets once more. She dug through the cabinet full of photography supplies and found a wooden box buried underneath a camera case and a tripod. Inside were two photo albums, one clearly much older than the other.

The first was full of black-and-white pictures from the forties and fifties, judging from the attire of the subjects and the cars in the pictures. She recognized a few people who looked like Georgie and guessed these were photos of her rich relatives. She imagined at least one of the children in the photos was Georgie herself. Many depicted old buildings in Laguna and some showed men and women in their swimming "costumes" enjoying the ocean. In one picture, Crescent Point, the site of Nina's murder, sat off in the distance.

The second album was more recent. All of the photos were color and taken during the seventies and eighties. Included were candids of Steve and Georgie's hippie-like wedding, with Steve sporting thick sideburns and wild hair and Georgie decked out in a lacy gown that reminded Ari of Stevie Nicks. The photos of them as a couple morphed into family photos that included baby pictures of Sam and Evan. Most were taken at events, such as birthdays and barbeques by the pool, and the Garritsons were surrounded by friends.

Other than the four Garritsons, the only other person she recognized was Scott Kramer, the teenager who cleaned their pool and became a family friend. He frolicked in the pool with the twins and apparently even took them out trick-or-treating one year. She couldn't imagine he would've enjoyed spending the evening with two little kids, but he wore his gigantic smile, the one she'd seen at the funeral. He was definitely a handsome man.

She flipped through the rest of the pages and sighed. There was nothing else to see. It was time to get back to the resort. Sam couldn't walk forever. She replaced the photo albums in the box and arranged the equipment as it had been. When she went to close the door, she glanced at the shoe rack hung on the inside. Instead of shoes in the rows of pockets, Georgie had stowed lenses. *Very creative*, she thought. Each expensive lens had its own lined pocket and was enclosed in a plastic bag. A small photo album was tucked behind one of the lenses. It only contained four photos, but the subject in them was the same—a young Scott Kramer.

The first was most likely a studio picture, perhaps his senior photo. The second was somewhat blurry and depicted Scott and Georgie, who couldn't have been more than twenty-two, putting hamburgers on the grill at one of the barbeques. Ari blinked at the third photo, which was much different, much more sexual. Scott stood poolside with the skimmer in his hand, his bleach-blond hair falling over his eyes and a cigarette dangling from his mouth. He wore only cutoffs, the top button undone. She guessed he was fifteen or sixteen.

"Interesting," she whispered.

But her breath caught at the last photo of Scott in the pool between Sam and Evan. In it all three of them smiling for the camera, their wet hair slicked back.

"Holy shit," she whispered.

Her phone vibrated. Biz had sent a text to her, Rory and Jane. "Get back to the resort. I've caught the murderer."

CHAPTER TWENTY-SEVEN

Jack knew a killer when he saw one. Bennett Mason, the security guard who sat across from him in Interview Room Two, was relaxed and affable—too much so. He'd willingly agreed to stop by on his day off after he finished his errands, which Jack knew had included a quick stop at the mall and the food court for a sandwich and a drink at The Miracle Mile Deli. He'd tailed him for most of the morning after re-interviewing Dean Horn, who'd broken into sobs when he'd seen Jack crossing the resort lawn to speak with him again. He'd known he was in trouble for falsifying his witness statement. What he hadn't known was how devastating his lie had been to the investigation.

After Horn had confirmed he hadn't been at his assigned post near the restaurant on the night Margarita was killed and Ian Patton reaffirmed he was positive he'd seen a security guard in the shadows, Jack had returned to his desk at four in the morning and reread all of the statements. Then he'd seen the answer. A whirlwind day had ensued as he returned to the resort and then followed Mason.

He hadn't slept in nearly thirty-six hours, and he was ragged, unshaven and disheveled, but he was running on the adrenaline of a cop with an answer, one that he was waiting to confirm by talking to the clean-cut American boy sitting across from him. Mason was twenty-four and a senior chemistry student at ASU.

Jack knew that Andre, Chief Phillips and David Ruskin were in the control room ready to watch the interrogation, which was also being recorded. He was grateful he wasn't in the same room with Ruskin, because he suspected by the end of the interview he'd be ready to throttle the lazy captain.

He cleared his throat and took a sip of water. "Mr. Mason, I appreciate you coming down here on your day off. I inherited this case just yesterday and I'm interviewing the key players."

Mason smiled congenially and folded his hands in his lap. "More than happy to help any way I can. Margarita was a great gal."

He picked up his pen. "So, you knew her?"

He nodded. "Uh-huh. The end of my shift coincided with the beginning of hers. I got off at three, and she would be going into work."

"She worked nights."

"Yeah, she got the money shift."

"The money shift? What's that?"

"Happy hour and the dinner rush," he explained. "Waiters and waitresses who work nights make the best tips. The money shift."

"Ah, I see. So you would see her as she was arriving and you were leaving. Did you guys pass each other at the parking lot, or how did you get to know her?"

Mason thought about the question for a moment before answering. "Well, I guess that's how we originally met, probably in the parking area, but I'd see her a lot on the patio. She'd usually arrive ten or fifteen minutes early because she wanted to be prompt, so she'd grab a soda and we'd chat after I clocked out."

Jack offered a slow grin. "Was there ever anything else?"

"No, no," Mason said, flustered. "We were just friends."

"But did you want to be more than friends?"

The easy smile disappeared into thin lips. After a long pause he answered. "At one point, for a while. Then Margarita made it clear she just wanted friendship so that was okay with me."

He pretended to read some notes. "Was it? Was it really okay?"

"Yes," he said firmly.

Jack stared into his unflinching blue eyes. "What if I told you that someone had seen the two of you arguing one afternoon?"

"Then I'd tell you that person was lying. Margarita and I *never* had an argument. Not once. Never," he said emphatically.

He leaned back in his chair and exhaled. "Okay, let's talk about the last day she was alive. Did you see her at the end of your shift?"

As if coming out of a trance, Mason snapped up. "Uh, no. I didn't. As I passed the patio, I looked for her to say hi, but she wasn't there."

"She was late, which was unusual."

He nodded. "Yes, it was very unusual."

"Do you know why she was late?"

"I do now but I didn't know then. Her car wouldn't start and so she borrowed a friend's car, a little Honda."

He picked up the file again and read through his statement. "And that was the car you had towed the next morning, right?"

"Yes. The lot has a strict nine-hour policy. It keeps the residents and visitors from parking there overnight and ensures there is enough employee parking. It's kinda cheap, actually," he admitted. "Management doesn't want to fork out the money for another parking lot, even though we need one."

"So you saw this car had been parked there for over nine hours and had it towed, not knowing it was Margarita's transportation that day."

He opened his mouth to say something and then closed it. "Yeah, that's it, really. The night security guard had chalked the tire so I had it towed."

"Which is the policy," he confirmed.

"Yes."

"And unfortunately by towing the car, valuable evidence was lost because the trucker—and you—trampled all over the ground surrounding the vehicle as you prepared it to be hauled away."

He slumped in his chair. "That's right. I've always felt horrible about that."

"I imagine," he sympathized. "Let me ask you. Where do you park your car?"

"I don't. I ride my bicycle. I live close and it saves a lot of money on gas."

Jack adjusted his glasses and picked up Mason's statement. "Oh, I see that now. Sorry. What kind of bike do you ride?"

"Cannondale, a CAAD Ten."

"Sounds like a really nice bike."

"It is. It's one of the best bikes Cannondale makes."

He scratched his head thoughtfully. "So where do you park a bike like that so it doesn't get stolen?"

"Well, I used to keep it in the employee break room, but some people started messing with it, so I started parking it over by the restaurant. The busboys are really cool and keep an eye on it for me. It's not in the way or anything and the manager said it was okay. I lock it up, of course."

"How many other employees ride to work?"

He shrugged. "A few, I guess. Not many." He snorted and said, "This is Phoenix. Everybody drives."

Jack laughed with him. "So true. What color is your bike?"

"Black and silver."

"But your seat is rather different, isn't it? It's very narrow and made of brown leather."

"It's actually called a saddle and it's much better for longer rides."

He took off his glasses and tapped them on the table while he thought of his next question. "Pretty distinctive, though, right?"

"Absolutely," he agreed. "It's from Brooks. That saddle set me back a hundred and twenty bucks."

"You don't know anyone else with a seat like that, I mean a *saddle*?" he asked.

"Of course not," he said with superiority. "Only serious riders would spend that much money."

"Was Margarita impressed with your bike?"

The question surprised him. "Um, we never talked about it. She told me she was glad I was helping out the environment."

He chuckled as if Mason had told a joke. "Do you think it was a turnoff, though? Maybe one of the reasons she wouldn't date you? I mean, who wants to date a guy with a bike? Where would she sit?"

Mason's face darkened and his body went rigid. "Margarita wasn't that judgmental. If we'd gone out, I would've borrowed my friend's car."

"Did you tell her that? Did you reassure her that you had wheels? Women have a thing for cars. How a guy gets around says a lot about his financial situation, his standing in life—"

"That's not why we didn't date." His pleasant tone had evaporated into an almost robotic voice.

"Then why?"

He swallowed hard. "She just didn't like me in *that* way."

"Did she have a boyfriend?"

"No."

"What about Julio, the patio bartender?" He frowned and Jack added, "Wasn't he the reason she kept arriving to work early? She wanted him to notice her. How did you feel about that?"

"Julio's fine."

He raised an eyebrow. "Is he? It didn't bother you that she'd rather be seen with an uneducated second-shift bartender than a college man who was going places?" Mason's face contorted into a sick expression at the thought. Jack leaned across the table and added, "She picked him to fuck and not you."

"I didn't care!" he cried. "Whatever she did with that illegal wetback was her business!" He pushed away from the table but didn't get up.

Jack glanced at the video camera in the corner and pulled a form from a folder. "Bennett, I need you to look at one more thing and then we'll be done."

He wiped his eyes and regained his composure. "Of course. I only have a few more minutes. I have a lot to do today."

"This is a page from the resort's call log. Have you ever seen one of these?" He shook his head. "Anytime a guest calls the customer service line, the information is documented by the representative who takes the call. On the night of Margarita's murder, a rep named Sarah took a call from a very distraught guest who had accidentally backed into a parked bicycle. Being a good citizen, the guest felt inclined to report it and offered to pay for the damages if the owner could be found. She described the bicycle very specifically, mentioning it was a Cannondale with a funny looking brown seat. That call came in at one twenty-five a.m." He tapped the page while Mason scanned it. "Unfortunately, the bike's owner never came forward." When Mason looked up at him, his eyes blazing, Jack asked, "Why were you at the resort at one in the morning?"

"I wasn't," he said indignantly. "I have no idea who this person is or why she's describing my bike."

"Where were you?"

"Home. In bed. I had to be at the resort by seven the next morning. You can check our records if you want."

"And I assume you rode your bicycle to the resort the next day?"

"I did," he said softly.

"Is that why a bus pass was charged to your credit card that morning before your shift started?" He pulled the credit card statement from the folder and shoved it at him.

A long pause ensued as Mason's gaze flitted between the statement and the call log. His head shot up and he glared at Jack. "There's no crime in buying a bus pass. Lots of cyclists alternate between types of transportation. I have no idea why this woman is reporting she hit a bike that looks like mine. My bike is perfectly fine."

There was a quick knock on the door, and Andre entered long enough to hand him a slip of blank paper and return to the video room. He pretended to read it, well aware that Mason's eyes were glued to him. He folded the paper in half and set it on the file. Mason glanced at the note before their eyes met again.

"Mason, what if I were to tell you that we just obtained a warrant for your bike and your apartment? We intend to have vehicle experts analyze every inch of that bike to determine if it's recently been in an accident or repainted. Those guys are so good. They don't miss a thing. They'll even be able to figure out which bike shop did the work or if you did it yourself."

Now it was Mason's turn to glance at the video camera. His expression became opaque and far away. "If you're charging me with something, I want a lawyer," he finally said, unwilling to look at Jack again. "Otherwise, I'd like to leave."

"Okay," he replied, "but I'd like to tell you a little story first. I think you had it bad for Margarita because she was a lot like you. She was pretty, in college and very smart. Just like you. You both came from good families, and I'm guessing you thought she'd want you for sure." He paused, but Mason ignored him and continued to stare at the camera. "But she didn't want you. She wanted the exotic bartender who was probably a little dangerous." He chuckled and added, "I've met the guy. He's definitely the Latin lover type."

Mason remained stoic.

"You finally couldn't take the rejection anymore. You showed up when she got off work. You knew the guard on duty, Dean, would be way busy entertaining Lisa at the guard shack in the west parking lot. You waited until Ian left Margarita and you followed her. Maybe you pleaded with her, or maybe whatever happened first was an accident. Maybe she made you so angry you just snapped. I'm guessing you threw her into the ravine and followed her down. That's where you raped and strangled her. Then you carefully covered your tracks to make sure no clues were left behind."

He thought he saw Mason's lips quiver, but he couldn't be sure.

"What you didn't count on," he continued, "was that Ian Patton actually saw a security guard as he and Margarita left, but it was too dark to tell who it was. Everyone assumed it was Dean Horn, but it was you. And I can't imagine how upset you were when you found your beloved bike nearly crushed. That must've been quite a long walk home, only to turn around again and be back at the resort by seven a.m. to have the Honda towed." He wagged a finger at him. "That was quite ingenious. Have the car towed immediately, which would give the police a reason to find your fingerprints all over it."

Mason's gaze slowly shifted from the camera to Jack. "I said I want a *lawyer*."

* * *

Chief Phillips' anger reminded Jack of the bright red and white coals of a campfire, the heat palpable but lacking the showy licks of fire that weren't half as dangerous. Ruskin was blathering about the shoddy work of Detectives Salt and Lawrence, not bothering to shoulder any of the responsibility for the botched investigation. They'd worked Escolido for two months and Jack had found the killer in less than two days. As Ruskin ticked off all the excuses he could think of for his lack of supervision, Jack resisted the urge to cut him off. Ruskin clearly wasn't recognizing the effect of his speech on the chief.

As he took a breath to start another paragraph, Phillips said, "Enough. Save it for the inquiry."

"What?" he asked.

"I'm opening an inquiry into the handling of this investigation. The family and the public will demand nothing less. *I'm* demanding nothing less. When my chief of detectives can't realize there might have been *two* security guards present..." She cut herself off and exhaled. "You can go. Juanita Baca is expecting you."

"Who the hell is she?" Ruskin demanded, dropping all decorum with his superior.

"She's down in HR. She handles retirements."

Jack's gaze dropped to the floor as Ruskin stormed out, muttering "fucking bitch" under his breath. When Jack heard the door slam, he looked up and found the chief staring at him. He shuffled his feet, suddenly uncomfortable, a feeling he wasn't used to. He was always smooth around women and he loved to flirt, but rarely had it ever been anything more. His heart still belonged to Ari's mother, but Dylan Phillips was a beautiful woman and he liked her behind Sol Gardener's big desk. She looked great. It *fit*.

She didn't dismiss him. She twirled a pencil between her fingers like a little wooden baton, deep in thought. "What do you want?" she finally asked.

"Me? Most people would say world peace, but I'm content with a great sunset over the ocean and a cold beer."

She cracked a little smile and dropped the pencil. "What kind of beer?"

His eyes widened. Was she flirting with him? "Pardon?"

"I need to know what to buy when we celebrate your *double* promotion."

He stammered, "What?"

"You're making lieutenant, *and* I'm appointing you the Chief of Detectives."

CHAPTER TWENTY-EIGHT

"I'm telling you this is a mistake."

Over the phone Molly heard the insistence in Sienna's voice. "You're probably right, but I can't let this go."

"I'm not saying that. I'm just against burglary."

She winced at Sienna's choice of words. She gazed up at Trombetta Dwellings and the dark window of Biz's condo. It wouldn't be breaking and entering in the purest sense. She'd acquired a key.

"Go home now and come back to my place tomorrow," Sienna whispered.

"Is your husband there?"

"Yes, he just got home from London and the answering service is calling him already. But *he* needs me tonight. *You* can have me tomorrow, as long as you're not in *jail*."

Sienna disconnected, having made her point. Molly pulled out Biz's key and security code, shame washing over her. She'd called her brother and offered to check on Ari's house, saving Brian a trip across town. He had been grateful, told her where Ari kept her spare key and never questioned her motives. She'd used the opportunity to search her office, and she was both dismayed and grateful when she discovered Biz's key and code. It probably meant they were sleeping together, but it also gave her a chance to find evidence linking Biz to Vince Carnotti or Wanda's death.

She parked two blocks away at the city bus terminal amid the vehicles of regular park-and-ride commuters. The lot was open until bus service ended at eleven, so her truck blended in perfectly. She'd already staked out the lofts and decided the parking garage entry was her best bet. Although she'd be subject to heavy scrutiny from the security crew manning the cameras, it was a better option than boldly crossing the main threshold and looking the front desk guard in the eye, possibly having to speak with him.

Years of police work had taught her about security cameras, blind spots and the limitations of technology. After her encounter with the lesbians at the pool, she'd come downtown and walked the block around Trombetta Dwellings, making note of camera type and placement, as well as barriers, plants and street lighting, all of which could work in her favor. Her conclusion was that the security was adequate but not top-of-the-line. *Maybe security consultation could be my next career step*, she thought, as she carefully avoided the shifting camera at the entrance and darted into the garage as a car exited.

She pulled up against a pillar and plotted a path to the elevator. She'd brought a paper bag disguised to look like groceries, and she set it down long enough to adjust her baseball cap and tighten her old Army jacket. No one could trace it, and any security guard watching the monitors couldn't tell if she was male or female. In fact, because of her height most observers would think she was a man—with brown hair. She'd found a cheap wig, letting dark wisps curl under the bottom of the cap.

One thing she'd learned from watching surveillance videos is that suspicious people drew attention to themselves with their odd behavior. As she crossed the parking lot to the elevator, she moved quickly as if the bag was heavy and she wanted to rid herself of the task, but she kept her stride casual, as if she did this every day. She made sure she constantly shifted the bag from left to right and kept her head down as the elevator headed up to Biz's floor and down the hallway to her condo. She made a production of fumbling for the keys, which gave her an excuse to stare at the lock until she was safely inside.

She quickly located the security keypad in the hallway and disarmed it. She took a deep breath. She thought she might throw up. She was shaking and her heart throbbed in her chest. She resisted the urge to run out and drive straight back to Ari's house and return the key. She'd come this far, and she needed to find out what she could about Biz.

She guessed Biz would never keep anything important at her office across town. The security could be easily breached and every abused woman who'd ever asked for her help had met her there. They knew her office and so did some of their shitty ex-boyfriends. If there was any evidence to tie Biz to Vince Carnotti it was here.

She quickly reconnoitered and was impressed by the loft. It was absolutely beautiful. She'd heard through the lesbian grapevine that Biz had remodeled it before she moved in. Now looking at the granite counters, the modern light fixtures and the Danish furniture in the master bedroom, she guessed she'd dropped nearly a quarter of a million dollars on the place, an impossible figure for a poor PI.

Judging from the clothes scattered about her room, she guessed Biz had left in a hurry on her way to meet Ari in Laguna Beach. She scowled, picturing the two of them together in the bed. How long had they been sleeping together? She imagined Biz's mattress was much more comfortable than the old one in her apartment, although Ari had always said the bed wasn't important, just the person next to her. A lump formed in her throat. *Stay focused*, she thought.

She returned to the living room, noticing there was no computer on the small desk built into a wall unit. A few random bills were stuck into a wooden holder, as well as her most recent bank statement. Her eyes widened at the balance listed at the top. Biz had over a hundred thousand dollars in the bank. Her gaze dropped to the transaction history, which listed a few deposits of a couple thousand each and a handful of electronic withdrawals to the utilities and the bank for her mortgage, which was more than all of Molly's monthly bills combined. Oddly missing were debit transactions. Whereas most Americans used their debit card regularly, Biz did not. She didn't write checks either, which meant that she dealt primarily in cash. *That's suspicious*, Molly thought. She's concerned with leaving a trail, but that could also be because savvy PIs hired by angry ex-husbands could follow her as well.

She put everything back and scanned the room. There had to be something, anything that could confirm her gut feeling that would justify the crime she was committing. She went into the second bedroom, which was a glorified storage space. Boxes were stacked three-high with clothes draped over them.

She went to the closet, which was stuffed with jackets, hoodies and coats. Biz owned a lot of clothes, but most of them were disguises, she realized. Her gaze dropped to the floor and she smiled. A small safe sat in the corner. It was certainly large enough to hold documents, guns and drugs—and judging from the position of the handle it was open. She couldn't believe her luck! Why would Biz be so careless? She was clearly too focused on getting to Ari, or she was too rattled after committing murder. That made more sense.

She crouched down and pulled the door open. Inside were three packs of cash wrapped in paper bands that said "ten thousand." She also had two passports, one legit and the other fake, under the name Sandy Chestwick. In that one she sported a short brown wig and garish makeup. It was quite a shock;

Molly had never seen her as anything but a butch. Somehow it reminded her of Lola, Wanda's alter ego.

Underneath the passports were a stack of presigned prescriptions for three different drugs. Not surprisingly, she couldn't read most of the handwriting and was only able to make out one word, oxycodone. All were from an Indian doctor and none of the prescriptions listed a date. *That's probably the point*, she thought. She's popping pills and doesn't want to bother with refills. There was nothing else, although she imagined this was where she kept her gun. She sighed. What did she think she would find, a Christmas card from Vince Carnotti?

An idea occurred to her. She flipped open the passport again and stared at the wig. She rummaged through the clothes, and not finding what she was looking for, headed back to Biz's room and the walk-in closet. All of her trademark concert T-shirts and faded jeans hung at the front. She fingered the clothing until she came to three garment bags. She unzipped the first one and stared at a sparkly evening dress. She rolled her eyes and unzipped the second one, finding a tailored Evan Picone suit she imagined Biz wore anytime she needed to go to court. The dress in the third bag looked familiar. Although it was a simple black cocktail dress, the neckline was unique and unforgettable—a deep square scoop. When worn with a pushup bra, the wearer would garner much attention from anyone at Hideaway, and she remembered her own gaze frequently dropping to Wanda's chest.

But she couldn't be sure. It was a dress and she was the last person in the world to judge fashion even if she was an expert on cleavage. Her gut wasn't satisfied. She noticed some shelves above the clothes and three wigs, each one perched on a Styrofoam head, one with long, red hair, the brunette one from her passport photo, and a long, flowing blond mane just like Lola's.

"That has got to be it," she muttered.

Now her gut felt better. She took a few quick photos of the dress and the wig with her phone camera and zipped up the garment bags. She made a sweep through the house, making sure nothing was out of place. Then she pulled out a change of clothes and a folded duffel bag from the grocery bag she'd carried in with her. She exchanged the Army jacket, wig and ball cap for a leather jacket, tight jeans and fedora. Now she looked as if she was ready for a date or clubbing, and she knew security paid less attention to someone exiting a building.

She stuffed the first outfit into the duffel. As she prepared to punch in the security code and leave, she heard the phone ringing. Apparently Biz still had an old answering machine, for after a moment she heard her voice instruct the caller to leave a message.

She was standing at the front door when the caller's voice made her freeze. It was Biz.

"Find what you were looking for, Molly?"

Her voice echoed through the house and although she'd asked Molly a question, she knew she wouldn't hear her answer. She'd obviously installed her own security system, one that was connected to satellite and allowed her to check her cameras, wherever they may be, through her phone. Molly thought about some of the decorative art she had seen in the living room and the childish stuffed bear in the bedroom.

"Don't worry. I'm not going to call the police. I wouldn't want to upset Ari. I wouldn't want to run the risk that she'd post your bail out of pity. I wouldn't want her asking a lot of *questions*. We know those questions, don't we, Molly? And we know the answers, too."

CHAPTER TWENTY-NINE

"I'm telling you we can go home," Biz insisted. "Bobby Arco is the killer. If you'd seen what I saw in that house, you'd know what he's capable of doing. He's a stalker and a child pornographer, and I hope his sorry ass fries in hell but not before some con makes him his bitch."

Jane and Rory were nodding furiously. Only Ari remained unconvinced. She pulled out Nina's last two journals. "Remember this entry? 'Valeria caught in secrets thanks to apothecary. Share with no one except H. Maybe Orlando? Must investigate! Can Benedick be trusted? Will it destroy? Cesario, oh, Cesario... It is Aguecheek.' I think I've figured it out."

She set the journal down and explained. "Valeria is Nina and the apothecary is her doctor, who told her something that made her realize the truth about Evan and Sam's parentage. I'm guessing Horatio is Evan and Orlando is Sam. Benedick is Steve, and she doesn't know if she can trust him because the truth could destroy him. Cesario is Georgie."

She looked at Rory and asked, "That character was a woman disguised as a man, right?"

She nodded. "Right. So Nina could've used it to reference a woman as well, particularly if she's Valeria."

"And Scott Kramer is Aguecheek," Ari continued. "She says 'Cesario, Cesario,' like she can't believe what Georgie has done. And when she finishes with, 'It is Aguecheek,' she's saying he's the dad."

"But how did Nina figure all this out?" Jane asked.

She shook her head. "I don't know. There are all kinds of tests during pregnancy, especially for women over thirty." She looked at Biz. "I agree that Bobby's scum, but I think both Georgie and Steve have a motive, a *strong* motive with these pictures."

Rory held up the photo of Scott with the twins in the pool. "It's not so obvious now that they're older. They've had time to fill out."

"Yeah," Jane said. "It's the forehead and the eyes."

She grabbed Nina's final journal. "And don't forget the last thing she ever wrote." She reread the lone entry. "'The secret will be revealed—DANGER. Poor Benedick! Poor Horatio! And poor Orlando—a pawn?'" She tapped the page. "She used the word 'danger.' This is the situation that threatened her the most."

"That's because she didn't know Bobby Arco was a sick perv who was stalking her," Biz argued.

The room grew silent as each of them pondered the possibilities. Biz knew Ari had a point. All of the Garritsons and Scott Kramer had a motive to keep the secret hidden, but she was sure about Bobby Arco. She knew criminals. She *knew* it was him and she needed to get home—and now. Too much was happening, flying out of control. Molly was somehow involved in Wanda's case and if she was communicating with Jack and Andre...

Ari looked at Rory, who'd spent the day talking up teachers at school about Evan. "You said Evan was distraught over the baby and Nina's choice, and he could've slipped out of the school music concert before the lights came up." She looked at Jane. "And you said Steve's alibi is flimsy."

"It is," Jane admitted. "There were two hundred people at that charity event, and he wasn't accountable to anyone for every single minute."

Ari looked back at Biz, almost pleading. "I just don't think it's so open-and-shut."

She took a deep breath. "The police are convinced. I spoke with Detective Justice after they raided the place—"

"From your 'anonymous tip,'" Rory said, pantomiming quotation marks. "I'm not sure I approve of your tactics, Biz."

"Tell me that after you're the victim of domestic abuse," she snapped. She looked back at Ari, unwilling to get into an ethics discussion. "Honey, what can I do to convince you?" She took Ari's hand and squeezed it. She couldn't leave if things weren't right between them.

"Come with me to Scott Kramer's house. Let's just stake him out for a little while and see if there's anything interesting."

"Do you think he's a suspect too?" Jane asked.

Ari threw up her hands. "Why not add him to the slate? Georgie was guilty of statutory rape. If Nina threatened to expose the relationship from thirty years ago, that's Georgie's motive, and she also has a flimsy alibi. She can close her store anytime she wants and no one would be the wiser. Steve had a motive to save his career. Would the governor really want someone on the task force whose wife had preyed on an underage boy? Evan wanted Nina for himself and was probably jealous of Sam, and if Scott knew she was about to expose him as the real father, it could certainly be embarrassing for him."

Biz sighed. "Okay, let's go."

* * *

Scott's house was located farther up the coast near Laguna Niguel. Though it was tucked away in a quiet neighborhood, Ari imagined it was still worth nearly a million, although it would never command the value of the Garritson place. He'd done well for himself, but he wasn't among the California elite.

His front yard was a masterpiece, a testament to his talent as a landscaper. Plants and flowers surrounded the entry and a stone pathway curved from the door to the driveway, each paver bordered by beautiful white flowers. A perfectly groomed hedge formed the property line, separating his Cape Cod-style house from the one next door.

They parked across the street, away from the glow of the streetlights. His garage was closed, but the blinds were open. He was moving in and out of the front room, setting out plates and silverware on the dining room table.

When he lit the candle sitting in the center, Biz said, "He's expecting someone."

"It looks very romantic," Ari commented, staring through the windshield.

Biz gazed at Ari's profile. She was so beautiful. Biz had never understood how the sight of someone could take a person's breath away until she met her. That first day when they'd been introduced, she'd stumbled over her words, instantly enamored and full of desire. She'd waited so long, so sure that Ari and Molly's relationship would eventually run its course, a victim of Molly's alcoholism.

However, she'd grown impatient and decided to give their breakup a little nudge, destroying Molly's personal and professional lives at the same time. She'd hated herself for that, but as she gazed at Ari, it was all forgotten.

She tucked Ari's hair behind her ear and grinned. She loved her new haircut and the way it framed her face. She massaged the back of her neck and Ari moaned.

"You're tense," she said.

Ari closed her eyes and murmured her agreement. She saw an opportunity and gently kissed her cheek. When she didn't protest, her lips wandered to her neck and her fingers slid deeper into her hair.

"We're supposed to be working," Ari whispered.

"We are," she answered before she nibbled her ear. "This is the best stakeout of my entire career."

They kissed. Ari's lips were magnets pulling Biz out of the driver's seat and into her lap. Ari's passionate kisses signaled permission and she stroked her breasts and her belly. A wave of euphoria swept over Biz with each flick of Ari's tongue and every undulation of her body. In her dreams this moment was like a fire in a cozy cabin, but as Ari directed her hand to her inner thigh, she realized how much she wanted it too. Instead of the cozy cabin a different image came to her mind, one that was much rawer—a bed of leaves under an enormous tree.

Biz pulled away and held her shoulders. "Baby, I can't wait much longer."

"You're not going to," she said with a grin.

Headlights flooded the street and they immediately hunkered down in the seats as a Mercedes cruised past them and pulled into Scott Kramer's carport. The car idled as the garage door slowly ascended.

Ari grabbed the binoculars and focused on the car. "Well, this just got more interesting." She lowered them to her chest, a smug look on her face. "The license plate says GRGY G. Georgie G."

They argued all the way back to Laguna Beach about the significance of an affair between Scott Kramer and Georgie Garritson.

"It doesn't make either of them a killer," Biz said adamantly. "It could just be they're in love and they've always been in love. Steve might even know."

"I doubt it," Ari disagreed. "If it was such an open affair, why would she lie about taking overnight trips to San Diego every two weeks?"

Biz held her tongue, frustrated by the turn of events. She still thought Bobby Arco was the killer. She *needed* Bobby Arco to be the killer, or at least she needed to convince Ari so they could go home and she could keep an eye on Molly. A fleeting thought occurred to her. Vince Carnotti might want Molly eliminated.

"I think we should just see what plays out with the police," she announced. "You said they had a second piece of evidence, whatever Nina grabbed when she fell over the railing, and Jane said that the patch from Bobby Arco's work shirt was missing when you saw him at the school." She gauged Ari's cynical expression and added, "If they have the patch they'll charge him with murder by morning."

She raked a hand through her hair and gazed out the window. "Then I guess we wait until morning."

They were forced to take a parking space in the back of the hotel. After she turned off the engine she made no move to get out of the car. Ari looked at her quizzically.

"You need to tell me what happens next," Biz said quietly. "We're going to your room and making love or I need to go down to the beach and take a very long walk. Which is it?"

She could see the debate raging behind her eyes, and she was surprised when Ari reached over, kissed her softly and whispered, "C'mon."

They quickly went to the room, giggling and holding hands. They found a note from Jane and Rory on the coffee table stating they were at a gay bar.

"Isn't that interesting," Ari mused while Biz groped and kissed her frantically from behind.

"Not really," she growled.

When she boldly unzipped Ari's jeans and yanked them from her waist, Ari cried out in surprise and the note fluttered from her fingers. Biz found an ounce of patience, long enough for them to stumble into Ari's bedroom before she claimed what was hers.

CHAPTER THIRTY

Ari awoke when the suite's front door slammed. Her eyes flew open and the sun momentarily blinded her, its white rays pouring through the open curtains. She sat up, conscious that she was naked. She never slept in the nude, but Biz had insisted. She looked around. Where was she?

Her clothes from last night had been piled on a chair but noticeably missing were Biz's things. Exhausted and somewhat disoriented, she pulled herself out of bed and saw a note sitting against the bedside lamp with her name on it.

Dear Ari,

Last night = amazing. The best! Our bodies were definately meant to be together. I'm sorry you'll wake up alone. I'd thought about rolling on top of u (I love sex in the morning) before I left, but we were up really late last night and u r a butiful sleeper. Got a text from Det. Justice. Bobby Arco was charged with 1st degree so I guess we're done. I've got to get back to Phx. I'll see u soon, baby.

Biz

She rubbed a hand over her eyes and read the note again. The use of text language and misspellings made her cringe, but she agreed with her sentiment about the evening. The sex had been great and exactly what she'd needed after nearly a year of abstinence. Biz was a considerate lover, even if she was a bit overbearing. When she'd tried to throw on her traditional nightshirt and boxers before they fell asleep, Biz had wrapped her in a bear hug and tickled her. She wouldn't let her leave the bed, cajoling her to remain skin to skin. She'd acquiesced but had fallen asleep slightly annoyed. She didn't like sleeping nude. She felt too vulnerable. She'd have to explain that to her before next time. She smiled. *Next time.*

Her thoughts wandered to Bobby Arco's arrest as she jumped in the shower and threw on some clothes. If he was arrested for Nina's murder, there had to have been another piece of evidence, something that tied him to the crime scene, like the name patch from his work shirt, but that didn't make sense. If that was the evidence, he would've been arrested before yesterday. She shook her head. How could Nina have misread the situation? She was trained to work with people and assess their threat level. How could she be so wrong about Bobby?

She found Jane filing her nails on the sofa. She raised an eyebrow and frowned, clearly in a bad mood. "Well, it's about time Little Mary Sunshine got out of bed. Biz is gone and Rory and I are *not* speaking to each other."

Ari poured herself a cup of coffee from the room service cart and joined Jane on the couch.

"What happened? I heard the door slam. It woke me up."

She glowered. "So sorry." She shook her head and threw up her hands. "That woman is the most frustrating person I've ever met."

"I get it. What happened?"

"Nothing! That's the point."

A headache was creeping across her skull, so she sipped the coffee faster, hoping it would bathe her system in caffeine, wake her up and save her from the inevitable hangover she knew was coming. Raiding the minibar after their second round of sex had probably been a mistake.

"Jane, what happened between you two? Did you sleep together?"

She slumped back and stared at the ceiling. "Somehow it got complicated. We went out to this bar, but we got so wrapped up in our conversation and our Words with Friends game that we never left the table. We spent the whole night laughing and making fun of each other's words. Then she suggested we have a match where we could only use dirty words or words found in a trashy romance." She paused before she said, "That's when it got complicated."

"How?"

"After about fifty letters we both got really turned on. I'd just spelled 'hungry' and then she spelled 'hungrier.' I told her that wasn't really a sex word and she said, 'It is if that's the case. Maybe I am hungrier than you.'"

"Then what happened?" Ari asked, pulling a cherry pastry from the cart.

"What do you think? That's one of the best come-ons I've heard given the context of a Scrabble game. I was all over her and she *loved* it. And *I* loved it." She stared at her incredulously. "Do you know how rare *that* is? And then she pushed me away. Said she wasn't hungry anymore."

"What?"

"She ran out of the bar and started walking down the street. I jumped in her car and followed her."

"Why did you have her keys?" Ari interrupted.

"We'd already been to one place…it's not important," she said. "Anyway, I was so angry I was screaming out the window and she was screaming back. Apparently there was a police car around the corner and they saw me driving five miles an hour down a busy street and the two of us screaming so they pulled us over." She paused and clarified. "Well, I guess it wasn't really pulling us over since he just walked up and told me to stop. Since we weren't drunk, the cops gave me a ride home and let Rory go. She wouldn't even look at me. She just jumped in her car and sped away. Thank God they were cool, or I could've spent the night with Bobby Arco."

"Did Biz tell you he was arrested for Nina's murder?"

She nodded. "It's not surprising. They must have more evidence, since Biz didn't hesitate to leave. Everything good between the two of you?"

"Yeah," she said with a shy smile. "It is."

"Better than Molly?"

Her smile faded and she said quietly, "Different." Before Jane could probe any further she asked, "So what was the door slamming about? Waiter upset with your tip this morning?"

"No, that was Rory. She showed up to apologize and explain her behavior from last night. She talked about commitment issues and a recent breakup and blah, blah, blah. Apparently *that* was why she'd been seeing Nina. I told her she needed to grow up. She got mad and stormed out. End of story. Glad she's gone."

She rose and clapped her hands together. "Let's get our things together. The Garritsons are staging an elaborate brunch to celebrate Sam's freedom and the catching of Nina's killer, although I don't think Evan will be joining us. Sam's so angry it could take years for him to forgive Evan for not telling him about the pregnancy."

She headed for the bedroom while Ari fretted.

"Honey, are you going to pack?"

"I will," she said, setting the cup on the table, "but first I need to tie up some loose ends."

* * *

Ari followed a uniformed officer down a long corridor of the Laguna Beach Police Department to Clay Justice's desk. When he saw her, his smile widened. She noticed he was wearing another Mexican wedding shirt, only in yellow this time. She pictured an entire closet filled with them in multiple colors.

"Are you here to compare notes? Do you want the secret to my great detecting ways?"

"I heard you had an anonymous tip, actually," she said casually.

His smile broke and he looked at her suspiciously. "Do you know anything about that?"

She shook her head honestly. "No, I only heard."

He murmured, "That Arco is one sick bastard."

"I don't disagree, but are you sure he's a murderer?"

"Absolutely. Slam dunk case. We found a critical piece of evidence in his house that linked him to the crime."

Her shoulders sagged as she worried what was coming. "Can you share with me what you found, you know, since I was looking too? I mean, I'm going home today anyway."

He chewed his lip and glanced about the empty squad room. Since it was Sunday, there was only a skeleton crew. "What the hell?" He leaned against the desk and said, "We found the shirt he was wearing that night. Hung in the back of his closet."

She was puzzled. "What? That doesn't make any sense. If you committed a murder, wouldn't you throw out the shirt you were wearing?"

He shook his head. "There's no understanding people. Maybe he only had one good shirt. Even with the pocket missing, he could still wear it with a jacket."

Her head snapped up. "What did you say?"

"I'm just sayin' that even though the pocket's gone—"

"Wait a minute. Are you telling me that Nina grabbed the pocket of a man's dress shirt on her way down?"

"Yeah."

CHAPTER THIRTY-ONE

Molly found Sienna huddled over a large cup of coffee at Lux Café. She was wearing her gym attire and a serious expression.

"You're a crazy woman, do you know that?" she said before Molly could sit down.

"I'm not crazy. I found the disguise that Wanda wore when she met me at Hideaway. Biz had it in her closet."

She started to berate her, but a waitress came by for Molly's order and she fell silent until the waitress headed back to the counter.

"And what if Biz finds out you broke into her condo? What if one of her neighbors saw you?"

She winced. "She already knows."

Her eyes widened. "How?"

"Apparently she has hidden cameras all over her place. She actually called her house and spoke into her answering machine *while I was there*. She was talking to me. I wouldn't be surprised if she was watching me while she was talking."

"Can somebody do that now? I mean, private citizens?"

"Oh, yeah. High-tech surveillance equipment is accessible to the general public. Look at all those nanny cams that your rich friends have."

"Most bought those to catch their cheating husbands," she laughed. "They weren't half as worried about who was handling their children as they were about who was *handling* their men."

"You weren't?" she asked.

"Nope."

"Really?"

"Really," she repeated and sipped her coffee. "Unlike most couples, Louie and I decided to talk about our sexual relationship before we ran into trouble. After he caught me with my maid of honor, I don't think we had any other choice. We decided to have an open marriage. Since I needed to be with women, I certainly couldn't ask him to be completely faithful."

"So he has other lovers?" she asked, fascinated by Sienna's lifestyle.

She shrugged. "Perhaps. Maybe not now but in the past. We don't talk about it. We just expect two things from each other," she said, wagging two fingers. "First, we take precautions with other partners, and we leave it as sex. There's no dating, no falling in love." She gestured at the table. "I'm actually making a huge exception for you, meeting you here for coffee. This is almost like a date."

At the mention of the word "date," Molly sat up, startled. "Date? This isn't a date."

"It's beyond my agreement with my husband," she said adamantly. "We're not naked and we're in a public place."

She leaned forward. "Then why are you here?"

She gazed at her thoughtfully. "Because my husband has nothing to fear from you. There's no way we'll fall in love. You're not a threat. You're still in love with Ari."

She frowned. "That's not true."

She reached across the table and took her hand. "Isn't it? I know this Biz person ruined your career and she may be a murderer, but aren't you worried about Ari? About her being with Biz?"

She pulled her hand away and crossed her arms. "You've got it all wrong. In fact, you probably won't like my motivations."

"Tell me."

Before she spoke she wrapped all of her anger into the tight little steel ball that sat inside her heart. "I can't wait for Biz to be arrested, that's true, but not because I'm worried about Ari. No, it's quite the opposite. I hope the police break down the door of her hot shit condo while they're doing it in bed. I hope the cops run into her bedroom with guns blazing just before they climax." She watched Sienna's face fall—and it pleased her. "I want Ari to suffer just like I suffered. I want her to know what it's like to lose the person you love the most in the world."

"How do you know she loves Biz?"

"Well, she left me."

"No," she disagreed, "from what you've told me, you left *her*. She was completely vulnerable after being kidnapped and nearly killed, and you caught her in a terrible moment of weakness, one that was probably orchestrated by Biz, I should add, and *you* ran out on her. Is that about right?"

Her face reddened. She'd twisted all the facts. *Or maybe she just untwisted them.*

"Still," she argued, "Ari's responsible for her actions."

"That's true," she conceded. "We all have to accept responsibility for our actions." She paused before she said, "I guess I was just lucky enough to find a partner who believed loving me was more important than punishing me."

"It's not the same," she snarled, "and why are we talking about this? My relationship with Ari has nothing to do with catching Biz. She's committed a felony and she's going to pay."

"What about her boss?" she whispered. "Wasn't she working for someone in the mob?"

She nodded. "Yeah, we've been trying to catch him for years."

"How do you think he's going to react when he finds out you know she's a killer?"

"He won't find out," she said without much conviction.

"Right," she said, taking one last gulp of her coffee before she stood up to go. "You're in over your head, Molly, and the person you love most in the world could get hurt or wind up dead. You think you feel awful now…"

She grabbed her purse and walked away.

* * *

Molly sat outside Ari's house, the truck's engine idling, studying the keychain shaped like a real estate sign, the words National Title Company stamped across it. She imagined it was a cheap souvenir Ari had received at some convention.

She glanced at the red front door that led into Ari's new life. She'd not yet returned Ari's spare key to Brian, and he hadn't asked for it. She guessed he was conveniently forgetting since he'd been by the house to work on the plumbing, probably using a key Ari kept hidden for emergencies.

She needed to return Biz's key before Ari returned from California, but she couldn't get out of the truck. The day before, she hadn't given a second thought when she'd hurried into the house and up the stairs on her mission to destroy Biz. The fact that she was technically breaking and entering didn't cross her mind, but for a reason she couldn't determine, entering Ari's house *this* time seemed more dangerous, as if there were more at stake.

Because I want to linger inside. If I can't be near her, I want to be near her things, and I really want to find that picture.

She killed the engine and hopped out of the cab. She strolled casually to the front door and slipped inside. The tile was dry and Brian had removed his equipment from the foyer. In the kitchen new plasterboard covered the site of the burst pipe. She guessed that the beautiful oak floors could be saved, but they would need to be refinished. Ari would be greatly relieved since it was the original hardwood.

She went into the solarium and gazed into the beautiful backyard, picturing her bending over to plant a flower, her cute little bottom tilting toward the sky. She blinked and took a deep breath. Maybe Sienna was right.

She scanned the room and noticed a small credenza in the corner. She searched through both drawers carefully, finding some old real estate awards, several knickknacks that she must have pulled out of storage and the framed certificate she'd received when she graduated from the police academy.

She headed upstairs and immediately returned Biz's key to the pigeonhole above Ari's desk. She opened all the drawers and chuckled at the superior organization. Every pencil, sticky note pack and paperclip was housed in some type of container and sat inside larger containers. She thought of her own desk and the middle drawer that wouldn't open because so many papers had been crammed inside. Ari wouldn't approve. She stepped back. There was nothing personal anywhere in the loft. It was her home office and nothing more.

She imagined she would find boxes in the guest room full of the things she hadn't had time to unpack, as well as the items that just hadn't found the right spot yet. So she was surprised when she opened the door to an inviting four-poster bed with complementary cherry wood furniture. She shook her head. Already she was ready for company. A few blankets were stacked in the closet, but the dresser was empty. She sat on the edge of the bed and plucked the maroon throw pillow from the pile against the headboard. She pressed it tightly against her chest. Ari had kept it on her living room sofa when she lived in the condo and would tuck it under her head when they lounged in front of the TV.

She contemplated whether Ari would really miss it if she took it, considering it was practically buried underneath two giant shams in a room that was hardly used. She rolled her eyes at her unbelievable thoughts. *I'm resorting to pillow theft.* She centered it on the pile and closed the door behind her.

All that remained was Ari's bedroom. She already knew there wasn't anything in one nightstand, so she checked the other one for good measure, finding only a stack of Sudoku books. The closet contained a modest collection of dressy clothes and very few pairs of shoes by most women's standards. She couldn't resist gazing at a few of her favorite outfits—the short pink miniskirt, the striped silk dress blouse Ari wore with her gray suit and her personal favorite, the black leather jacket.

A stack of large red IKEA boxes sat in the corner with neatly printed tags on the front. She knew their contents, which had been a discussion point at various times during their relationship. Ari saved all memorabilia, believing every experience deserved to be chronicled. The first box was simply labeled "Cards" and contained every greeting card she'd ever received, but she hadn't included the ones from Molly. Underneath was a box labeled "Entertainment," followed by "Photos," then "Letters," and the most interesting one in her opinion, "Miscellaneous." Inside were the screwiest of the odds and ends she'd acquired throughout the years, including weird pencils, her pressed corsage from her senior prom and her first baby tooth. But there was nothing from their relationship.

The only place left to look was the dresser. Her hope faded as she realized the unlikelihood of Ari relegating the mementos of their relationship to a dresser drawer. Still, she needed to find that photo and anything else Ari may have kept since she had never put her "Molly Things" in the IKEA boxes.

She pulled open the drawers one after the other, her disappointment growing with the revelation of each drawer's contents: sweaters, T-shirts, socks and, as titillating as it was, underwear. Six drawers and no mementos and no photo.

She sat on the edge of the bed and shook her head. What was she thinking? Why was she here? Her phone fell from her pocket to the floor. She leaned over to retrieve it and her gaze settled on a long plastic box under the bed. She got down on all fours and pulled it out, expecting to find all of her gift wrapping supplies, probably color-coded by hue. Instead several memories burst forth at once and competed for her attention, each triggered by an object in the box.

She immediately reached for the framed photo, the one she'd been hoping to find. She smiled at the significance of it being on *top*. They had been so happy. Ari had protested when Jane asked for a picture, insisting that her hair was a mess. She'd pulled it up with a clip and several strands had escaped throughout the day as they'd trolled the antique shops and taken a short hike. She looked so fresh and alive. She was the most beautiful in her most natural state.

Molly inhaled to ward off the tears and the urge for a scotch, which suddenly overwhelmed her. She thrust her hand in her pocket and clutched the familiar stone, her lifeline to sanity. She closed her eyes and waited for the moment to pass, willing herself forward as if she were passing through a mountain tunnel. She visualized the exit and saw the continuing highway at the end. Light appeared and she rounded the corner. She opened her eyes and dropped the stone back into her pocket.

"Great," she whispered, reaching for a scrapbook with a nondescript black leather cover.

A newspaper article was glued to the first page. It was the coverage of her first big case, the murder of a prominent businessman. One of Ari's best friends had been accused; it was the case that brought them together and ignited their relationship. She flipped the pages and read the headlines of subsequent articles that created a timeline of the case and its eventual closure, which included Ari being shot.

She noticed all of her important cases, the ones worthy of news coverage, were chronicled in the scrapbook. Although her name was never mentioned specifically, Ari was cataloguing her career. Interspersed were several articles about crimes the police suspected were the work of Vince Carnotti, the man most likely to have been behind the end of her career.

A lump formed in her throat as she glanced through the pages devoted to the last murder she'd investigated, the one that ended with a terrible explosion only a dozen yards from where she was. No one had been arrested in the end. No one needed to be.

The rest of the pages were blank like a story with no ending.

She put everything back inside carefully and shoved the box under the bed. She stood, full of resolve, marched into the guest room and yanked the maroon pillow from the bed.

CHAPTER THIRTY-TWO

Cars lined the Garritsons' driveway and Jane brazenly pulled the rental up next to the fountain creating her own makeshift parking space. "I doubt anyone will tow it," she said.

Music and boisterous laughter rolled through the open front door. "This is quite a party," Ari murmured as they headed up the walk.

"They're celebrating," she replied. "Wouldn't you? I'm sure they want everyone who is anyone to know Sam is innocent. Steve's appointment to the task force depends on it." They had barely stepped across the threshold before a waiter presented a tray of champagne. Jane handed her a flute. "I'll hand it to Biz. She got the job done."

Jane raised her glass in salute, and she met her toast silently. Laguna's A-group milled about the great room in expensive suits, fine jewelry and designer dresses. She spotted Steve and Georgie greeting people near the French doors. Both wore broad smiles as they accepted the congratulations of their friends and admirers. Georgie constantly dabbed the corners of her eyes, unable to control her emotions.

Sam approached with his arms outstretched. "I'm so glad you came." He hugged both of them and said to Jane, "I owe you so much."

"Not us," she corrected. "Biz. She's the one who got you out of this."

He looked around. "Where is she?"

"She had to get back to Phoenix. She said to tell you good luck with the rest of your life."

Tears filled his eyes and he couldn't reply. She imagined he was thinking of the life he *wouldn't* have—the one with Nina and his child. His expression fortified Ari's resolve to do what needed to be done.

"Come say hello to my parents," he said, guiding them toward the French doors. "I don't think I've ever seen them so happy."

Georgie flew into Jane's arms while Steve pumped her hand vigorously. "You two are the best friends Sam could ever have!" she exclaimed. "I had my doubts…"

"Hey, what are friends for?" Jane asked, still caught in Georgie's strong embrace.

"Well, you always are welcome to visit Laguna," Steve said. "I'm sorry Evan isn't here," he added.

"Dad, don't start," Sam warned. "It's going to be a long time before he's forgiven. If he'd told me about the baby, none of this would've happened. Nina never would've been out jogging alone—"

"Sam, your voice," Georgie said in a harsh whisper. "This is a *party*. Let's not discuss such tragic things today."

His face filled with contempt. "If not now, when, Mother?"

He stalked off and Georgie sighed. "It's going to take a long time for him to get over this, I'm afraid."

Ari realized Sam still had no idea that Georgie had known about the pregnancy before Nina's death. "I don't know if he'll ever get over it," she said. "I have some disturbing news, unfortunately. They're dropping the murder charge against Bobby Arco this afternoon."

"They're what!" Steve shouted. Everyone turned toward him, but he quickly regained his composure.

"How can they do that?" Georgie asked. "He's a horrible human being."

"He is," she agreed, "but like Sam, he didn't kill Nina. Her killer is still at large."

A commotion at the front door caught their attention. Scott stood between an angry Sam and Evan, who was pleading for forgiveness. Standing together, she saw the uncanny resemblance between the three of them...and her mistake.

"You have no right to be here!" Sam shouted. "You as much as killed her yourself!"

"Don't say that, Sam! I loved her too!"

"You son of a bitch!"

Sam went for Evan and several well-dressed men pulled them apart.

"I need to find the bathroom," she whispered to Jane, who only grunted a response.

Mesmerized by the confrontation between the two brothers, no one noticed her slip down the main hallway. Evan and Sam's shouting was barely audible as she entered Georgie's studio. She headed to the closet where Georgie kept the smocks, aprons and old dress shirts, no doubt cast-offs from Steve's closet. She remembered wearing one of Big Jack's shirts in kindergarten during art class. It was the cheapest and easiest way to protect her school clothes.

She pulled out the three Oxford-cloth button-downs, only one wasn't so old, and it was missing a pocket. Whereas the other two were covered in paint and seemed threadbare at the neck and sleeves, the third was perfect except for the missing pocket.

"How did you know?" Steve asked from the doorway.

"I didn't at first. I thought it was Georgie. She was the one I'd seen wearing the shirt."

"No, she would never stoop to such levels." He puffed out his chest and pointed his index finger in the air. "Preserving the family name, Steve," he said, mimicking her. "It's all about the family."

"That's why Sam dumped Nina."

"Of course."

"When I saw Scott, Sam and Evan standing together at the door, I knew you had to know that Scott was their father. How could you not?"

He didn't answer, which was an answer in itself. She gauged his casual stance. She was safe—at least for the moment.

"So if you thought Georgie was the killer, how did you jump to me?"

"Actually it was something Detective Justice said to me today. Some people might keep a dress shirt that was missing the pocket, if it was their only dress shirt, but you have several. I realized this shirt, though, was too new. I can see you typically give Georgie your old shirts, but this one is fine, and when I saw her wearing it, I noticed it didn't have any paint on it."

He chuckled and shut the door behind him, locking it. "You're more observant than the police. When they came to search the house she was wearing the damn thing under her smock, but no one noticed."

"Why didn't you get rid of it? Throw it in a Dumpster or burn it?"

He shook his head. "I didn't realize the pocket was gone. I was just too shaken up when I got home...*afterward*," he said slowly. "I just changed and threw it in the hamper. Next thing I knew, Georgie was wearing it two days later. The housekeeper must have decided I wouldn't want it anymore so she put it there." He motioned to the closet. "When they searched the house later that day, I couldn't understand why they kept looking in odd places like the cedar chests and the dryer. It all made sense when I heard Nina had been discovered with something in her hand."

"But yet, once you figured it out, you still didn't run up here and take it. Why?"

He stared at her blankly. "I figured the danger was past, and then Bobby Arco was arrested…" He sighed. "I don't know. Why didn't Nixon burn the tapes? Maybe I wanted to get caught. I'm not a killer."

"Yes, you *are*," she said as gently as she could.

Rage crossed his face and she saw a different man. The affable city councilman with a smart, sensitive nature vanished. "Only because I had to! I've put up with my coward of a wife loving another man for our entire marriage and never having the decency to come clean about it. How many holidays and barbeques have I sat through with *our good family friend* or, as the boys call him, Uncle Scott? Would you like to take a guess? And those pretend weekend trips to San Diego to check out the inventory," he said sarcastically. "I know what inventory she's checking on. Our whole marriage is a sham! And then when Nina got pregnant the thought of having to stare at Scott's grandchild while everyone congratulated me and called me *Pops*?"

She couldn't believe it. "Georgie still thinks you don't know? She's spent your marriage letting you think you were Sam and Evan's biological father? How can that be? Anyone who looks at them has to know."

He laughed out loud. "Oh, Ms. Adams, you are naïve and obviously not wealthy. Let me explain everything to you." He strolled to a patio door that opened onto a small balcony. "Money smothers common sense, and you will believe *anything* if it protects your status, your home and your career."

"So essentially she blackmailed you. You said nothing and got to keep all this."

"And a spot on the city council," he added. "Don't forget that. Politics is all about money." He flung the door open and the sea breeze wafted into the studio. "I'm not a fool, Ms.

Adams. I know my limitations. We needed each other. Georgie's powerful father never would have tolerated her loving the lowly pool boy, who was underage, by the way. But she got to have it all by marrying a hardworking Yale graduate *and* shtupping the pool boy on the side. It worked out for both of us. If we hadn't married, I'd be some mid-level manager for a mediocre company having a turkey on rye for lunch and planning Saturday barbeques. Yale can't change a man's personality. I'm not what you would call executive material." He paused and added, "My only regret is that we never had another child. Georgie always said two was enough." He gestured to the open door and the small balcony. "I don't suppose there's any chance you'd join me out here? The view is lovely. Georgie calls it 'inspirational.'"

"I don't think so."

"I guess my reputation precedes me," he said with a crazy laugh. He raked his hand through his hair and paced nervously.

"Does Scott know?"

He snorted. "I'm sure he does now. Back then he was just a kid. Young people notice so little."

"But Nina's pregnancy was about to ruin everything and expose your family secret," she said. "I spoke to her doctor this morning. She was Rh negative and there was a concern about incompatibility if Sam was Rh positive. It could be dangerous to the baby. She found out through the tests that the baby was type A, and Sam had told her he was type O, like her. It was a complete impossibility for her baby to be type A if both of them were O."

He offered her a little round of applause. "Give the lady a prize. I'm type O, as is Georgie, but good old Uncle Scott is AB positive." He grew wide-eyed and blurted, "Do you know how freakin' rare that is? He's like the blood bank's wet dream! Only something like nine percent of all white men are AB positive. He's a damn rock star! No wonder Georgie's always wanted him so bad."

She could tell he was starting to lose it. She backed up closer to the door, and he took three giant steps toward her and belly laughed. Her heart pounded and she tried to picture the doorknob behind her. If she turned and ran, he'd grab her for sure and pitch her over the railing, regardless of the consequences.

"So you killed her before the secret got out. If everyone learned that Scott was Sam and Evan's father, you'd be disgraced."

"Worse," he argued. "I never would've been appointed to the governor's task force. Under the law, Georgie raped Scott all those years ago, which is as far from the truth as it could be. *He* actually seduced her, but that doesn't matter. She was the adult. There was no way the governor would appoint the husband of a statutory rapist."

She heard voices coming down the hall—*Jane*.

"We're in here!" she called, hoping they could hear through the locked door.

"Ari?"

"Jane! Get the door open!"

She ran to her right and managed to put Georgie's worktable between her and Steve as the pounding and shouting increased. He cocked his head like a dog deep in thought, listening to the commotion outside. Suddenly a childish grin spread across his face.

"They're coming," he said in a sing-song voice. He darted to a cupboard and pulled a small handgun off the shelf. She instinctively ducked behind the worktable. "Georgie insisted on protection," he said, facing the door, the gun at his side.

"Gun!" she shouted as loud as she could, unsure if anyone could hear her over the screech of the wooden door splintering away from the lock.

Clay Justice and two uniformed officers trained their weapons on him. She saw Jane, Georgie, Evan and Sam behind them.

"Ari, are you okay?" Jane cried.

"I'm fine."

"Mr. Garritson, put down the gun," Justice said.

He ignored him and looked toward Georgie. "Honey?" he bellowed.

"Mr. Garritson, put down the gun. Then you can talk to your wife."

"*You* are not in charge here, detective! I'm calling the shots, so to speak." Realizing his own play on words, he giggled. "Honey? Answer me!"

"For God's sake, Steve," Georgie cried from the hallway, "put down the gun. What's going on? What are you doing?"

"What am I doing? What am *I* doing? For the first time in my miserable life I'm doing something for *me*. It's finally all about me. Instead of perpetuating your lies, licking your ungodly ugly pointed pumps or cleaning up after you, I'm doing something for myself, and this is all on you, baby."

"Mr. Garritson, put down your weapon," Justice repeated in a firm, even voice.

"I will not," he said in a child-like voice, and a vision of the PEZ dispensers floated through Ari's mind. He cleared his throat and in a deep, manly tone said, "Boys, your mother has something to tell you."

Then he raised the gun.

CHAPTER THIRTY-THREE

Biz was the type who hated the last day of vacation. She wanted to savor every minute of her life away from *her life*, which was usually full of darkness and problems. If she was flying to a destination, she always booked the earliest flight to start her trip and the latest one for the return. She maximized her time away and the journey home was always bittersweet and somewhat sad.

Such was not the case coming back to Phoenix from Laguna. She'd pushed the speedometer to ninety during the long stretch across the desert, knowing it was highly unlikely a highway patrolman would stop her. She had to get back as fast as possible and check out her apartment. The idea of Molly snooping through her things enraged her, but she'd managed to sound cool and calculating on the answering machine even though she wanted to scream.

At first glance everything seemed to be in its place. She rushed to the bedroom closet and dropped to her knees in front of the safe. How careless she'd been! She couldn't believe she'd left it open, but she'd never killed anyone before. Her mind had stopped the moment Wanda gasped and fell through the air. The slice of time between her death and nearly toppling her bike outside Quartzite didn't exist.

She surveyed the rest of the apartment. Nothing was missing and she wasn't surprised. Molly wasn't a thief. *She just wants to see you arrested for murdering the woman who ruined her career. YOU ruined her career.* She returned to the kitchen and poured a shot of tequila. She needed to calm down.

So what if Molly knew everything? She couldn't prove it. Even if she'd taken photos with her camera phone, they wouldn't hold up in a court of law, and Biz would press charges for breaking and entering. Molly had as much to lose.

She pulled the receipt from her wallet—her insurance policy. She wasn't in Arizona when Wanda was murdered. She was at a mini-mart in California. It was flimsy, but it was enough proof to get any charges against her dropped unless they found something else at the crime scene, another mistake she couldn't remember. The tequila went down her throat slowly as she contemplated the idea of Jack Adams finding a clue.

Her cell rang and Ari's number popped up. "What? No FaceTime?" she asked when she answered, her mood already shifting. "I like to see you when we talk."

"I'm not really interested in seeing you right now," she said coolly. "I'm pretty upset, actually."

"Why?"

"We caught the real murderer, Steve Garritson. The police are dropping Bobby Arco's murder charge."

She poured another shot, suddenly feeling exposed and vulnerable. "Steve? Really? I thought it might be Georgie or Evan."

"No," she said flatly. "It was Steve. He's dead. The police killed him after he pointed a gun at them."

"What?" She couldn't believe any of it. "Are you okay, honey? You sound funny."

"I'm fine. It's been a rough afternoon."

"I still can't believe it was Steve."

"No, you *knew* it was Bobby," she said tersely. "Remember? Open-and-shut case?"

"Yeah," she said weakly.

"But you're the one who shut it. Somehow you found out about the dress shirt and you put a matching one in his closet so he'd be charged with murder in addition to child pornography."

"He deserved it."

"That doesn't matter! It's not right. You can't manipulate justice. You can't be a vigilante."

She bit her lip. Ari was the last person she ever wanted to fight with. "I know. You're right. I'm sorry. When are you coming home? I really need to see you. I need to hold you."

Ari sighed. "Biz, I don't know what to think right now. I'm not sure us being together is a good idea. We see the world too differently."

Anger flared inside her heart. She'd waited so long. "You mean how in your world justice and truth always win and in mine they usually don't, at least not without a little help?"

Ari didn't reply and she slapped the counter. She shouldn't have said it, but the tequila was stripping away her patience. She hated do-gooders like Ari, but she loved her because she was so good. It didn't make sense.

"Look, just come home and we'll talk," she pleaded. "I know I screwed up."

"Jane and I are going to hang out for a while. I'll be back in a few days and we can talk then. Okay?"

"Yeah. Sure. No problem."

She disconnected and finished her third shot of tequila. It was over already. She didn't see that coming. She thought Ari understood. She'd had enough pain in her own life to recognize the means justified the ends. Biz was certain Ari would do *anything* to bring her brother's murderer to justice, even if it meant resorting to devious or illegal tactics, but Bobby Arco and Steve Garritson weren't Richie Adams. In Ari's world there were two standards, but Biz saw only one for everyone, which is why she'd stopped by the police department and found a sister in the evidence department who gladly showed her the dress shirt pocket for the promise of a date. After a quick stop at the mall and a little help from her pocketknife, she'd left a piece of evidence the police wouldn't miss.

Only slightly inebriated, she pushed Ari from her mind and returned to self-preservation and her plan. She grabbed a trash bag from the pantry and went to the bedroom closet to retrieve the blond wig and the slinky black cocktail dress, her only remaining connections to Wanda. She had hurled the highball glass from Wanda's apartment into the desert on her way to California so once the wig and dress were gone, if the police searched her apartment, they would come up empty-handed. She just needed to dispose of the bag.

She donned her favorite baseball cap and took the Subaru keys from the peg in the laundry room. She was desperate for a shower but removing Wanda completely from her life was a priority. She was sorry to lose the wig. It was one of her favorites. *Damn that Molly*, she thought.

The parking garage was half empty, most of the residents still enjoying the end of their weekend. As she waited for the gate to scroll up, she debated where to dump the bag and decided to keep it simple. She'd drive over to the east side and find a garbage bin on the perimeter of a strip mall. No one would ever know, and it would be impossible to trace.

She'd just pulled out of the garage and was waiting to turn left when three black and whites converged on her, sirens blaring and lights flashing. She was too stunned to move. She took some deep breaths and glanced at the bag next to her. *It doesn't matter*, she thought. *It's private property. It means* nothing.

Jack Adams and Andre Williams approached, motioning for her to get out. *Keep it together*, she thought, as she rolled down the window. She'd make them work for it.

"What's going on?" she asked perturbed.

Andre pulled a warrant from his breast pocket and handed it to her. "Sorry, Biz, but we need to search your vehicle and your condo."

She read the search warrant implicating her in the murder of Wanda Sykes. "This is crazy." She looked at Jack, who wore a stony expression. "Jack, c'mon."

He squatted, his enormous frame filling her window. "You need to think, Biz. The last thing Sol Gardener told me before he died was that Ari was still in danger. Someone could still hurt her. I'm guessing that someone is you."

"I could never hurt Ari," she said sincerely.

"Maybe you couldn't push her off a balcony, but Vince Carnotti wouldn't hesitate to take her out."

He paused and she realized what he said was true. Eventually Carnotti would use Ari against her if he felt threatened.

"Now, you need to come with us for a little chat. On the way to the station you need to think about what should happen next, about what's important and how to save yourself." He checked his watch and added, "We've been here a little over a minute. How long will it be before Carnotti knows you're in police custody? Think about that."

She peered through the windshield looking for the dark Escalade. He was right. Carnotti's people listened to police scanners and had cops on the inside. If he didn't know about the search warrant he would soon, and he'd wonder what Biz would say or what she possessed that might incriminate him. Then he'd worry. Jack knew it.

Ever the gentleman, Andre opened the door for her. "I'll run this back down the ramp to your parking space. Which one is it?"

"Forty-eight," she mumbled, already sensing her life was shifting.

She walked with Jack up the street to his sedan. She glanced back at the lofts, wondering if and when she'd return. She suddenly realized it didn't matter whether the police could prove a case against her. She'd taken painstaking precautions to kill Wanda and sifted through garbage to gain an alibi, but she didn't need insurance against them. They were the good guys. If she wanted to stay alive, she needed insurance against Vince Carnotti, and she guessed that was what Jack and the DA would propose. They were the good guys—and she wasn't. Despite all of her years helping women, she was a thief, a burglar and now a murderer.

As the car pulled away to join the downtown traffic, she noticed a red truck parked on the other side of the street. She glanced into the side mirror as they passed. She may have been mistaken, but she was almost positive Molly Nelson was leaning against the steering wheel, flipping her off.

CHAPTER THIRTY-FOUR

Jack reached for a bottle of Maalox he'd found in Molly's old desk and took a hefty swig. His stomach was doing somersaults and he couldn't relax. Who would have imagined he'd get stage fright the first time he conducted morning briefing as the interim Chief of D's? He'd been going to briefings for decades, never contemplating what the poor guy at the front might be experiencing. Now he knew, and it had turned out okay. The officers actually seemed to *like* him in the position.

It wouldn't be official for a few more weeks, since he'd be getting a promotion to lieutenant, but according to Phillips it was a sure thing. He was definitely the hero of the hour for solving Escolido and getting an indictment on Vince Carnotti. It had been a great week.

"Have I told you how great you make me look?" Dylan asked, strolling into his office and folding herself into one of the small chairs. Today her hair was pulled back with some clips and he could see her high cheekbones. She was smiling. He liked it when she smiled.

"You have," he said. "Thanks."

"I want you to see this through with Elizabeth Stone. You know, work with the marshals, act as the go-between. Are you up for that?"

He nodded. "I was going to insist, actually. She was involved with my daughter."

She didn't hide her surprise. "Your daughter's gay?"

"Yes," he said evenly. "She's a lesbian. Her previous girlfriend was Molly Nelson, whose help on this case, I may add, was critical to the indictment."

She held up a hand in surrender. "I'm sorry. I take back everything I said. I was wrong, and I look forward to meeting her and shaking her hand. Satisfied?"

When she looked up, he saw a dimple on her chin. "Mostly," he said, grinning.

She pointed at the darts on his desk. "Are you any good?"

"I'd like to think so. I became really good during my retirement, but I imagine I'll get rusty really quick."

She picked up a dart and fired it into the board on the opposite wall. It didn't hit the bull's-eye, but it came close.

"Beat that."

His landed directly across from hers. "I'd say we're evenly matched."

She looked momentarily flustered, and they exchanged a long look before she sprung out of the chair. "I need to get back to work."

He watched her go, enjoying her lingering perfume.

* * *

The music inside the apartment delayed his knock. He'd never heard Molly play, but Ari had said she was amazing. He listened to the lively and brisk melody. He knew nothing about classical music or the composers and had cringed the few times Lucia, Ari's mother, had forced him to the symphony or, worse, the ballet. Violin music *and* dancing.

"She's really good, isn't she?" a nearby voice asked.

He peered over the rosebush and saw Molly's neighbor sitting on her porch. She was a typical little old lady with her hair in curlers and wearing a duster.

"I love to come outside and listen to her," she continued. "I can hear the music a lot better outside than through the wall."

"I agree. She's excellent."

"Who are you? I'm not tryin' to be nosy. I'm Dorothy Lyons, the head of neighborhood watch. So I'm watching—and listening to Molly."

"I'm Jack Adams," he said with a wave.

Her face lit up, and he realized she didn't have her bottom dentures in. "Ari's dad?"

"Yeah, Ari's my daughter."

"Great gal," she said. "The best. We need to get those two back together as soon as possible. Molly's turned into a grumpy Gus without her."

"I'll work on it. It was nice meeting you, Mrs. Lyons."

"You too, Jack. You got a girlfriend? I can set you up. I know a lot of women, and all of them still have their original teeth."

"That's okay. I'm good."

Before she could ask any more questions, he knocked, and the music instantly stopped followed by a commotion as if she was picking up things before she opened the door.

"Jack? What are you doing here?"

"I thought I'd come and give you an update on Biz."

They went to her small kitchen table, and she brought them each a can of diet ginger ale. "I hope this is okay," she said. "It's the strongest I've got these days."

"This is great," he replied. "So, Biz agreed to immunity and witness protection in exchange for her testimony against Carnotti."

She looked dumbfounded. "Are you serious? The DA's going to let her get away with murder?"

"She's not getting away," he said. "She's losing her life as she knows it, and we're getting the biggest criminal in the city."

"She *should* lose everything regardless! She's a killer!"

He reached for her hand. "Molly, hear me. Biz knows the game. She knows how to play hardball. She doesn't have to give us anything, and she's also saying that Carnotti as much as ordered her to kill Wanda."

"What?"

"She corroborated your story about the day at the apartments. The waitress who saw Biz in the coveralls was right. Biz and one of Carnotti's goons went out the back way, and according to Biz, Carnotti told her to kill Wanda—or else."

"She was already planning on doing it—"

"No," he interrupted. "She was planning an accident, and it probably wouldn't have worked."

She shook her head, not liking any of it. "You don't know that."

He leaned back in the chair. "It doesn't matter. The deal's made. She's out of here and Carnotti's in custody."

"And Wanda's dead."

"Yes," he agreed, "she's dead. The woman who ruined your career is dead. Have you forgotten that?"

She looked away. "She didn't ruin my career. I made my own choices and I've spent the last nine months coming to terms with that." She met his gaze with sincerity. "I'm an alcoholic. The only person who destroyed my life is *me*."

CHAPTER THIRTY-FIVE

Ari and Jane spent the next two days walking along the ocean, enjoying the hotel's spa and relaxing by the pool as a way to forget Sunday's traumatic events. By Monday, Steve Garritson's death and the newly revealed family secrets were plastered across all of the California newspapers. Evan, Sam and Georgie had gone into seclusion, one paper reported, and another showed Scott Kramer leading the Garritsons out of the funeral home.

"I can't even imagine how they must be feeling," Jane said, clicking off the TV remote and pulling her last suitcase off the bed. "They watched their father die."

"I feel horrible for Clay Justice," Ari said. "It's never easy to shoot anyone."

"He was clearly a very sick man," Jane concluded on her way into the bathroom to gather her toiletries. "Are you done packing already?" she called.

"Yup. I hardly brought anything, remember?"

Jane's retort was inaudible but no doubt sarcastic. She stirred her tea and lingered at the patio door, watching the waves. After returning from the Garritsons' on Sunday night, they'd switched rooms to gain an ocean view, deciding they needed a real vacation before returning to Phoenix.

The minute Justice had mentioned the dress shirt pocket, Ari had guessed the killer was Georgie and showed him the pool picture of Scott and the boys. After explaining the ramifications to their family and Steve's appointment to the task force, he agreed to get a search warrant and expedited the lab's review of Arco's shirt, which she assumed Biz had planted. He'd managed to show up with the unis just in the nick of time, or she guessed she'd be dead. She shivered for a second and gulped the warm tea. She'd been cold since Sunday and she knew it wasn't the November air.

Jane looked around the suite and counted her four suitcases. "I think that's everything. Did you call the cab?"

She smiled sheepishly. "No, I made other arrangements."

Her face lit up. "A limo?"

"Nope."

Someone knocked and Jane looked at her suspiciously. "It better not be who I think it is."

"Answer it," she said innocently.

She went to the door and shouted, "Go away! I don't want to see you!"

Ari couldn't make out the reply, but she groaned and set down her mug. "Jane, don't be an idiot."

She let Rory in and gave her a hug. "I'm glad you're okay," Rory said. "How scary that must have been for you."

"I'm fine."

"I'm fine, too," Jane announced. She glared at Rory with her arms crossed.

"I didn't ask you," Rory replied.

She sensed another fight brewing. It was probably a mistake to ask her for a lift to the airport.

"I've got something I want to say to you," Rory said.

"What? Are you going to humiliate me like you did the other night? Or maybe you'd like to insult my vocabulary or mock me with words I don't know?"

Her lips curled into a smile. "Tempting, but no. I want to be very clear so I'll keep it simple."

"Well, if you avoid too many multisyllabic words, I might be able to get it," Jane said, scowling. "What do you want to tell me? I'm ready."

"You're amazing."

The scowl vanished as Jane saw the earnest look in her eyes. "Oh," was all she could say.

Rory pulled her into an embrace and kissed her softly. She seemed to be swooning. Rory's strong arms were the only thing keeping her upright.

"I haven't enjoyed anyone's company like this in a long time. I love sparring with you, and one of these days, Jane, I'll be ready. Then I'm going to show up on your doorstep. Okay?"

"Uh-huh."

"Until then I'm just going to keep whippin' your ass at Words with Friends."

Her challenge reignited the sexual tension that had swirled between them for the entire trip. Jane practically jumped in her arms for a kiss that demanded privacy.

"I'll meet you guys downstairs," Ari said, grabbing her bag. Now she was ready to go home.

* * *

Swinging the pickax felt good. Ari loved the steady motion and the thrill of the steel flying over her head before it punctured the ground. She'd soaked the large rectangle that would be her vegetable garden for two days so the stubborn Arizona soil wouldn't break her pick. Her old sneakers were covered in mud and felt like cement blocks. She wiped the blade again, enjoying the dirt on her skin. Ironically, being outside cleansed her after a terrible week.

When she and Jane had returned home, her father had been waiting on the porch. He told her of Biz's arrest for murder and her involvement in Molly's dismissal. She'd been too stunned to cry at the time, but the tears came later that night. So had the shame. She felt like a co-conspirator and she didn't think she could ever face Molly again. If she'd known...

She hefted the pick over her head again and walloped a fresh piece of earth. It helped her forget everything. She added a slight grunt with each motion and put more force behind her swing. It was going to be a damn good garden.

After another row she took a break and dropped onto a pile of bricks, nearly panting. This was much harder than planting flowers.

She heard the back gate close. Her dad or Jane was coming by to ask her to go out, no doubt. She quickly formulated her refusal. She just wanted to be alone.

The woman coming across the garden path wasn't Jane, and for a split second she didn't recognize her. She looked so different, so *healthy*. Her beautiful blond curls were styled in a blunt cut, and she'd lost a lot of weight. She looked fabulous in a tight T-shirt and jeans. She came to the edge of the tiny grass strip and stopped, not wanting to muddy her sleek black boots.

They hadn't seen each other for nine months, three-fourths of a year or nearly two hundred and seventy days, depending on how you counted it. On some days, she'd counted every way imaginable. She'd lost track of how many times she'd thought of her, of their life.

She couldn't speak. She only stared. Molly was always beautiful but now she was... She looked at the ground. She was losing control of her emotions.

"I rang the bell, but I didn't think you heard me," Molly said.

She shook her head. "No, I can't hear anything out here. That's why I leave the back gate open. I don't think anyone would want to steal my garden."

"That's not really advisable," she replied, sounding like a cop. She stood with her weight on one leg, her thumb looped in her front pocket. Typical Molly.

"You're right. I'll get a padlock for the latch."

"Good." She nodded and they returned to the awkward silence until they both started to speak at once. Then they stopped and then they started. Finally, they just laughed. It felt so good to hear her laugh and even at a distance her crystal blue eyes shone.

"Sorry, go ahead," she said. "What did you want to say?"

"No, you first," Molly insisted.

She realized she must look ridiculous. Her hair was matted against her head and she was covered in mud, wearing her most tattered cutoffs and disgusting T-shirt, the mud on her face like war paint. She was a sight.

"I just wanted you to know that I had no idea about Biz. If I'd known—"

She held up a hand. "I get it. It's okay. I know you weren't involved."

The corners of her mouth turned up in a consoling smile and her voice was soothing, calm. She had never heard this tone. Molly was usually gruff. She spoke in clipped sentences. She was a cop.

"What did you want to say?" she asked. "Why are you here? Not that I mind," she added quickly. "I'm just surprised. After the email you sent..."

She shifted her weight uncomfortably. "I was angry. I guess I still am, a little."

She bristled and Ari prepared for the outrage that usually followed, but instead, her shoulders sagged and she looked at her meekly. "Do you remember the night I was so drunk I tripped and we fell down?"

She looked perplexed. There had been *many* nights that fit that description. "I'm not sure."

"I wanted to go bowling and you wouldn't go. You sprained your ankle in the fall."

She nodded. "And I called Jane to pick us up. Yeah, I remember. What made you think of that?"

She swallowed hard before she said, "I just wanted to say I was sorry, and I think your hair looks great. You look great. That's what I wanted to tell you." She offered a little wave and headed to the gate.

She'd said what she came to say and that was it.

"I'm sorry too," Ari whispered. She jumped up and clomped across the overturned earth. "Molly?"

She turned slowly and Ari saw she was crying. "Yeah?"

"Could we go to lunch next week?"

Bella Books, Inc.

Women. Books. Even Better Together.

P.O. Box 10543
Tallahassee, FL 32302

Phone: 800-729-4992
www.bellabooks.com